A forbidden love..
jeopardy... a

Then There's Trust

Susan Gray

All characters and events in this publication, other than those clearly in the public domain, are fictitious and any resemblance to real persons, living or dead, is purely coincidental.

Editing, design, typesetting and publishing by UK Book Publishing

www.ukbookpublishing.com

ISBN: 978-1-918077-61-2

Then There's Trust

ALSO BY SUSAN GRAY

Spanish House Secrets

Blossoming of Truth

Hope on Hope

THE SMALLWOOD FAMILY TREE

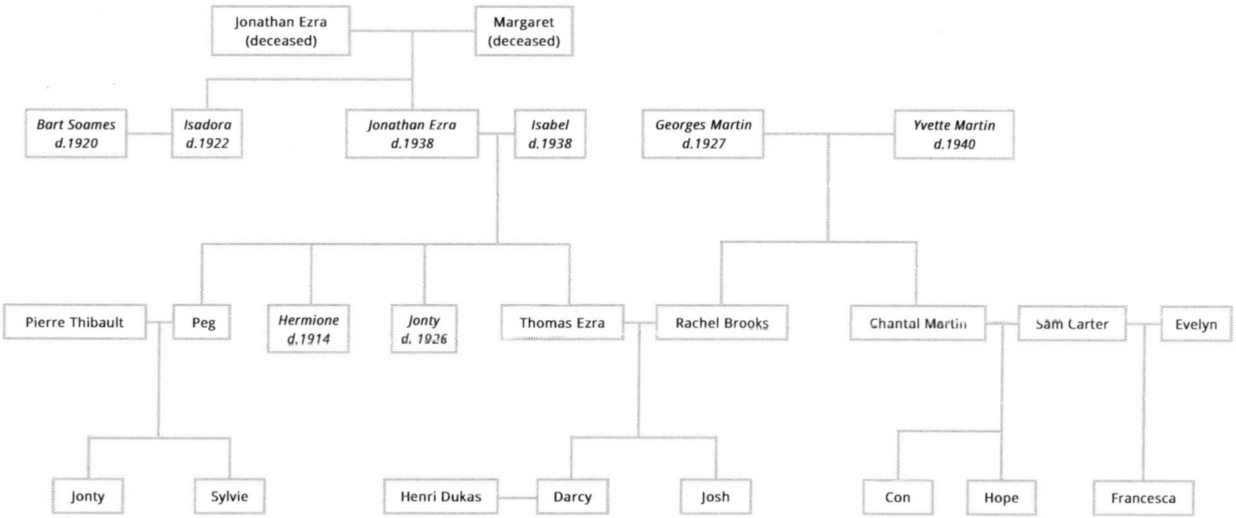

To my husband, Vic.

'Never be afraid to trust an unknown future to a known God.'

Corrie Ten Boom

Chapter 1

NORTHEAST ENGLAND
SEPTEMBER 1952

Noise tickled at the edges of her dream...a cry...a newborn's cry... was she dreaming? Leaving the cosiness of her bed, she walked clumsily to the adjoining room. The primrose yellow drapes were drawn back, as daylight pricked the horizon with the promise of early morning sunshine. A surge of excitement rushed through her, as her unborn child wriggled and gave a kick.

"Hello little one," she greeted, smiling and placing her hand on the neat bump. "Are you preparing me for early mornings?" She sighed...four more weeks to go!

"Chérie," whispered a deep voice from behind as two strong arms enveloped her.

"I heard a baby crying... but of course, I was dreaming," she replied, resting in her loved one's embrace. Together they surveyed the prepared nursery.

"Aujourd'hui, we will add the final touches," he indicated with a nod towards the newly framed pictures.

Darcy stepped forward, lifting the sketches of a giraffe, then a lion, drawn from memory by her own hand. Her eyes drifted to another framed sketch…not an animal this time but the first verse of a poem.

Encased in a border of tiny, fluffy feathers it read…

'Hope is a thing with feathers, that perches in the soul,
And sings the tune without the words, and never stops at all'

Emily Dickinson

With oneness of heart, Henri read his young wife's mind.

"Our baby is the first step towards our hope-filled future, my darling."

Gently, she moved her hand to touch his side. "Then we will trust for our second step of hope, Henri…your future hip surgery."

Hope and trust would take them forward.

The wider family at Meckleridge House were eagerly awaiting the birth of this baby – a symbol of hope and trust…but two days later…

***

"Please," she exhaled "…do something…please…please, Tallie…help me." The anguished cry escaped from the young mother's lips. She gasped for breath as the second wave of pain elapsed. Her distraught husband stood at her side, mopping her brow, beaded with perspiration.

"Sssh, ma chérie, soon it will be over," he urged, trying to sound calm.

CHAPTER 1

Darcy grabbed Henri's hand as another pain engulfed her.

"No, no," she shouted, screwing up her eyes and tightening her grip.

"Don't push, Darcy. "Pant…pant." The midwife's experienced voice sliced through her niece's wailing. Tallie, the midwife, beckoned over her shoulder to her sister, the mother of the distressed young woman.

"Make the call, Rachel…it's time."

Rachel needed no second bidding and raced along the landing to the top of the stairs.

"Quick, Tom…phone for help," she yelled to her husband, pacing the floor in the hallway. Tom leapt into action. Lifting the telephone, he shouted into the receiver. "Flying Squad, Mary, it's Meckleridge House, we need them now."

The stunned telephonist obeyed his command, engaging the wires to make the connection. "Doing it, Tom," she responded.

"Thank you, Mary," Tom uttered, replacing the receiver, and putting a strong arm around his petite wife, squeezed her. Pulling away, Rachel ran back to the anxious expectant parents and her sister, the midwife.

Minutes later, the bell on the Flying Squad ambulance was sounding its distinctive 'ding-a-ling-a-ling', as the skilled driver raced up the driveway leading to Meckleridge House. The emergency response ambulance, accompanied by another midwife and doctor, screeched to a halt at the front door. Henri, Tom and Rachel stood in bewilderment as their darling Darcy was transferred into the hands of the medical team and taken to the local Malhaven Hospital.

"I must follow," declared Henri, leaning heavily on his walking stick.

"I'll drive," indicated Tom.

Sitting in the hospital waiting room, the trio remained silent. It was a beautiful September day, but no sunlight penetrated the windowless cubicle. Each was lost in their own thoughts. Henri felt numb. He wanted to be at his young wife's side in her hour of need, but hospital protocol forbade it.

Chantal, almost unrecognisable in hastily adorned theatre garb, had assured him Darcy was receiving excellent care, before she disappeared behind swinging doors. However, it did little to assuage his fears and anxiety; hospitals in Henri Dukas' experience spelt one word …trouble.

"She's strong and brave," declared Tom, to no-one, but somehow, he felt it was his duty to fill the silence with reassuring words, as they awaited news from the theatre.

"But two lives are at stake," uttered Rachel's feeble voice. "Our dear daughter…and our first g-g-grandchild." She began to sob uncontrollably, as Tom placed his arm around her. Henri and his parents-in-law continued to sit… and wait…and worry.

It was just over an hour since they'd arrived at the hospital and Chantal's facial expression was bland as she entered the waiting area. As a midwife with many years' experience, she was struggling to remain professional. She'd performed this daunting task before…but not to her own flesh and blood. This was cruel…heartbreaking and unfair, but it must be done. She stood in front of her family.

CHAPTER 1

"I am so sorry, Henri," she whispered to the young man, taking his hand. "The little one is so beautiful...but he did not breathe. Come with me and see." She turned, as Henri stood.

Rachel was aghast. "But...Darcy...what about Darcy?" she called, as her sister and Henri walked towards the door.

"Exhausted, Rachel, but she is strong," Chantal responded.

Rachel collapsed against her husband's chest and let out a wail.

Henri was shown into the clinical room. His beautiful wife was propped up on pillows, cradling a tiny, lifeless bundle in her arms. Tears coursed down her cheeks. Henri reached out and embraced her.

"He...he's...so perfect, Henri," her voice strained. "Perfect and beautiful...I can't believe it," she gulped, as Henri stroked his tiny son's white face.

"Welcome, Leon Henri Dukas...and farewell, my precious boy. May God look after you, little one," the young father declared, his voice sounding like cracking glass.

The attending midwife approached the bed, anxious to perform her duties.

"Wait," called Tallie, from the doorway. "Can my sister see him?"

The midwife looked dubiously at Chantal.

Her reply was curt. "This is not the district, Sister Carter...we have our rules on the maternity ward." Her tone was sharp, as she reached to take the baby, but Darcy pulled him close to her body. After a brief hesitation, the midwife sighed. "Perhaps, we can make an exception."

Chantal opened the door before the midwife changed her mind, returning minutes later with Darcy's parents. She stood back and observed the family group. Grief was etched across all their faces…so much hope, cruelly snatched away.

***

The gravel pebbles crunched beneath his feet. Josh Smallwood stopped, dropped his bag and surveyed the view – his family home…Meckleridge House, devoid of colourful bunting.

"Welcome home, Joshua Ezra Smallwood," he said aloud to himself cynically, shaking his head. So much for his mother's promises – *"We'll hang out the flags when you return home for good,"* she'd declared, when he wrote giving his demob date from National Service.

Retrieving his haversack, he continued up the sweeping driveway.

His home, a large house, had been a hotel in his childhood, before the war. But his memories of those days were scant. He'd arrived by train over an hour ago. The twenty-minute walk to his home was normally no problem. However, carrying his baggage – a heavy haversack, crammed with the contents of his National Service days – was no mean feat. He'd expected his dad to be waiting in the car to collect him. But with no sign of the family's Austin car, he asked the station master if he could use the telephone…but there was no reply.

"Probably forgotten the date of my arrival," he'd commented to Jim Corrigan, who was hovering in his office. Jim was acquainted with the Smallwood family.

CHAPTER 1

"Not like your dad to forget dates and times, young Josh – sit yourself down and try again in five minutes. It'll be a hike to your place with all your kit," he chuckled, eyeing Josh's baggage.

"Yes, Jim, that's the end of my National Service…now to face the real world." Josh walked over and looked out into the station yard.

"Got any notions what you're going to do next?" enquired the older man, flicking his cap off his head and running his hand through his ginger hair.

"In a word, Jim, no. I haven't a clue. I guess I can always help on the farm in the short term while I consider my options."

His mind wandered to the substantial enterprise surrounding his family home – a farm, a market garden and a horticultural business.

"Well, you're a lucky lad, Josh, plenty of scope for you at home. Your dad's quite the businessman." Josh was silent, none of the prospects his home environment afforded appealed to him. He looked at his watch.

"Can I try to phone again, please?" Jim nodded.

That was half an hour ago.

Josh dropped his bag and jogged over to the front door – it was locked. "What is going on?" he queried to himself. This was most unusual. Normally, his fastidious mother 'laid out the red carpet' when he came home for a few days' leave – not allowing him to lift a finger, spoiling him with his favourite foods and supplying him with culinary treats to take back to his barracks. Yet here he was…home for good, his army days behind him… no reception party and the door locked…something was up!

He walked around to the back door, tried it to no avail, slung down his bag and headed off towards the greenhouses. Surely Henri would be hard at it, engrossed in his plant propagating work. But there was no sign of his industrious brother-in-law anywhere.

He wandered over towards the neatly mown lawns and stood hands on hips. He was sweltering. The rich autumn hues, abundantly evident in the extensive grounds, should have signalled a cooler day – but the warm sun, plus the exertion of his walk, rendered him gasping for refreshment.

Returning to the building, he peered through the windows…everything looked shipshape and normal. He considered his choices…sit it out, seek out Ivan in the market garden or jog over to the farm – Nancy, the farm manager's wife, would provide him with a cuppa. The latter choice appealed and, knowing Nancy, there would be food to accompany it. Decision made, he set off for the farm.

Where was everybody? Meckleridge House was an extended family home – it was rarely empty. His parents, Tom and Rachel; his sister Darcy and her husband Henri; his aunt Chantal, Sam and their little twins Con and Hope, all lived in this sprawling house.

Just then he heard a rumbling noise – the all too familiar chug of Bennie's truck. He smiled…at last signs of civilisation! The rusty red pick-up truck ground to a halt in front of Josh.

"Eeeh, Josh lad, I'm so sorry," declared the burly farmer, his elbow balanced on the open window. "I was supposed to collect you from the station, but I didn't get the message until I got back from the mart. I figured you'd be home by now. Hop in, my Nancy will give you a brew and explain." Josh opened the passenger door with its distinctive clunking hinges and sat down on the tatty bench seat. Bennie cranked the gears and swung the old truck around, driving towards the farmyard.

"What's up, Bennie…where is everyone?"

"It's grand to see you, lad. Bet you're pleased all that boot bashing's behind you. Now you can get to grips with real life back here at Meckleridge."

Josh noticed the farm manager's avoidance of his question, but the look on his tanned face caused a flutter of panic to ripple in Josh's stomach. Arriving in the yard, Bennie yanked on the handbrake, and they alighted the vehicle.

"Like I said, Josh, Nancy will fill in the details. When I got back from the mart, she gave me a garbled message while I was having my bait. I had to eat up quickly and get on over to the station to collect you off the train. They're all at the hospital, lad. It's your sister and her baby. They had to get the Flying Squad."

Josh's jaw dropped. The panic ripples now turning to fear in the pit of his stomach. He knew next to nothing about babies – but was aware calling the Flying Squad… wasn't good.

The farmhouse door opened and Nancy, Bennie's wife, appeared. Snuggling into her generous bosom was his blonde curly haired cousin, Hope, and at her side a male replica with shorter hair.

"Uncle Joshy, Uncle Joshy," whooped the little boy running into his big cousin's arms.

"My, Conrad Carter, haven't you grown since I last saw you." Indeed, in the seven months since his last visit home, his toddling cousins had transformed into young children.

"We go to school now," announced Hope, pertly.

Nancy chuckled, "And don't we know it…this little miss thinks we haven't been educated, Josh. So, watch your 'p's and q's'."

"A pea is a vegetable and the name of a letter, did you know that, Joshy?" remarked Hope, wriggling free from Nancy's arms.

Josh stifled a grin, and lowering Con to the ground picked up Hope, tickling her as she dissolved into a fit of giggles.

"Who does she remind you of?" Josh asked Nancy as he followed her retreating figure into the farmhouse kitchen.

"Aye, she's the model of your sister…in looks, attitude and actions. But sit yourself down, Josh, this is a poor homecoming for you, not what your mother planned but… well… I need to be telling you what's going on."

In between being assaulted by his cousins, devouring two sizeable portions of homemade corned beef pie, a chunk of freshly baked bread and washing it down with a cup of tea, Josh gleaned the happenings at his family's home that morning.

"It was a right old 'tizz was', Josh. Typical of my Bennie to be at the mart. Your sister went into labour early this morning. She was a month early…not a good sign, but your aunt was in charge, and she being a sister midwife on the district… well, it was ideal. It was all going to plan …until it wasn't. Another pot of slosh?" she asked, homing in on Josh with the large, heavy teapot. He nodded and watched as she 'sloshed' the thick brown liquid into his mug.

"Thankfully, Sam dropped these two at school and I got on with me jobs. Next thing I knew your dad was on the phone asking if I could collect the rascals from school and could my Bennie fetch you from the station, because they'd had to call the Flying Squad. Darcy was having difficulties…and…" The words were tumbling from Nancy's mouth at a fast rate of knots.

"Slow down, woman. You're going to get Josh, and the kiddos, all worked up with your ramblings," chastised Bennie.

"Has there been any news from the hospital yet?" Nancy went over to sort the twins, squabbling over some building blocks on the clippie mat in front of the range cooker. At that moment the telephone rang.

Bennie returned from taking the call. "They're home, so off you go, Josh. But, Nancy, we must keep the twins here, for a bit longer."

***

Fortified, Josh jogged over from the farm to Meckleridge House. His mind was all over the place. He knew his sister's baby was due in the autumn. On his last visit home in February, Darcy and Henri had announced their news. During the celebration meal, the night before Josh returned to his base, his sister had rattled a spoon against a glass.

"Listen, everybody. Henri and I want to make an announcement…we are expecting our first child in the autumn." It was welcome news. They'd been married for just over two years and during that time she had suffered a miscarriage. Josh wasn't sure about the details – women's stuff, not really his scene. But the news was certainly a cause for celebration. His mother's letters over the summer, when he was doing his stint overseas in Cyprus, mentioned how well Darcy was keeping – so this was an unexpected turn of events.

He ran into the house through the back door, kitchen and hallway into the conservatory, coming to an abrupt halt. He could see, taste, feel and hear the sorrow in the room. His dad jumped up from the chair beside the fireplace and wrapped his arms around his son.

"Welcome home, Josh…sadly, it's not a cheerful homecoming for you," he exclaimed.

Josh gawped at his parents, and Chantal and Sam. "What's happened?" he asked, sensing an ominous reply.

It was Sam who answered. After shaking Josh's hand with a firm grip, he said, "Good to see you home, Josh, but unfortunately, we have some sad news. Your sister's baby was stillborn when she gave birth this afternoon. Darcy is well, but exhausted and will remain in hospital for a few days."

Josh swallowed. "Stillborn?" he asked, embarrassed by his own ignorance.

"He died during delivery, Josh. The medical team were unable to revive him. They've named him Leon Henri, after Henri's father and grandfather. Henri is at the hospital comforting Darcy," explained Chantal.

Josh snivelled into his cuff – this was heartbreaking. Henri suffered from a disease which affected his hip, requiring him to use a walking stick. He often spent days in bed unable to walk about. This baby would have been such a blessing to Henri and Darcy and to the wider family.

"But surely she can have more babies?" Josh asked tentatively, not sure if it was an appropriate comment to be making.

"In time, Josh…in time. She will need to give herself an opportunity to recover both mentally and physically. Meanwhile, it's good to have you here," Chantal commented.

Josh walked over to the settee where his mother, Rachel, was sitting, seemingly staring ahead at nothing. He knelt in front of her, and they hugged. Then he stood and walked to the door.

A loud rattle at the front door broke the tense atmosphere. The family looked at one another questioningly; standing nearest to the door, Josh responded.

"I'll go."

It was the telegraph boy from the Post Office, a stranger to Josh.

"A telegram for Doctor Samuel Carter," he said. "Is he available?"

Josh nodded and reached out to take the envelope as Sam emerged from the conservatory.

"I'm Doctor Samuel Carter," he announced, approaching the front door.

For the first time since entering the house, Josh noticed how much older, thinner and greyer Sam Carter appeared. His hands were trembling as he took the envelope and closed the door.

Tearing open the telegram his eyes scanned the brief missive. Chantal walked to Sam's side. He coughed and placing his arm around her shoulders they walked together into the conservatory, as Josh followed.

"It's from Francesca," he indicated and proceeded to read the script to the assembled group.

'Gramps died STOP Come quickly STOP Francesca.

Chapter 2

"Oh Sam…I'm so sorry," Chantal articulated, draping her arms around his neck.

He embraced her tightly, then resting his forehead against hers, sighed deeply saying,

"I must go, Chantal… let's hope this will be the beginning of the end."

Chantal understood and nodded.

The passing of John Conrad Carter, aged eighty years, was not unexpected. His wife, Pauline, had passed away two years previously. But the demise of Sam's father heralded the advent of tricky, unpleasant developments.

"It's not a surprise," added Sam. "He suffered a stroke not long after Mother died. Francesca has been sending me regular updates – she was close to her grandfather, and he seemed to be improving."

Tom stood and shook Sam's hand. "We are sorry to hear of your loss, Sam. No matter how anticipated, it is still a wrench. I guess you will be the only one to sort the arrangements."

"Yes, I must speak to the hospital. I'll need to take leave of absence." He went to make the call. Minutes later he returned.

CHAPTER 2

"That's settled. I'll drive up tonight," Sam decided. "I know it will be late when I arrive, but it will give me a full day to begin the arrangements tomorrow."

Chantal gazed into her beloved Sam's face.

"If you go over to the farm to collect the twins, I'll start packing your case. That way you can spend some time with them, as you will be away for at least a week," remarked Chantal, in her usual organised fashion.

"I'll make something to eat, then you won't need to stop on the journey," added Rachel, jumping into action.

Josh stared out of the window…what a homecoming! Thankfully, he was home…he could assist wherever he was required. Within minutes the family rallied around, helping each other with various tasks.

"Do you want me to attend the funeral, Sam?" Chantal asked, as they were saying their goodbyes, later.

Sam gazed adoringly into her eyes…this was awkward. As the mother of his two youngest children, her place should be at his side…but…

"No, my darling girl, I know you want to support me, but it's the end of an era. Your presence would give rise to too many questions, which will be answered in due course. Anyway, you are needed here to support Rachel, Darcy and the twins." The enormity of the situation hit him afresh.

***

The three-hour journey north afforded Sam Carter plenty of time for reflection. He knew he'd been an ostrich…weren't they supposedly known for burying their heads in the sand to avoid unpleasantness? He chuckled to himself, doubting if it was true. Amazingly, he felt light-hearted – he shouldn't …he was en route to sort his father's funeral. But yes, the day of reckoning had arrived…no matter how hard he had tried to avoid it.

Four years ago, he was a 'dead man'…he did not exist… on paper. He sighed – if he'd maintained his obscurity, then he would not be facing this mess. But it was never meant to be …was it? The last four years with his beloved Chantal and the product of their love, their twin children Conrad and Hope, had been such a blessing. He could never have anticipated such outcomes when he set foot on English soil again in 1946.

Sam glanced around at the countryside he was passing, leaving County Durham and onwards into Northumberland. Twilight was pricking at the edges of the canopy – rolling hills and farmlands dotted with dirty sheep and trees tinged with the golden hints of autumn. The foliage was resplendent, crowned in September glory. He sighed, changed gear and negotiated a set of winding bends. Northeast England…it felt more like home than his native Scotland.

He'd moved here over twenty years ago to train as an orthopaedic surgeon at the Royal Victoria Infirmary in Newcastle – and quickly adapted to his surroundings. Back then he was escaping…fleeing from the wreckage of a disastrous marriage. He'd expected his wife, Evelyn, would divorce him in time…but he was still shackled to the woman. The marriage was a complete sham. She'd inveigled him into believing the child she was carrying was his – the result of an irresponsible, misguided lifestyle. Their mothers were friends and the marriage was encouraged. When it transpired Francesca was not his own 'flesh and blood', Sam could take no more. Yes, Francesca was his daughter on paper, so dutifully he'd provided for her until her twenty-first birthday. He'd always regarded her as his daughter, and the strong paternal love bond was reciprocated...but now...what would happen?

Oh, he loved Francesca – she was the innocent party, he did not want to hurt her. She was ignorant of the fact that her biological father belonged to her mother's 'set' of friends, having been a married man all those years ago. The whole scenario sickened Sam.

Now, on his father's death, Sam had inherited the Matthison 'pile'...a sizeable residence in its own grounds along with many lucrative investments.

There was no doubt in Sam's mind this fact was pivotal in Evelyn's refusal to divorce him. As his wife, she and Francesca continued to live in Matthison Hall, enjoying a status and unearned income...but now it belonged to Sam!

He dreaded meeting his estranged wife. She'd refused to speak to him at his mother's funeral. Thankfully, Francesca had maintained a strong communication with him.

He hoped, perhaps misguidedly, Evelyn would be amenable – agree to a divorce and vacate the premises. But, if not... he had a back-up plan.

The train was about to run off the track...and Sam would be the driver, because the pair could only continue to live in Matthison Hall if Sam allowed it. Samuel Conrad Matthison Carter as the new heir of Matthison Hall was about to give his estranged wife and daughter their marching orders. His intention was to sell the property!

***

As Sam was crossing over the border into Scotland, Josh was driving his mother to the local hospital for the 7.30pm – 8pm visiting slot. Josh hated hospitals, but fortunately he had avoided them during his twenty years of existence on this earth. He parked the car and escorted his mother, Rachel, into the stark building, the smell offending him.

The hospital was large, offering full general services to the inhabitants of Malhaven, Bronhill and Malsett. The Ironworks in Malsett were thankful for its presence. The Burns Unit boasted eminent surgeons, frequently called upon to practise their skills, due to the dangerous nature of ironmaking. Sam also worked at this hospital on the orthopaedic ward.

"It's a good job you are back for good, Josh," remarked Rachel, in her south country accent, linking her son's arm. Rachel was not a native of the northeast, having been raised in the south of England then moving north for work, before marrying Tom.

"There will be extra duties for you," she continued.

Josh sighed. He was in danger of being catapulted into work he did not want.

"I'm not sure I'll be staying at home for much longer, Mother." The words escaped Josh's mouth before he realised. He felt his mother tense as they negotiated some stairs.

"But you've only just returned! You've been away for two long years – why do you want to go away again?" Rachel exclaimed, shocked by this revelation.

Josh realised he'd just put his size ten boots slap bang into the mix of circumstances. He hastily tried to redeem himself.

"Just passing the comment, Mother, I'm not sure where my future will take me…but I'll stick around to help out under the present circumstances." Their conversation ended as they approached the maternity ward.

Josh greeted his sister and brother-in-law …both looked distraught. Darcy was such an attractive young woman and seeing her look so bedraggled, with damp, lank hair and a red blotchy face, pulled at his heart strings. He stood back while his mother fussed. Henri vacated the chair adjacent to the bedside, to allow Rachel to sit.

The two young men hugged.

"Mon frère, so good to see you home," Henri remarked.

Josh felt tongue tied, "Hello Henri…I'm s-so sor-r r-y," he stuttered.

The Frenchman looked close to tears, but quickly checking himself, smiled faintly. Josh approached his sister and enveloped her in a hug.

"Josh Smallwood, you've filled out since I last clapped eyes on you. Foreign climes must suit you," Darcy declared, attempting to greet her brother appropriately.

Josh looked down at his bulky frame…a far cry from the lanky young lad who left Meckleridge two years ago. He raised his forearm to flex his muscles, only just visible under his short-sleeved shirt.

"Stodgy food and lots of exercise," he muttered. "I'm sorry to hear about the baby," he added.

Darcy attempted a weak smile.

"It's life, Josh…it happens…but it hurts…badly," she uttered, almost choking on her words.

A young nurse appeared, to take Darcy's temperature, curtailing further discourse.

"Only two visitors allowed," she announced, sticking the thermometer into Darcy's mouth and grabbing her wrist to take her pulse.

"I'll step outside," offered Henri.

Josh observed the nurse, something about her seemed familiar...it couldn't be...surely not. Beneath the stern façade, the pristine, pale-blue uniform, overlaid with starched white apron and teamed with the most ridiculous looking flouncy head covering, black seamed stockings and flat black laced shoes... was a shape Josh Smallwood had admired in bygone days!

He watched with fascination, checking to see if his recollections were correct. As she plumped up the pillows and straightened the counterpane, Josh cleared his throat.

"Judy Dempster...is that you, hiding behind that uniform?" he enquired quietly, with curiosity.

There was a pause – Darcy and Rachel were talking, oblivious to the encounter.

The young nurse pulled her back straight and picked up the thermometer dish from the bedside locker. As she walked past Josh, she said sternly under her breath, "You've got a nerve, Josh Smallwood," and strode across the ward leaving a bewildered Josh in her wake.

The handsome young man was flabbergasted...what was the meaning of that brusque retort? He was baffled. His mother and sister stared at him, having observed the final exchange.

"You've ruffled somebody's feathers, dear brother," remarked Darcy. "Who is she? She must have just come on duty; she wasn't here earlier."

Josh shook his head.

"Honestly, sis, I don't know what she means…I vaguely remember her from school," he remarked.

But strictly speaking that wasn't the truth. Josh's vague recollections amounted to fancying Judy Dempster since fifth form – a fancy which continued to 'tickle' him until the present day!

Josh Smallwood was blessed with normally wavy blond hair, blue eyes and a tall broad frame. Army rules, however, reduced his fair locks to the regulation 'short back and sides'. His endearing manner and quirky sense of humour afforded him no hardship befriending a beautiful girl.

During his National Service days, he'd accompanied many attractive young ladies to the pictures or a local dance. He was quite the heartthrob, but his encounters were mostly innocent.

Josh shrugged his shoulders as his weary brother-in-law returned to the ward.

"I'll wait in the corridor," he announced, squeezing his sister's hand. "Better not aggravate the uppity Nurse Dempster," he chuckled, with a cheeky grin. "Chin up, Darc, you'll soon be back home, and I'll be around to attend to your every wish," he added, then left the ward.

***

"Did you remember?" shouted Darcy urgently, as Henri slowly ambled and limped towards the bed. Her impatience was evident.

"I've been sitting here all morning…waiting. It's up here," she announced tapping her head, "and it needs to be in there," she exclaimed in exasperation, as Henri pulled a sketchpad and pencil case from his shoulder bag.

It was the day following the birth and Darcy was not taking too kindly to being treated as an invalid.

"These stupid rules," she grumbled, snatching her sketching tools. Henri was exhausted but had slept well, eager to return for afternoon visiting.

"Did you manage to sleep?" he asked, bending to kiss his wife.

"Huh! Fat chance of that in here. Too many moaners and groaners and babies crying." She grabbed Henri's arm.

"This is cruelty…being in here…without my baby." Henri saw the anger in Darcy's eyes. He looked around the ward. Most mothers had cradles at their beds or were in final pregnancy stages. Darcy fitted into neither category…it was heartbreaking. He gave her the bunch of late summer blooms, carefully selected from the gardens at Meckleridge House.

"For you, ma chérie, with my love," he pronounced, but Darcy was agitated and thrust them onto the bedside cabinet, eager to begin her task. Henri sat down heavily and watched as she selected a pencil.

"How do you feel today, ma petite fille?" he enquired in his heavily accented voice. Although having lived in England for five years, with an excellent command of the English language, he still retained his native tongue for phrases of affection.

Darcy sighed, rubbing her still extended stomach.

"I'm sore, hot, aching, exhausted, upset and sick of being made to stay in this bed. The nurses around here should be in the army. The rules and regulations are ridiculous. I'm going to write an article about it. 'Do this, Madame Dukas… don't do that, Madame Dukas'. They are infuriating, the lot of them!" Darcy placed her hands on her head.

"I don't see why I must stay in hospital when I've got my own personal midwife at home. Tallie probably knows more about looking after a bereaved mother, than all these silly nurses put together."

Henri smiled and grasped Darcy's hand. His young wife's frustration was no surprise to him. He listened daily to her ramblings on all sorts of topics. She would probably give vent to this issue in the way she always did…writing an article for a newspaper or magazine.

"Patience, ma chérie, you must have patience…you have been through an ordeal. The staff, they know best. Chantal is busy, Sam's father has died, and he has gone to Edinburgh to sort the arrangements. Her attention is for the twins. In here you can relax, recuperate and regain your strength."

Darcy looked perplexed. In all the trauma of the previous day no-one had informed Darcy of Sam's family bereavement. She stared wide-eyed at her husband.

"Oh, gosh, that is going to put the cat among the pigeons."

Henri shook his head at another of Darcy's descriptive phrases. He frequently struggled to follow their meaning.

"I mean that's going to trigger a lot of unpleasantness up in Edinburgh for Sam."

Henri knew some of Sam's story, having helped Darcy to trace Sam's family background when he was missing during the war.

"How?" he asked innocently.

"Because Sam's wife and daughter live in Matthison Hall. Sam is his father's heir. Now, it all belongs to him. That is going to create problems."

Henri nodded, recalling how Sam was discovered living rough in Tom and Rachel's country shack, years after the end of the war, when he was thought to have died. He was reluctant to declare his existence, but after reuniting with Chantal he was persuaded to return to civilisation.

"I'm sure it will all resolve itself," he remarked, as Darcy lifted her pencil and sat back, closing her eyes.

He looked on in fascination and adoration as Darcy's slender fingers guided the pencil across the page. She was entranced…completely absorbed in her task. Henri knew from experience to refrain from comment. Once Darcy Dukas was coaxing her pencil to recreate the image in her brain, she was immersed in deep thought. She worked skilfully with speed and in minutes she was finished.

She lay back against her pillows and stared at the image she had generated. She gulped. A single tear trickled down her pink cheek.

"My baby…my beautiful baby." The tears oozed from both eyes as she passed the image to Henri. He stared incredulously at the portrait of his infant son who less than a day ago had entered this world, but failed to breathe, his life snatched away during the birth process. The sketch was perfect…an exact representation of their offspring as he lay at peace in his mother's arms.

"Ma chérie …it is so beautiful. How did you remember so much detail?"

Darcy shook her head. Her gift for creating portraits was something so natural, she took it for granted. This portrait would take pride of place in their bedroom, alongside a one she sketched of Henri after their first meeting in France.

"We will frame it, ma chérie, sign it please."

Darcy lifted her pencil and in the bottom corner wrote *'Mon fils' D.D.*

Chapter 3

TEN DAYS LATER

Sam was sitting alone in the kitchen of Matthison Hall when he heard footsteps approaching. He tensed and continued to layer the butter onto his toast, anticipating another 'ear bashing' session. To his surprise it was Francesca who opened the door.

"Good morning, Dad," she murmured, stooping lovingly to kiss him on the cheek.

"The same to you, my dear," Sam replied, in his cultured Scottish accent. "And where are you off to bright and early, this fine morning?"

Francesca was already wearing her outdoor coat. She was a tall, elegant young woman, in her mid-twenties, with brown flowing locks. She retrieved a glass from the cupboard and began to run the tap.

"I have a few routine home visits this morning, but I need to check into the surgery en route," she replied.

Sam smiled. His daughter had recently commenced working at a local surgery as a junior general practice doctor. After filling her glass, she turned and rested against the sink, sipping the contents.

"What's on your agenda, today?" she enquired, then chuckled. "Apart from avoiding another 'run in' with mither," she added. Sam always queried why Evelyn stuck to the old Gaelic term for mother. But after twenty-five years the endearing term still stuck.

"I doubt if I'll achieve that," Sam remarked, wiping his mouth with a monogrammed napkin… CC – even ordinary items carried Evelyn's presence. It was one of Sam's many dislikes. CC stood for Conrad Carter.

"We have an appointment at the solicitors at eleven o'clock to draw up the interim plans after the 'will reading' yesterday," he remarked. "Then I need to spend the rest of the day in your grandfather's study. I've decided to put all the paperwork in boxes and take it back home to sort at my leisure."

"When are you going back home?" Francesca asked.

"On Friday. I'm due back at the hospital on Monday. I need to spend time with Chantal and the twins over the weekend – two weeks is far too long to be separated from them."

Francesca nodded, then reaching over Sam's shoulder, she picked up the remaining half of his buttered toast.

"Hey, leave it be, young lady; if you'd asked, I'd have made some for you, but you usually skip breakfast."

Francesca grinned. "I know…got to watch my figure… but it looked so tempting, just sitting there."

A cough from the hallway curtailed the friendly banter.

"Bye Dad. Watch out for the fiery darts," she whispered in Sam's ear, then picking up her briefcase, she left the kitchen.

"Bye, mither," she trilled, almost colliding with Evelyn Carter as she left.

"Bye," called Sam to his daughter's retreating figure.

Was it Sam's imagination or did the temperature drop a few degrees, as the graceful figure of his estranged wife walked elegantly into the kitchen. Her hair was silver grey and seemed to match her icy matronly persona.

"Good morning, Evelyn," Sam attempted a civil start to the day.

"Is it?" snapped Evelyn. "And can I remind you for the umpteenth time it's 'Eve' now."

Sam raised his eyebrows in annoyance at Evelyn's latest 'fad'. Apparently, according to Francesca, Evelyn's current escort referred to her as 'Eve' and she had adopted the term.

Quite frankly, Sam couldn't care less what her new beau called her...he only wished the chap would ask her to marry him, then their divorce would appear attractive to her.

"What can possibly be 'good' about a morning when I am to learn the detailed procedure of the eviction from my marital home?"

Sam wisely refrained from rising to the bait; he did, however, vacate the table and carry his dishes to the sink, keeping his head bowed. He focused on the task of handwashing his utensils and heard a sigh of frustration emanating from the mouth of the discontented woman.

"It's a formality, Evelyn. There will be no more surprises."

The contents of John Conrad Carter's will afforded Evelyn ample provision with which to purchase a suitable house, bungalow or apartment and live modestly off the remainder – if invested wisely. Francesca was to benefit from a lifetime annuity set up by her grandfather. The will stipulated Matthison Hall, and the remaining investments, were left solely to Sam.

When the solicitor read the document, after the wake, a few small beneficiaries – the housekeeper, cook, gardener and valet – vacated the room, as Evelyn asked a leading question.

"Did Father indicate if I would be allowed to retain my living quarters…my home…my daughter's home?" Evelyn's voice had gained crescendo as she spoke…the question heralded a blast of cold air.

"That is not included in the will, Mrs Carter. Your husband is now the sole owner of Matthison Hall. I suggest you both attend my office at 11am tomorrow morning where the details of the arrangements can be formalised." This meeting had been requested by Sam, anticipating Evelyn's reaction.

Sam finished his drying task and turned to face Evelyn, who was now seated at the kitchen table, her head in her hands. Her neat tweed skirt and cream lambswool twinset did not concur with the woman who would now be required to make her own breakfast

"To think I have come to this!" she moaned, sweeping her hand across the breakfast table.

Sam had informed the staff they were to take a day off today, as a 'thank you' for their extra work surrounding the funeral wake. He chose to ignore the demeaning retort.

"You will be given an adequate amount of time to make alternative arrangements, Evelyn. The meeting today sets out a rough timetable for the affected parties. I'll see you in the hallway at 10.30…we may as well travel together." Then he escaped the chilly atmosphere.

Climbing the stairs two at a time, he flopped down on his bed with decided relief. The sooner today was over, the better things would be. After the solicitor and guests had departed the previous day Sam spoke to his wife and daughter.

"It is my intention to sell Matthison Hall," he'd announced. The look on Evelyn's face could have sent an army into retreat…'shock and horror' were understatements.

"But you can't…it's unspeakable…it's my home…my marital right…my daughter's birthright," she exclaimed.

Over the years, Sam had learned to blank Evelyn's outbursts, and this was no exception. She'd continued, as father and daughter listened to her wailings.

"What will people say?" she ended.

"Oh… 'Matthison Hall is up for sale', I expect," he replied, with sarcasm.

Francesca had stifled a smirk, receiving a stern look from her mother.

"This house is surplus to my requirements. I neither work nor live in Scotland. The proceeds will enable me to buy a house in County Durham for my family."

"For your French floosy and your bastard children, you mean," she almost spat the words in Sam's face.

"That's enough, Evelyn, haud yer wheesht," he responded, admonishing her in his native dialect. He'd prepared himself for this scenario and true to form Evelyn Carter did not disappoint.

He sighed and lay down on the bed. The comments about his English family rankled him. In essence it was the truth. But his darling Chantal and his delightful twins did not deserve those references. His life was a mess…he had created it...but now, with his father's passing, he had the chance to rectify the situation.

If all went to plan... the solicitor would draw up a timetable outlining significant dates. The date by which Evelyn and Francesca needed to vacate Matthison Hall; the date for a house sale of furniture and effects – Evelyn and Francesca would be given the opportunity to take whatever they wanted – and the date for the house to be put on the market for sale.

Then, and most importantly...the date for the commencement of the divorce proceedings.

Sam had instructed the solicitor with these details. Under no circumstances, was Evelyn Carter being allowed to remain on the premises to thwart a potential sale. Once she left the property, she would hand in her keys...it would be final.

Sam sat up, then stood. Yes, the day could not come quick enough. Francesca had already begun looking at houses...she intended to set up her own home – another bone of contention with her mother.

However, these things took time. It may be weeks, months or years before his family home sold. But today was the first step into Conrad Samuel Matthison Carter's happier future.

***

NORTHEAST ENGLAND

Josh was restless, ten days after arriving home and he was agitated – looking for adventure. Oh, there was plenty to occupy his time. One thing about life at Meckleridge

House – it was never dull. As a young child, Josh was used to sharing his home with others – hotel guests when he was a young child; wounded servicemen when the house was requisitioned as a convalescence home during the war; and latterly as an extended family home for various members of his family. There was always work for idle hands.

He seemed to have been crowned 'honorary favourite uncle' to Chantal and Sam's twins, although truthfully, they were his cousins, but 'Uncle Joshy' was a refrain he could not ignore. The absence of their father, who was in Scotland following their grandfather's death, meant Josh's presence was required…constantly.

By now, he was adept at guiding spoons full of food on make-believe aeroplanes into the mouths of two youngsters.

"You're a godsend, Josh Smallwood," his Aunt Chantal commented, praising his playful abilities. Bathtime was another duty he'd perfected – splashing about, ducking and diving with toy boats and corks. Even daytime romps down the grassy slopes of the grounds, and hide and seek downstairs after tea, produced squeals of delight and joy from Sam and Chantal's offspring.

Josh was amazed how exhausting these two little bundles of joy could be!

"How does Sam manage to relax after a demanding day at the hospital?" asked Josh wearily.

"He adores spending time with them, but you have been so helpful, Josh. I appreciate the way you have stepped into Sam's shoes in his absence."

Nearly two weeks back home and Josh Smallwood was still none the wiser what to do with his life.

CHAPTER 3

"If the farm and market garden don't interest you, then apply for an apprenticeship at The Works," suggested Rachel. The nearby Iron Works in Malsett provided work for most of the young men in the surrounding area – but Josh was reluctant to make enquiries. During his National Service he'd trained as a mechanic. It was a useful skill, and he was considering buying an 'old banger' and restoring it, in his spare time; but he needed to apply himself to finding a 'proper job'.

"Josh," called Darcy, in her winsome way, as he was descending the stairs the following morning. "Can I ask you a big favour, please?"

Josh went in search of the voice posing this question. He found his sister lounging on the settee in the conservatory and pulled a face.

"Depends," he replied, shoving his hands in his trouser pockets and standing with his back to the fireplace.

"You know how you are unemployed at present…" his sister began.

"Try telling that to Chantal…I think my new job is being a child minder," he guffawed.

Darcy grinned.

"Apart from that …you are available to assist…to help… you did say that night in the hospital…"

Josh was beginning to wish he'd kept his mouth shut. In the unfolding upheaval on the day of his return, maybe he had offered to help if needed…but Darcy had a husband to look after her needs.

"What are you after?" he asked, emitting a sigh of frustration.

Darcy sat up. "I need a chauffeur."

Josh looked perplexed. "Why do you need a chauffeur – when you own a car and can drive?" he asked.

Darcy stood up. "I know that, stupid – but I can't drive for another four weeks to ensure I've healed after the birth."

Josh felt his cheeks redden with embarrassment. "You've got a husband – why can't he be your chauffeur?"

Darcy shook her head. "Not really…it's work and technically I'm not supposed to be working. I resigned from my job intending to be a mother…" She paused then continued, "But…I'm not…so I've decided to pick up on something I started investigating a few months ago."

Until recently, Darcy had been a reporter at the local Malsett Guardian, a small weekly newspaper. Reporter was an exaggeration of her duties. Most of her time was spent typing, filing, answering the telephone and making tea – yet Darcy Dukas held an ambition to become an investigative journalist. She had written and published two items for the regional papers, The Journal and The Northern Echo. She'd also won a national competition in a Young Writer's Award…but she longed to widen her scope.

Darcy wandered over to gaze out of the window. Josh stared at her – compared to Chantal no-one would guess she'd recently been pregnant. He recalled his aunt still looking pregnant for months after the twins' birth.

"Now I'm no longer employed at the Malsett Guardian…I can be freelance. Take on whatever assignments I fancy, then if I'm successful…write a scoop and sell it to the highest bidder."

Josh let out a low whistle. "Darc, you are crackers, what kind of 'scoop', as you call it, could you unearth…be real, your head is always in the clouds."

Darcy stood with her hands on her hips, staring at her handsome brother. "Listen to me, Josh Smallwood, if my family think I'm going to sit around and vegetate just because my baby was stillborn...then they better think again. I might have failed at my first attempt of being a mother, but I'm going to make a name for myself as a reporter. Right now, I need a chauffeur...Henri is busy with his horticulture work, and you are unemployed! Here's the deal. If I manage to get a story printed, I'll get paid and I'll give you a percentage of my earnings. I provide the car and petrol ...and you get to drive our sports car ...does that sound fair?"

Josh grinned – driving his sister and brother-in-law's sports car appealed...and if there was a chance of some earnings – well, why not agree?

"Okay...it's a deal," he replied.

***

EDINBURGH

The atmosphere in the car was tense. Sam was driving. His head was pounding. The allotted one-hour appointment had stretched to over two hours, causing the patient solicitor to alter his schedule.

Eveyln could have won an Oscar for her performance... drama, hysterics and a fake faint, all played their part. Sam was ashamed of the woman he once thought was the mother of his child. She was milking him for every penny – but the terms of John Carter's will, restated by the family solicitor, gave no leeway for Evelyn's demands.

"I wish to remain in my home," she lamented. "I have lived there for over twenty-five years…where will I go? I have no-one to help me. I can't be expected to cook and clean and take taxis…it is below my status in life." Her voice became a wail…rising to a high pitch, culminating in a fake faint. Sam took delight in slapping her face, knowing she was pretending.

"Stop this now, Evelyn," he demanded. "You have adequate funds to employ staff; no-one expects you to manage on your own."

"But I need Elsie and Guy…they know me. Francesca must stay too…I need her."

The solicitor was used to family histrionics at the reading of a deceased person's will, but this client was proving manipulative.

After a cup of tea – to calm her nerves – Sam agreed to approach Elsie and Guy Smails, his father's former employees, and negotiate Evelyn retaining their services. He also ended up bestowing on Evelyn, the use of his father's old Rover, which Guy had polished and pampered for years in his duties as John Carter's valet. Evelyn, however, was to be responsible for the maintenance. Sam saw an opportunity.

"If I agree to this, Evelyn …you must agree to begin the divorce. The car and the retaining of the Smails' services will be the only negotiated settlement. The finances are clearly stated in Father's will."

"Yes, but the divorce settlement is different. You deserted me over twenty years ago – I need recompense for that."

At this juncture the solicitor interjected. "Mrs Carter… John himself told me, before his demise, you would be amply provided for out of the estate. He wished for a peaceful settlement for Conrad – your husband has kindly donated far and above this requirement. I think the time has come to move on to the main part of our meeting today …the timetable for your leaving Matthison Hall."

Eventually, a timetable was arranged and Evelyn reluctantly agreed to begin the divorce proceedings. The solicitor wisely had his secretary put everything in writing and both parties signed the corresponding paperwork.

There was, however, one salient point yet to discuss, but not in the solicitor's presence. Much as Sam told himself to avoid opening more difficult conversations, he knew he needed to raise this issue.

"When we inform Francesca of the timetable tonight, I suggest we tell her about her biological parentage. Now the divorce process is underway, she needs to be told."

He manoeuvred the car out of the city of Edinburgh. This was going to be hard.

Francesca was unaware that Sam was not her biological father. To Francesca her father was the man who worked in England. His only appearances throughout her childhood amounted to two weeks in the summer and two weeks at Christmas. The summer visit coincided with her birthday. She'd always believed they were related by blood. Evelyn's deceit as a young woman had resulted in him being named on the birth certificate.

As she had now attained the age of twenty-five and in view of the forthcoming divorce, it was Sam's intention to make Francesca aware of the facts. As a medical doctor he knew the importance of genetics. To his knowledge there were no problems, but he felt it was the ethical thing to do.

Evelyn let out a moan. "Why? Tell me why she needs to be told. She's your legal child – why burst her bubble? She's always adored you – heaven knows why – so let it be!"

Sam knew exactly why Evelyn wanted the true parentage kept quiet. It held the potential to damage Evelyn and Francesca's relationship. It portrayed Evelyn in her true colours, especially as the man was already married when conception occurred. Divorce was becoming more acceptable since the war, but in the circles in which Evelyn moved, divorce still carried a stigma. Separation, on the other hand, was tolerated and acceptable.

As things stood, Sam was the guilty party, deserting his wife and their young daughter. Sam had lived with the situation for years. No-one, other than Sam and Evelyn, knew the identity of the real father. Sam's gut instinct was to tell Francesca who the man was…tonight. But Evelyn held other ideas.

"Conrad," Evelyn gulped. "You can trust me over this…I won't contest anything else to do with the divorce… but only if you will grant me, this one last thing. Let Francesca believe you are her real father…please."

Sam shook his head…had he heard correctly? Trust her? Could he? But if he did, Evelyn would not stand in the way of their divorce. After all these years, it was unbelievable.

He sighed heavily as they arrived at Matthison Hall, and he made a snap decision.

"Very well… I'll agree. I only hope I don't live to regret it," he replied.

Chapter 4

"Daddy's coming home today…Daddy's coming home today," Darcy's sweet voice chanted the phrase as her voice echoed along the landing of Meckleridge House. She was firmly clutching the hands of Con and Hope who were attempting to keep the rhythm with their cousin.

"Where's Daddy?" squealed Hope.

"He is in his car, Hope, he will be back by teatime," Darcy replied. But the little girl stopped in her tracks and stamped her foot.

"I want Daddy NOW," she demanded.

Darcy crouched in front of the angry child. "It takes a long time to travel in his car, Hope, so why don't we go for a walk and explore, while we are waiting. We might find some conkers."

Hope pulled a face as her twin brother stuck his tongue out at her.

"Okay you two, we'll put on our coats."

The little group descended the stairs into the square hallway, as Rachel emerged from the back lounge.

"Just where do you think you three are going? Have you forgotten you are supposed to be resting after your confinement, Darcy?" her mother enquired, pointedly.

"Oh, Mother…let it rest…I am not a fragile invalid. All this old-fashioned thinking about a confinement. It's two weeks since it happened and I'm sick and tired of lying around. Fresh air and a stroll around the grounds will do me no harm! Come on, troops…left, right, left, right."

Rachel shook her head – there was little point arguing with her tempestuous daughter.

As they marched towards the front door, it opened.

"Mammy, Mammy," screeched Hope, flying into her mother's arms.

"Where are you going?" asked a subdued Chantal, enveloping her daughter in a loving embrace.

Rachel noticed her sister's blotchy face. "What's wrong?" she asked, raising her eyebrows as Chantal lowered her child to the ground and tried unsuccessfully to tame the mound of bouncy, blonde curls the young girl had inherited.

"Oh, nothing." She hesitated. "It's a lovely morning but decidedly chilly out there…where are you going?"

Con stared at his mother. "Conker hunting," the little boy announced. "We'll put them in our pockets."

"Well don't stay out too long, remember Darcy is poorly. She mustn't get too tired."

Darcy was ready to explode. "Not you as well," she huffed, buttoning up her jacket.

"Exercise is good for you, Darcy, but don't overdo it. A little each day…remember?"

Darcy led the way, and the conker hunting party left the house.

CHAPTER 4

Rachel headed for the rear lounge, as Chantal hung up her coat, having walked back from her shopping errands.

"Kettle's on. What's happened? I can tell you've been shedding a tear."

Minutes later, the two sisters were facing each other, sitting by the glowing fire in the rear lounge. Fourteen years separated them. Chantal always regarded her older sister as a mother figure. Rachel had been left in her aunt's care when her parents fled to France prior to the First World War. For years she assumed they were dead, until Tom unearthed her mother's whereabouts in Bordeaux, France, just after their marriage. Rachel was re-united with her mother and discovered the existence of her younger sister, Chantal.

"Right…what's upset you?" Rachel asked, as she drank her cup of tea. Rachel still insisted on using her Royal Albert china cups and saucers even for morning cuppas.

Chantal waited, composing herself, tears still pricking at the edges of her eyes. "It was the woman in the post office when I was buying Tom's stamps," she gulped, "she knows, Rachel, I'm sure of it. It's the way she looks at me…as… if…I…were…a piece of dirt."

Rachel straightened her back.

"Come, come, Chantal. How can Freda Dawson possibly know? You're paranoid over the situation. Anyway, it's none of her business. As far as she is concerned, you are Mrs Carter. Goodness me, you are known as Sister Carter to many young mothers in Malhaven."

Chantal lifted her head. "Oh, Rachel…I'm tired of living under this stigma. I long to be Sam's legitimate wife and hold my head high as I go around this town visiting my patients." She lifted her fine bone china cup to take a drink.

Rachel remained silent, giving her sister space. Anguish shrouded Chantal's face as she recalled her morning visit.

An hour earlier Chantal had entered the town's post office to purchase stamps for Tom. As she was paying for them, Freda Dawson, the postmistress, spoke.

"A moment please, Sister Carter." The tone of her voice and the emphasis on the surname sent a shiver down Chantal's spine.

"This letter has arrived with a French postmark." Anxiety clutched at Chantal's stomach. "The address is Meckleridge House, but the name is strange." She reached into a drawer and retrieved an airmail envelope. Then holding it in her hand she read the addressee's name.

"It is addressed to Mademoiselle Martin…who is she? I thought it best to wait until yourself or Tom came in, to deliver it in person…in case it is wrongly addressed."

She paused before handing the envelope to Chantal – carefully watching for a sign of reaction. Chantal felt the blood drain from her face as she took the post from the curious postmistress.

"Do you have a French visitor staying with you at Meckleridge House?" she probed.

Chantal looked at the strange handwriting – for a fleeting moment she was tempted to say something about it but quickly stopped herself…better not to add fuel to the already smouldering fire.

"Oh, it's quite alright, Mrs Dawson…it is correctly addressed," she added and placing the envelope in her basket, she left the building, without further explanation.

Once outside, she quickly turned and headed out of the town in the direction of Meckleridge House, tears trickling from her eyes. She knows, she thought…I am an imposter… I'm not Chantal Carter…I'm Chantal Martin, unmarried mother of two young children. She felt weak and vulnerable. It was out of character. Chantal Martin who had stood by, as a Nazi soldier had searched her midwifery bag containing a coded message, during her days in the French Resistance Movement, was being demeaned for her marital status by the glare of an English postmistress!

Once clear of the town, she sat down on a low wall and ripped open the letter. It was written in her native French. It was a brief letter informing her of the death of her friend and former landlady, Margot. Chantal had rented rooms in Margot's house before moving to England after the war. It was sad, but not unexpected – the lady had a serious heart defect.

Margot had often written to Chantal, but knowing the complicated situation, she always addressed her letters to 'Mrs Chantal Carter'. Margot's brother, however, who shared the house with his sister, was unaware of the subterfuge so, on the sudden passing of Margot, he'd written to inform Chantal…using her correct name.

It was an understandable mistake. Chantal was sure Freda Dawson had deliberately retained the letter until a time she visited the post office…just to see the French woman's reaction.

Chantal relayed the incident to Rachel and finished a second cup of tea.

"Chantal," remarked Rachel, "forget it…it's happened and appears to have had the desired effect…but your marital situation has nothing to do with busybodies like Freda Dawson. Remember… there was a time when I was the topic of their gossipmongering, when Tom and I were first engaged." Rachel recalled the outcry of some townsfolk when Tom proposed to Rachel after she had betrayed him.

"There are still folk who look down on me and it's nearly twenty-five years ago!" She shook her head at the recollections.

"Chantal, you have a loving 'husband' and soon you will have the paperwork to prove it," she declared. "Life throws these bricks at you… just keep trusting …it's a season and it will end." Rachel paused, watching her sister dab her eyes with her embroidered handkerchief.

Life had thrown more than bricks at Chantal…more like boulders. The years she'd spent hoping against hope she would one day be reunited with her beloved Sam. Even Sam's 'missing in action' status during the war, did not rock her steadfast hopeful belief. Finding Sam alive and well after the war, was a miracle, which still astounded Rachel.

She and Tom had welcomed the couple to live in their home, while Sam began the legal process of returning to civilisation. The birth of the twins brought the couple and the extended family such joy. Once Sam was 'legal', he retrained in his former occupation as a doctor, and Chantal took up the reins of her former profession as a district midwife.

Chantal deserved to be legally married to the father of her delightful twins and see this stigma lifted.

Chantal stood and looked into the mirror hanging over the fireplace.

"Yes, Rachel…you are right …at last the divorce proceedings have begun. It will not be long now until

Matthison Hall is sold, and Evelyn will be out of our lives. But until then, I must trust all will end well."

Rachel stood and hugged her dear sister.

The telephone rang and Chantal went to answer it.

"Sam's just about to leave – he'll be home later," she announced after taking the call.

***

Josh took a final glance in the mirror. Thankfully, his blond hair was growing again. It felt good to be free from the regulation 'short, back and sides' compulsory haircut he'd worn during his National Service days. He'd toyed with the idea of growing a beard over the last two weeks, hoping to add an air of maturity to his looks, but he'd become so accustomed to being 'clean shaven', he dismissed the idea.

Tonight, he was meeting his two pals, Sid and Ricky from schooldays. Like him, they were newly returned from fulfilling their national duties. They'd arranged to go to a dance in the town's Free Mason's Ballroom.

Before his army training, he'd spent most Saturday nights engaging in these pursuits. The object was simple – to 'eye up' an attractive girl and ask her to dance. If she 'floated his boat', he'd ask to walk her home and arrange a future date at the local cinema.

The process had proved successful prior to his stint in His…no…Her Majesty's Service. It was just over six months since King George VI had died and the beautiful Princess Elizabeth had succeeded him – her coronation was set for the following year.

Josh meandered down the stairs, grabbed his jacket off the coat stand in the hall, and popped his head around the back lounge door. "I'm off," he called to the void…no-one was around. He'd eaten an hour earlier, making his own meal, guessing the rest of the family would be eating according to their individual schedules.

Evening mealtimes at Meckleride House were usually fixed at 6.30pm except for Sunday lunch after church, and Saturdays, when everyone 'did their own thing'.

He sauntered off down the sweeping driveway. He felt awkward about tonight. It was only after bumping into Sid at the garage, the other day, he discovered his pals were also back home. Josh, Sid and Ricky had not met up in over two years and the three young men were 'new' to the local dating scene.

Josh took the cream and red Venture bus from Malhaven up to Malsett. He noticed a group of young women board the bus in Bronhill; guessing by their attire, they were headed to the same venue. He failed to recognise any of them and surmised they were a few years younger.

It was a weird feeling. He was well acquainted with picking up a girl at a dance. On the rare occasions they'd had a night out from his base, he'd been quite successful. No doubt his tall, broad build, blond hair, blue eyes and engaging manner, all played their part, but these one-night conquests had been innocent affairs, except for a girl called Mandy Fisher – she'd been the exception. He'd taken her out several times and well…she'd 'taught him a thing or two', but although she was attractive and he'd partaken of the offerings without hesitation – he'd known when to call a halt to their relationship.

CHAPTER 4

Looking back, he felt he'd had a lucky escape – pleased he'd parted company with her before they became too involved. At twenty years old, Josh was quite relaxed where the female species were concerned, but now he was home things might be different.

A local band was in full swing as Josh, Sid and Ricky entered the venue. Popular tunes along with loud singing, whistling and high-pitched squeals pervaded their ears.

"What a racket," declared Sid, as they picked their way across the dance floor, carefully avoiding spilling the beers they'd purchased at the bar. With difficulty they managed to find a corner bench seat, sandwiched tightly between some courting couples.

Conversation was impossible, so Josh used the opportunity to scan the dance floor for potential talent. The beat was infectious, and he found himself tapping his foot.

Suddenly, his eyes alighted on a shapely brunette. He twisted around for a better view...was it her? His self-imposed question was answered as the young nurse he'd met at his sister's bedside the day he arrived home, turned. Their eyes locked. Okay, thought Josh...time to explain yourself, Nurse Dempster. He downed his beer, signalled he was 'going on the prowl' to his pals, then weaved his way towards his target.

Within seconds he was standing opposite the young lady who had first caught his attention during fifth form days; back then she was being escorted by another lad, so he'd observed from afar. Tonight, she was 'dancing', or rather mooching around, with a group of girlfriends.

With plenty of experience behind him, he gave her 'the eye' and within seconds he was swinging and spinning her around the floor, as they distanced themselves from her friends. They moved alongside other bopping bodies. He attempted a smile, but it failed to work. She stared at him in a disconcerting manner, causing an uneasiness to fill him. What was her problem?

Out of the corner of his eye, he noticed both Sid and Ricky pair up with girls wearing poodle skirts. Judy's attire was more conservative – a plain green dress with short sleeves and a scooped neckline. The style enhanced her tiny waist and flared into a full skirt. Everything about her ticked his boxes. Her hair was flowing, released from the severe style of her nurse's attire. Her make up was minimal – a pale pink lipstick, which he felt a sudden desire to taste. She looked 'classy', more mature, Josh decided...now how do I get her to talk? He mused.

As if by magic, the music slowed, heralding a slow foxtrot. As convention decreed, he placed his right hand on her waist and the other at shoulder height, clasping her hand. They swayed, stepping forward, to the side, back and side again. Judy's left hand was on Josh's shoulder. He dared to move his head closer to her cheek and Josh felt the tension ease in his partner's grasp.

"Can we be friends?" he attempted to whisper in her ear.

She stopped abruptly.

"Tomorrow...bandstand...three o'clock," she murmured, then turned on her heels and disappeared into the sea of swaying bodies.

He stared after her in disbelief... something told him not to follow her, so he slunk back to the corner he'd occupied earlier and watched.

He observed her chatting to her friends. She avoided making any eye contact with Josh...peculiar, he thought.

Sid returned to their 'corner' along with the info that Ricky had 'clicked'. The evening progressed without either young man finding a date. Josh kept the interchange with Judy to himself. Sid was a good mate…they'd been pals since elementary school. He would tell him…but not yet.

***

Sunday lunch at Meckleridge House was like a 'well-oiled machine' after returning from church. Rachel cooked the vegetables to accompany the large leg of lamb which had been slowly cooking in their absence. The preparation process was traditional, and everyone knew their role.

Before breakfast, Josh's mother attended to the main event. The lamb was reared on the adjoining land, having munched the lush grass before its final journey to the local abattoir. Tom had collected it from the butcher's the previous day. While Tom and Darcy peeled potatoes and carrots, Sam and the twins shelled the peas and Henri whisked up the batter for the Yorkshire puddings. Chantal's role was to lay the table in the dining room.

Only Josh felt redundant.

"Get yourself out into the garden and pick some mint leaves, Josh Smallwood. Everyone has a chore on a Sunday morning…have you forgotten?"

Josh chuckled and grinned…who had been on 'mint sauce duty' in his absence? He pondered.

"Have you remembered what to do?" his mother called after him. "Wash, chop and soak in vinegar with a teaspoonful of sugar. Henri makes delicious mint sauce."

Question answered.

But the perfections of mint sauce making were far from Josh's' mind, as he plucked the pungent leaves. After lunch, he would excuse himself and take a walk up to the local park.

He'd admired Judy from afar since they'd worked together on a school geography project. A field trip to the North Sea coast, travelling in a small hired bus afforded him plenty of time to observe her. Of course, she hardly noticed him, because she was making gooey eyes at Keith Shotton that term. Judy had left school at the end of the fifth form. Josh stayed on to do his 'Highers' before doing his National Service. He now knew Judy was training as a nurse.

The two occasions they had crossed paths since his return, satisfied Josh he'd been right to carry a torch for the brunette, and he trusted that their rendezvous today would pave the way for a future date…if …he could find out why she was being so evasive towards him.

Chapter 5

A Sunday afternoon in September and the townsfolk of Malsett were set to enjoy the last of the Salvation Army Band concerts of the season. It was a tradition in many households in the town, to take a walk in the park and listen to the band playing a variety of popular tunes alongside hymns. Visiting the bandstand on a Sunday afternoon had not been a practice adhered to by Josh's family, but he was aware of the event.

As he approached, he heard the brass band tuning up. A good-sized crowd were in attendance and Josh loitered around its perimeter. He sensed Judy's presence long before he heard her voice. A flutter of delight twirled in his stomach as she came to stand behind him.

"Don't turn," she instructed. "Give me a few minutes and meet me at the seesaw," she added.

Josh was perplexed. This girl was certainly different.

In less than five minutes he was standing at the opposite side of the ancient seesaw to Judy. No words were spoken as she pushed off creakily, up into the air, enabling Josh to climb on the other end.

For a few minutes they 'seesawed'…why?... wondered Josh. Breaking the silence Josh asked, "Do you come here regularly?"

"Occasionally," she replied, leaving Josh even more puzzled. This was not what he'd envisaged. Searching for something to fill the silence he spoke above the creaks of the playground item.

"I see they've added a few more play items," he commented, nodding towards two newish swings and a roundabout. Judy made no response. A father with two youngsters about Con and Hope's age walked towards the seesaw.

"Puzzle Tree," said Judy, placing her feet on the ground as the seesaw came down. By the time Josh returned to the ground and politely held the seesaw for the young girl to climb on, Judy was nowhere to be seen. He vaguely recalled the 'puzzle tree' from years ago, playing 'chasey' with his French cousins, Jonty and Sylvie. He shook his head. Why this ridiculous game of cat and mouse, or rather mouse and cat? It was absurd but also intriguing.

Catching up he stood beside Judy under the sweeping bows of the old tree. Time to bring this chase to a close, he thought.

"Back to my question last night at the dance…can we be friends, Judy?"

The young woman turned. Once again, she was smartly dressed in a crisp white blouse and flared navy skirt. She looked very attractive.

"Never, Josh. We can't be friends. My family forbid it!" Then she strode off, leaving Josh mystified.

***

Henri cradled his beautiful wife in his arms as they lay down to sleep. At last, the house was silent. Sam's return from Edinburgh on Friday had given rise to a noisy weekend. Naturally, Chantal and the twins were delighted to be re-united with him. News of the commencement of the divorce proceedings and the impending sale of Matthison Hall was welcomed by the family. Tomorrow, Sam would return to his job at the hospital, Chantal to her midwifery duties and the twins would be back at school. Normality…Henri hoped.

Henri stroked Darcy's face. How could their lives return to normal?

"Ma chérie, you seem distracted. Apart from the obvious reason…is anything else troubling you?"

Darcy sighed. The obvious reason…her eyes fell on the sketch of their baby son, which Henri had framed and mounted on the wall before his wife was discharged from hospital. The dim lamplight cast a ghostly shadow around baby Leon's portrait.

"I'm restless, Henri, I want to do something useful. All this sitting and lying around is driving me crazy." Henri reached down and gently kissed his darling wife.

"Yes, Darcy, but you must give your body and mind time to heal. I can't imagine your level of grief. My grief is huge, but it's in my head and heart. Your grief is both mental and physical. I have my daily routines to distract me. But for you – it's a void…a chasm. It's an ache I wish I could fill for you. But give it time. The doctors told us to wait before…you know."

A tear trickled down Darcy's face. At twenty-two years of age, she was ready to become a mother. She'd yearned to bring their baby into this loving environment and raise him. Life could be so cruel. Henri's debilitating, physical condition *osteonecrosis,* was a burden, but they had learned to live with it. The limitations it brought were difficult yet not insurmountable. They continued to hope for a medical cure, in due time.

The arrival of their son should have brought hope and joy to their young marriage. Yet, it was not to be – his life cut short before he could breathe.

"You must give yourself time to grieve, ma chérie. Cry, scream, shout at me if necessary. I have experienced grief and disappointment before. I have what the English call 'the thick skin'...I will understand."

Darcy reached up to caress her young husband's bearded face.

"I love you, Henri Dukas...you are so understanding... but you are also suffering." She hesitated, then coughed. "Henri... I have something I want to ask you about."

They lay in silence for a while then Henri extinguished the bedside lamp. He knew his young wife, so gave her the space to formulate her words, but instead a waterfall of tears engulfed her. Darcy sobbed...and sobbed and sobbed. Pent up grief and emotion escaped the invisible wall she'd erected since the birth of her stillborn son. Henri held her close, surrounding her with a physical and emotional strength upon which to lean.

Soon the tsunami of grief ebbed, and her heaving body stilled.

"Ssssh, ma petite fille...let it go...unburden yourself." In the stillness of the late-night hour, Henri wiped the residue of tears from his loved one's face.

"I needed that, Henri...it's threatened since I was discharged last week. I felt it was a sign of shame and weakness to give way to my emotions. The hospital staff showed no compassion whatsoever."

Henri smoothed her hair and kissed her blotchy cheeks.

"Tears are natural and necessary. We cry to express ourselves when words are too painful. There is nothing shameful or weak in having a good cry," he remarked, squeezing her gently. "Now what did you want to ask me?"

Darcy blew her nose and rested her head on Henri's chest.

"If I can't be a mother...then I want to have a career," she added. "I hope to be a mother in the future...someday... but for now I want to resume my career."

"What's on your mind, my darling?"

Darcy pulled from Henri's embrace and sat up. Swinging her legs over the side of the bed, she stood up and bent to turn on the lamp. Henri gazed on in adoration at her petite figure. She'd carried their dear baby boy in a neat bundle and apart from full breasts there was no lingering evidence of her eight-month pregnancy. She moved around to Henri's side of the bed and sat down.

"I want to explore the possibility of becoming a freelance investigative reporter, Henri."

It was no surprise to Henri. From leaving school her ambition was to become a recognised journalist. She'd taken a shorthand and typing course after leaving school, then was successful in securing a job at the local weekly newspaper office, one year before their marriage.

Until her pregnancy, she'd enjoyed her role and Henri hoped in the light of her loss, the newspaper would be willing to re-employ her. Yet somehow, Henri doubted if this was her intention.

"Will you seek to return to The Guardian office?"

Darcy shook her head. "No, my work was interesting, but really, I was a secretary. I typed up other reporters' articles, filed archives, answered the telephone and made endless cups of tea. Apart from reporting on the Women's Institute's visit from an African missionary and attending a garden party held by Lady Compton, the MP's wife...that's all the reporting I've done for The Guardian."

She looked so animated, Henri could watch her all night.

"All that has been good training…but it's not the kind of journalism which interests me," she exclaimed, her voice rising. She stood and walked over to the window, pulling back the drapes. The glow from a large Hunter's Moon penetrated the bedroom.

"I want to unearth stories with human interest and sell them to a local or national newspaper. The sky's the limit, Henri," she explained, holding out her hands towards the autumnal moon. "I possess basic skills and I'm a quick learner. We don't need the money, you earn a good salary, and our living costs are modest. Then you have your father's money invested." Her voice trailed off as she became lost in her thoughts.

Henri always knew there was limited chance of Darcy settling in a humdrum job…and now motherhood was on hold…well! She shut the drapes and walked over to her husband.

"Do you understand my need to explore this idea, Henri? I've been given a chance…it will help to take my mind off Leon's death. Seeing The Carter family and their happiness hurts me, Henri. One day…that will be us – we'll have our own little brood…but for now, I must do something. Will you trust me on this, Henri?"

He sat up and reached out his arms to envelop her.

"I understand what you are saying, ma chérie …but how will you achieve it? Where do you begin?" he asked.

"I have things in mind. The way mothers of stillborn babies are treated is wrong. People don't know what happens. I intend, in time, to disclose the mental cruelty… but it's too real and raw at present, so I have another idea."

Henri lay back and Darcy snuggled up beside him.

"Last spring I typed up an article about a local farmer who found a chest of valuable items hidden in his barn. It was a straightforward account reported on by the senior reporter at The Guardian, Alec Grundy. It was assumed the chest was hidden during the war. It transpired that a local man's aunt was so fearful the Germans would ransack her house and steal her precious antiques, that she instructed her nephew to hide the chest of items in a barn on an isolated farm. The aunt died and the farm was resold. But when the chest was returned to the nephew some items were missing…four valuable miniatures… painted cameos. No-one was accused of anything, but the question remained. What happened to Aunt Lydia's miniatures? Were they stolen, sold on, hidden or mislaid?" Darcy paused, momentarily.

"No investigation was launched but the mystery fascinated me, so I approached the nephew in my own time, and asked him to describe the cameos. Well, you know how I can visualise things and sketch them. The man was astounded when he saw the representation. I still have the drawings in a sketch pad. He said if I ever uncovered their whereabouts – he would reward me financially. I fully intended to scour the antique shops around the area, but then I discovered I was expecting Leon and forgot about it...but now..." she sighed.

"Now, you want to resume your investigation. But what's that got to do with reporting, Darcy, you've lost me along the way?"

Darcy smiled. "If...and it's a big if...I do find them then the case can be passed over to the police and I could pen the reporting article. Strictly speaking, it would be the Guardian's scoop, but it's not the reward I'm after...just the thrill of the kill. Josh is willing to drive me around if you'll let him drive our sports car."

Henri watched Darcy's expression. He was apprehensive, but he knew his wife...perhaps it would benefit her to investigate something like this.

"I'm a little concerned as to your welfare, ma chérie, but if your ex-army brother is willing to go with you as your chauffeur and protector – then I won't stand in your way."

Darcy reached up and hugged Henri.

"Trust me over this, Henri. I can begin next week and use the next three weeks of my 'confinement' doing something interesting."

***

"Mother, when you are up in Malsett, could you get me a couple of things from Lamb's Stationers, please?" Darcy asked at breakfast the following morning.

"I've got an appointment at the hairdressers at 11.30 today – why don't you come with me and get them yourself," Rachel suggested.

Flabbergasted, Darcy reacted. "Mother...are my ears deceiving me...have I been handed a 'get out of jail free card'?" She asked in amazement. It was almost three weeks since Leon's birth and to date everyone had pussyfooted around Darcy.

"A little browsing in our local bookstore and stationer's is hardly going to tax you, Darcy. Why don't you get your items, then go into The Carlton Café and have a cuppa. I'll join you when my hairdressing appointment is finished."

Later that morning, Darcy entered the Stationer's shop. After completing her purchase of a new sketch pad and a reporter's notebook, she turned from the cashiers' desk and came face-to-face with someone familiar. There was a whoop of delight from both parties.

"Chrissie!" shrieked Darcy.

"Darcy!" bellowed Chrissie.

The two old friends hugged.

"What are you doing here?" asked Darcy, knowing her friend had moved to Yorkshire, a couple of years ago. Darcy noticed a look of sadness cloud her former schoolfriend's face.

"Long story...but how are you? I heard you lost your baby, Darcy, I'm so sorry for you and Henri." Darcy hated the phrase 'lost your baby'. It implied they'd been careless and mislaid him.

"Our baby, Leon, died during the birth process, Chrissie...we didn't 'lose' him." Fortunately, Chrissie had known Darcy since infant school days and was used to her verbal admonishments.

"I'm on my way into The Carlton for a cuppa – do you fancy one?"

Chrissie checked her watch. "I just need some writing paper and envelopes…I'll catch you up, okay?"

Within ten minutes, the two former friends were sitting at a round table in the local café, catching up.

"So, tell me about married life, Darcy. I haven't seen you since your wedding day," commented Chrissie.

Darcy shook her head in disbelief. Where had the years gone? She gave her friend a potted version of her blissful existence with the heartthrob Henri Dukas. Chrissie had envied her friend's romance and subsequent marriage. They'd tried to keep up a correspondence, but it was soon limited to birthdays and Christmas cards bearing a scribbled 'hope you are well' on the side.

Chrissie asked about the pregnancy and what plans did Darcy have regarding another baby.

Darcy sighed. "Not yet. The doctor says I'm well and young, but a miscarriage and a stillbirth play havoc on your emotions. So, we've been advised to wait for at least another year before trying again."

Chrissie looked preoccupied, then asked. "Will you go back to the Guardian?"

Darcy's eyes lit up. "No, I've got a new project in mind…becoming a freelance reporter. It's only an idea at present, but I would like to write about the injustices of mothers who experience stillbirth. It was horrid, Chrissie. All stiff upper lip… 'you'll get over it'… 'pull yourself together', sort of stuff. It's got to change, and I intend to do my part to make it happen. Meanwhile, I'm going to launch myself into something I began when I fell pregnant and it had to go on hold. Josh, my brother, is going to act as my chauffeur because I can't drive for three more weeks.

Anyway, what about you? Why did you go off to Yorkshire so quickly?"

The waitress brought the tea and scones. Darcy explained her mother would be joining them and the waitress set an extra place at the table.

"My mother went to help her sister nurse our grandmother," Chrissie explained. "Aunt Maggie and my cousin live in a village just outside of York. I got a part-time job as an assistant in a grocery store in the village. Hardly a career choice, but it helped to pay towards our upkeep."

Darcy recalled how Chrissie had fancied becoming a hairdresser when she left school but ended up working in the family business – the local florist, Leveridges.

"So, what happened to your floristry skills…did you abandon them?"

Chrissie cut her scone and began to butter it.

"Only for a while, and that's why we've moved back… well that's not the main reason. I'm working in the florist shop and being an understudy to Aunt Ada, who should really be retired. She's the maiden aunt in the family. She knows her stuff but is quite blunt. I hope when I'm fully trained, I can bring a bit of empathy to the role. Ada makes the choices regarding the funeral flowers and she's so formidable … people dare not cross her, so they just agree," she chuckled. "I'm learning to drive, so I can do deliveries in the van."

Just then, Rachel appeared with her hair neatly curled after a cut, shampoo and set.

"Oh, you look smart, Mother. You remember Chrissie, my old school friend?"

"Of course, I do…how are you Chrissie – are you up here visiting?"

Chrissie greeted Rachel Smallwood, who was surprised to learn Chrissie Leveridge and her mother were living in Malsett again.

"I'm just off to powder my nose, girls...ask the waitress for my tea, Darcy," Rachel added and walked off to the ladies' room. Darcy's reporter's nose had detected a comment Chrissie had made.

"What was the main reason you have returned to Malsett, Chrissie?"

The colour drained from Christine Leveridge's face. She replaced her cup in the saucer, reached out and touched her friend's arm. "I have a secret, Darcy, but I'm ashamed to tell you."

Darcy sensed shockwaves approaching. Chrissie turned to check on Rachel's lingering absence.

"I became entangled with a man. He rented two rooms for me in a house in York. I took a new job in a fashion shop in the city centre."

Darcy's eyes widened. "Oh, Chrissie, were you engaged to this man?"

Chrissie shook her head. "No... I hoped that would happen...but it didn't. He didn't live there, just visited. I was flattered and so relieved to leave my aunt's overcrowded house and secure a job in the city."

Darcy suspected there was more.

"But Darcy... you know him... keep all this to yourself, please."

Darcy nodded, then hearing her mother's approaching footsteps, she asked under her breath, "Who was he, Chrissie?"

CHAPTER 5

It was only a faint whisper, but Darcy heard the name clearly…and it sent a shiver down her spine…Henri's former adversary… Darcy's old boyfriend…Grady Forrester!

Chapter 6

Darcy stepped inside the office of the Malsett Guardian. When she'd last been here, her future centred around the advent of motherhood…but now?

"Well, hello, Madame Dukas, what a lovely surprise to see you!" Audrey Nesbit, the office manager jumped to her feet and enveloped Darcy in a hug. "I was so sorry to hear about your loss, Darcy. How heartbreaking for you and Henri."

Darcy smiled and shrugged. "These things happen, Audrey…it's life. I'm young, so maybe there will be another baby in the future. Now, what's new in Malsett? Any grisly murders and burglaries at gunpoint to report in my absence?"

Audrey chuckled. The two women had worked together for a few years and were relaxed in each other's company. While Audrey's role was purely secretarial, Darcy undertook occasional reporting tasks in the locality. Audrey often sensed the younger woman's desire for 'meatier' assignments.

"No, Darcy, northwest Durham continues to enjoy a trouble-free existence on the crime front… unlike other parts of the country." It was true and thankfully serious crime was a rare event.

"Are you hoping to return to your job? His Nibs hasn't interviewed anyone for your replacement yet."

Darcy shook her head. "No, Audrey, no plans to return, but it doesn't mean I've lost my reporter's nose. In fact, I'm here to ask a favour please." Darcy took a seat and explained.

"Do you recall that case we reported on a few months ago at Cromarty Farm?"

Audrey looked thoughtful then sprang to life. "Er... yes...some miniature paintings went missing – is that the one?"

Darcy nodded. "Any chance of you letting me take a peek at the file to check the address, please?"

Audrey walked over to a large filing cabinet, returning a few minutes later with a buff folder. She handed it to Darcy.

"Here... you did the paperwork, so you know what you are after."

Darcy hastily flicked through the file and noted a few things in her jotter, as Audrey watched on with curiosity. "What are you up to, Darcy?" she enquired.

Darcy tapped the side of her nose. "A hunch, Audrey... nothing more...but if I unearth anything I'll pass it on for The Guardian to report. I'm bored just sitting around and thought I may as well engage in some 'freelance work' until I see what transpires."

Audrey smiled, she was fond of Darcy and admired her enthusiasm.

"Best not mention it to His Nibs – he might not approve - but I bet he'll welcome a story if I uncover one!"

Audrey laughed, His Nibs as they affectionately called the owner of the Malsett Guardian, was a friendly chap who carefully guarded his little empire.

"Your secret mission is safe with me, Darcy. It'll do you good to go sniffing around for a story."

The two women continued to chat and eventually Darcy left the office. She'd enjoyed the camaraderie of the office work at The Guardian but found the work humdrum. She longed to uncover a bigger story and the prospect of being freelance excited her.

***

Chantal and Sam were sitting at the table in the dining room. Sam was filling in the divorce paperwork which had arrived from the Edinburgh solicitor that morning, while Chantal was reading the accompanying letter.

"Well, this sounds promising," Chantal remarked. "Three interested parties have made appointments to view Matthison Hall as soon as the date is finalised. And you thought nobody would be interested. It was only advertised a few days ago."

Sam looked thoughtful. The date for potential viewings was dependent on Evelyn's departure from the house.

"I hope Evelyn keeps to her side of the bargain. She must vacate the premises by mid-October, earlier if possible. Francesca reckons she's viewed a couple of places, but I expect she'll drag it out. Once she leaves, I'll need to go up and check things over."

Chantal stood up and walked to stand behind Sam, placing her arms around his neck.

"Not long now until you are free from Evelyn. Do you intend to keep in contact with Francesca?"

Sam dropped his pen and clasped Chantal's arm. "She's my daughter, Chantal. We may not share blood, but our bond is strong. Until Francesca finds a home of her own it won't be easy, However, there's another problem."

Chantal stiffened and sat down on the chair adjacent to Sam. "Problem?" she repeated.

Sam sighed. "Evelyn wants to keep quiet about Francesca's parentage. Technically, there's no reason why she should know, but I feel uncomfortable about withholding the fact from her."

Chantal pursed her lips. "I agree with you, Sam. I know it won't make any difference to her as she's always regarded you as her father, but she's an adult, I think she needs to know. Tom and Rachel would agree... it's concealing the truth and truth is important."

"It's also ethical, Chantal; as a doctor I look to potential hereditary factors. But Evelyn has put me on the spot and indicated she would not contest the divorce or the move date... if I agreed to refrain from informing Francesca."

Chantal reached out and squeezed Sam's hand.

"Perhaps...in the future...when you are divorced and the house is sold...then you can tell her."

Sam smiled. "I'd like to invite Francesca to visit us here at Meckleridge. I want her to meet you and the twins."

Chantal smiled. "I'd like that, Sam. She sounds a lovely person."

***

"Come on, spill the beans, Josh Smallwood...what's eating you?" Darcy confronted her brother as he put his foot down on the throttle of Henri's sports car.

They were travelling to Corbridge, about twelve miles from Malhaven, to visit the soldier at the heart of the missing miniatures mystery.

Josh shrugged. "Don't know what you mean," he responded.

Darcy threw back her head and chortled.

"Josh, you always put on a Mr Moody face and act all 'huffy' when something is bothering you – so out with it. I can keep secrets …is it a girl? I'm surprised you haven't been 'snapped up' since your return home."

Josh remained quiet. Should he impart Judy Dempster's comment to his sister?

"I'm waiting," Darcy nagged. "I'll keep on asking until you tell me."

Josh snorted. "There's nothing much to tell…but it stays between us, okay?"

He glanced sideways at his older sister.

"Of course, I promise," she remarked.

Two years separated them, but they had always been close. This was the second time in two days she'd been asked to keep a secret.

"Do you remember the nurse who attended to you at the hospital when you lost the baby?" Josh asked.

Darcy swallowed her usual retort to her brother's choice of words. The days after the birth were painful to recall, so she'd drawn an invisible curtain over them.

"Not sure…it's all a bit of a blur and I don't remember much," she responded.

"When I came to visit you that first night I recognised one of the nurses – she was in my year at school."

Darcy looked thoughtful as Josh continued.

"Anyway, she was a bit offhand with me when I spoke to her."

Darcy nodded. "Yes, I remember her now ...very pretty and not given to small talk."

Josh liked the description. "Well, last Sunday afternoon I met her in the park, after dancing with her on Saturday night at the Masons. She's called Judy Dempster."

"Oooo my romantic brother wooing a girl at the local dance," Darcy remarked, snidely.

"Fat chance of that happening. I'm afraid she led me on a sort of runaround at the park when I met her on Sunday – I asked if we could be friends." Josh paused.

"Her reply was bewildering – she said, no.. because her family forbade it! Then she just walked off."

Darcy stared wide eyed. "Why...what have you done?"

"I haven't a clue, but it's bugging me because...I fancy her."

Darcy smiled – her little brother pursuing a girl...when did he grow up?

"Come on, Josh, think. Have you upset her recently or in the past...maybe at school?"

"Nothing, Darc. I've racked my brains, and I know I've done nothing. I've never even asked her out. At school she had a boyfriend, but I'm assuming that's over now. The more I dwell on the subject, the more I like her."

"Then corner her and ask her. It's unfair to make a statement like that and not offer an explanation. Or ask around your mates ...they may know something."

Josh shook his head. "I'm not about to do that - it makes me look guilty of something. I'm trying to forget about it... there's plenty more fish in the sea."

Darcy pondered. Chrissie's situation was so sad – how had she become entangled with Grady Forrester? She'd had a crush on him at school she remembered, but the last she heard about Grady was when he went off to university in York. Oh gosh, she thought…she must have met up with him when she moved to live near York with her mother. And now here was Josh wanting to befriend a girl who appeared 'off limits' …problems …problems…problems.

Darcy looked at the road sign. "That way," she indicated, and Josh manoeuvred the red sports car into a country lane.

***

Cromarty Farm lay in a basin beside the River Tyne, located south of Corbridge. It was attached to a hamlet called Hywell. The road was narrow and rugged, and the little car bounced around.

"This could kill the suspension…Henri won't like it."

Darcy paid no heed. Cars served a purpose – they transported you from A to B. The mechanics were alien to her.

"What's the suspension?" she asked.

Having trained as a mechanic, Josh launched into an explanation, only to be shouted down by his impatient sister.

"Put a sock in it, Josh. I don't understand, so spare me the detail."

Josh brought the car to a halt at the side of a stone-built house. "This is it …Hywell House and over the road is Cromarty Farm where the chest was hidden in a barn," Darcy remarked.

It was a cold call, and Darcy knew from experience that unless it was a straightforward reporting task, like a garden party, a reporter was best served with an unexpected arrival.

"You stay here, if I haven't returned in half an hour – come and find me," she called as she alighted from the car.

"But what if…?" Josh's words flew into the breeze as his sister opened a little white picket gate leading to the front entrance of the large house.

A metal knocker provided a distinct call to the occupants. Josh watched on as an older lady opened the door.

"Is Colonel Simpson at home please?" Darcy enquired.

The question was answered with an audible grump, as the woman turned and spoke into the void of the dark panelled stairway. Darcy tapped her foot and reached into her shoulder bag for her notebook and pencil. An approaching whistle descended the stairs.

"Who's asking?"

The question came from the lips of a man in his late forties. Before Darcy could answer a little dog sprang through the door at the far end of the passageway and bounded along towards the front door.

"Catch her," called the lady. "She's desperate to be outside but she's got pups to look after."

Darcy bent down to apprehend the small, brown and white long-haired dog.

"Oh, she's adorable…what's her name?" she asked, as the little dog danced around, enjoying the attention.

"Betsey," replied the woman. "Mother to four little pups, soon to be on their way to a new home…well, at least three of them are off to new homes."

She bent down, picked up the dog and retreated into the kitchen as the whistling man arrived at the front door.

Darcy looked up. She remembered Colonel Simpson. She'd interviewed him on a cold January day, before she knew she was pregnant.

"May I help you?" asked the man. His dark brylcreemed hair was plastered to his head. "I know you, don't I? I never forget a pretty face. You're that newspaper girl, aren't you?"

Darcy smiled sweetly. "Yes, Colonel Simpson, Darcy Dukas, I'm pleased you remember me."

"Drop the Colonel, luvvie, my army days are past...just call me Brian."

"Hello Brian, I was wondering if there had been any developments regarding the missing miniatures. They caused some curiosity amongst our readers, and we do like to keep our readership informed."

It was basically true – there had been interest, people claiming to have seen them and wondering if a reward was being offered, but at the time Brian was happy to let things go.

"Well, as I said at the time I think they were pinched and sold on, but I was newly home from my army career and couldn't be bothered to have the police poking around, so I just left it."

He ran his hand across his jaw thoughtfully. "But on reflection, now I'm settled, maybe you could offer a reward. I would like them returned for sentimental reasons – they remind me of my aunt."

Darcy lifted her notepad.

"Come into the parlour and I'll think what to say," he invited.

Brian led the way into the parlour. It smelt musty. Darcy doubted if anyone had graced it with their presence since

Brian's aunt left this earth. She took a seat on the edge of a dark green chaise, as Brian stood with his back to the stark, cold looking fireplace. Flicking open a page Darcy began to write.

"Now shall we do an article saying you are appealing for information regarding the whereabouts of these missing miniatures...a treasured family heirloom?"

She opened her bag and retrieved the sketch of the items she'd made back in January.

"Eeh, lass, that's so life-like...you're a fair old artist. I just described them to you, didn't I?"

Darcy felt herself blushing but remained business like.

"We would print the sketch, give a brief background, saying how the items were mislaid during the war – that way we don't expect any police involvement. Then offer the reward. We would refrain from mentioning your name, asking people to contact the newspaper office." Darcy fleshed out a rough draft of the article, then handed it to Brian for his approval.

"If you could just sign at the bottom, Brian, that confirms what we have agreed," she added, knowing she was flying by the seat of her pants, as no agreement had been sought from the newspaper...but she was freelance now – she could make up her own rules!

Brian read the account, signed and dated the draft.

"I can't be sure when or even if my boss will decide to print this, but we will remain hopeful, Brian, and your miniatures may well be returned anonymously" Where did she get her nerve? Darcy asked herself.

"Do you have any suspicions who might have known about the chest and its hiding place?" Darcy asked as she returned the sketches and pad to her shoulder bag and stood up.

"Aye, lass, I do …but there's no proof. If they read the article, they may be conscientious and return them for the reward money."

Brian was offering a £5 reward which Darcy thought was attractive. She walked over to the door and Brian followed.

The kitchen door opened, and the little dog appeared again, keen to receive more adoration from the visitor.

"Betsey, kitchen," commanded Colonel Simpson severely, in his stern army voice. But Darcy's attention was too inviting for Betsey to ignore.

"Oh, she's a darling," Darcy exclaimed, bending to pat the fussing dog.

"Do you know anyone who wants a Cavalier pup?" Brian asked.

"Why?" asked Darcy, in surprise.

"Well, there were four pups in the litter, three are spoken for and I can't be faffed with advertising one pup. The others are dogs and are leaving this week. I don't want to be left with one bitch."

Darcy sprang to attention.

"Can I see the puppy please?" she asked.

Brian's domineering voice boomed down the passageway. "Iris, bring that bitch puppy out here, please."

Betsey scampered along the hallway as if sensing the impending threat to her offspring.

Iris Simpson appeared carrying a miniature replica of silky delight. Darcy's eyes enlarged. She dropped her bag, opening her arms to envelop the gorgeous three-month-old puppy.

CHAPTER 6

"Oh, Mr Simpson, she's beautiful, she looks like a thoroughbred...I'll take her ...how much do you want for her?" Darcy asked in anticipation.

"No charge, Miss – as I say, you'll be doing me a favour. She is a thoroughbred, but she was the smallest in the litter. Iris, fetch a blanket," he instructed to the lady, whom Darcy assumed was his sister, judging by the shape of their noses.

"Have you had dogs before, Miss?" he asked, as the puppy snuggled contentedly into Darcy's arms.

"Always, until a couple of years ago when our Golden Retriever died."

"This is a King Charles Cavalier Spaniel...a Blenheim. Her name will be your choice."

Iris returned with a blanket, a toy and a bag of tiny meat scratchings.

"She's just been weaned, so is ready for a new home." Brian picked up Darcy's bag and handing it to her, opened the door.

"Got a posh car, I see, for a reporter." He nodded towards the car, where Josh was patiently waiting.

Darcy refrained from replying to the comment.

"Well, Mr Simpson, thank you for your time and for the gift of the puppy. I'll be in touch if we decide to run the article. Good day."

Darcy walked across to the car. Josh jumped out to open the door for Darcy.

"What may I ask is THAT?" he enquired briskly, eyeing the bundle of fur.

"This, Josh, is Lady, my new puppy."

Josh started the car and revved the engine, noting the occupant of the house watching him from the doorway.

"Are you mad? You came here to find out about missing miniature paintings and you've ended up buying a miniature pooch instead."

"Josh, don't offend Lady please, she's not a pooch …she's a Cavalier King Charles spaniel and she didn't cost me a penny, as she was the last of the litter."

Josh raised his eyebrows. "And the missing miniatures?" he asked expectantly.

"Well, The Malsett Guardian has a new story to publish offering a reward… but not until I've had a try at tracking them down myself!"

Josh looked at his sister and shook his head. Just what was Darcy up to now?

Chapter 7

ONE WEEK LATER

"That sounds like a bag of old bones," Henri declared, as Josh brought his newly acquired purchase to a standstill in the rear yard of Meckleridge House. Henri stood shaking his head with a look of amazement on his face, as Josh jumped out of the driving seat of his pride and joy…an old Ford 8 motor car.

"It might sound a bit grim, Henri…but the potential is great!" Josh remarked, opening the bonnet for Henri to survey.

"It'll need quite a bit of attention – engine, brakes, steering and ultimately bodywork. It's going to be a long-term project, but I'm in no hurry to finish it." Josh grinned.

Henri perused the inner workings of the old jalopy.

"Rather you than me," he chuckled.

"Well, we don't all have money to spend on a swanky sports car, Henri, so £10 paid for this *bag of old bones* will do me nicely."

The two brothers-in-law laughed.

"Yes, but you don't have a wife with expensive tastes to please," Henri replied. "Could you see Darcy riding around in that?"

Josh was silent then a slow smile spread across his face. "I'm going to call her Beryl, and just you wait… in a few months even Darcy will want to take a spin in her."

"Oh, good grief, what have you wasted your money on, Josh, my boy!" exclaimed Tom, emerging from the back door of the house. "A Ford 8," he muttered, walking around the rusty green vehicle.

"Brakes, my lad – the first thing to tackle. These old girls were notorious for their poor brakes."

Josh raised his eyebrows.

"Yes, Dad, I know, but as I've just been saying to Henri, I'm in no hurry. I'll park it in the bottom shed, then I can leave all my nuts and bolts around and not be in anyone's way."

Tom nodded.

Fortunately, Meckleridge House boasted several old outhouses and garages. The two closest to the main building were used to house Tom and Henri's cars. Sam's car rarely saw the inside of a garage. A few minutes' walk down a slope led to a large outhouse, big enough to take three cars. This was where Beryl would call her home, while the restoration process was taking place.

Squeals of delight caused the men to look up as Darcy and the twins rounded the corner of the house. Con and Hope were both holding the leash of the excitable puppy who was bounding towards the male group, tugging the young children in the process.

"Uncle Joshy – we've just taken Lady for a walk."

Darcy stood with her hands on her hips. "What is THAT?" she declared.

Josh turned towards his sister and smirked.

"That… my dear sister, is 'Beryl' and don't go offending her by calling her a THAT!" remarked Josh, snidely, in retaliation – reminiscent of his sister's comment when she showed Josh the new puppy a few days ago.

Darcy began to laugh.

"Really? Oh, Josh…how will you ever attract the female population of Malsett driving around in that, sorry, I mean, Beryl."

Henri walked over and placed his arm lovingly around his young wife's shoulder, giving her a peck on the cheek.

"Careful, you two," shouted Darcy, as Tom opened the car door for the twins to climb in.

"Stop it, Hope," rebuked Josh, as the little girl poked her finger into a hole in the leatherwork on the back bench seat. Hope proceeded to bury her head in her hands, sensitive to her cousin's reprimand. Josh reached over to comfort the tearful girl.

"Joshy is going to make this car look shiny and new – just like your daddy's."

Hope nodded and sucked her thumb, just as Darcy tapped her brother on the shoulder.

"Are you free tomorrow?" she enquired.

Josh pulled a face. "Not really…why? I wanted to get started on Beryl."

Darcy grimaced. "She can wait…I want you to drive me into Newcastle. I've listed six antique shops I want to visit – so an early start – okay?"

Josh sighed. Drat – he'd been hoping to spend the day on his car. He'd already spent an afternoon chauffeuring his sister around Hexham, as she scoured antique shops for these miniatures and now, she wanted to continue her search in Newcastle. But he'd made a promise, so reluctantly agreed.

***

"Please, Mother, it's just for today. Normally, I intend taking Lady with me, but she's not properly trained yet."

Rachel sighed. As she'd anticipated, training the little puppy would end up being her job...Darcy did not possess the patience.

When Darcy had arrived home with the unexpected canine bundle, now known as Lady, Rachel was cautious. "There's a good reason why we refrained from having another dog after Jess died, Darcy. Babies and dogs aren't the best combination. We all love having a dog, but we thought it sensible to wait until the twins were older and then you fell pregnant..." As soon as the words fell from Rachel's lips – she regretted them. "Never mind, the deed is done, but a puppy is a responsibility – you'll need to spend time training her."

Of course, Darcy was full of good intentions, but Rachel knew her daughter and now one week later...Rachel was being charged with 'puppy minding' while Darcy and Josh went off on another escapade.

Rachel scooped the puppy into her arms as Josh revved the car engine and Darcy sat in the passenger seat.

"Where are they off to?" asked a voice from behind. Rachel turned to see her sister descending the stairs, closely followed by the twins.

CHAPTER 7

"Oh, another one of Darcy's journalism expeditions. And guess who is left holding the puppy!" Lady rushed towards the children, as Rachel put her down on the mat. Already the twins and the puppy were good friends.

"Both the dog and the journalism thing will help to take Darcy's mind off the stillbirth, Rachel. Darcy was never going to sit around for long. It's been four weeks, so only two more to go and then she can drive herself around. Where did you say they were going?"

"Off to Newcastle apparently to scour some antique shops. Darcy is hoping to find some miniature paintings which went missing during the war. They belonged to the guy who gave her the puppy." Rachel looked at her sister, dressed in her uniform.

"I completely forgot you were working this morning – it must have slipped my mind – what with the new puppy and news of our French visitor coming tomorrow."

Chantal looked at her sister, dressed pristinely, as always. "I'm sorry, Rachel, we all seem to rely on you so much at present. Did you say a French visitor?"

Rachel walked towards the back lounge. "Yes, a telephone call this morning from Jonty's friend, Marcel – do you remember Jonty mentioning him when he was here in the summer? He's coming to live and work in Durham."

"No, I don't remember, but it will be good to speak my native tongue again. Henri and I rarely speak in French," she chuckled. "What's his age?"

"I'm guessing mid-twenties, if Jonty befriended him at university. I understand they are still quite friendly." Rachel sat down heavily in the fireside chair, as the twins patted the puppy.

Chantal watched…her sister looked unusually weary today. "Rachel, you do too much. I feel so guilty leaving the twins on a Saturday."

"Chantal, get yourself off to work. Two young children, a new puppy and a French visitor – surely, I can manage that…I used to run a hotel before the war, so how hard can this be in comparison?" Chantal gave a hollow smile.

"You were a lot younger in those days, Rachel."

Chantal knew how capable and fastidious Rachel was, but two young children and a puppy could be demanding for her fifty-year old sister. She did feel guilty – perhaps she should give up her midwifery duties? But Rachel had insisted Chantal should return to work two years ago, saying Meckleridge House did not need two full-time women to run the extended family home.

"I'll enjoy being an aunt," she'd declared…but secretly Chantal was concerned her sister was doing too much. She hoped when Sam's family home sold, they could buy their own house, then she would leave her job and care for Sam and the children, giving Rachel a quieter life.

"What time is this French visitor arriving tomorrow?" she asked, checking her watch.

"Lunchtime. Tom gave him directions and suggested he arrived about half past twelve, which should coincide with our return from church."

Chantal bent to kiss her offspring goodbye. "Be good for Auntie Ray, you two, and don't overexcite the puppy. She's just a baby and needs lots of sleep."

Chantal left the house to walk into the town. Her visits were all nearby today.

CHAPTER 7

The arrival of the French guest in northeast England had been forgotten until his phone call that morning. Rachel was feeling tired today and could nicely have done without the dog and the twins to oversee. But as was her way, she got up and busied herself, making some tea. Tom would be in from the greenhouses soon for his morning cuppa and would hopefully take the twins and the dog for a walk, allowing her time to do some baking.

Tom and Henri's horticultural business had become a fast-growing project. It was five years since they'd developed a new breed of pink rose, which they'd named 'Darcy Rose', in honour of Darcy. The early trickle of orders was now a steady flow. Recently, Tom had negotiated contracts with five stockists from other parts of the country.

Rachel decided to begin making a chocolate cake to keep the twins occupied and began assembling the ingredients.

"Con, Hope, wash your hands please. We have a French man coming to have lunch with us tomorrow and I thought we'd make a lovely cake. When Uncle Tom comes in for his elevenses you can ask him to take the dog for a walk." The twins loved baking and were soon helping their aunt with the preparations.

French guests were normal at Meckleridge House. Tom's sister Peg had moved to France as a young woman, married the handsome Pierre Thibault and raised two children – Jonty and Sylvie. Apart from the war years, the French family visited Malhaven every year. Last summer Jonty told them about his friend Marcel Duval, who was coming to live and work in Durham city in the autumn.

"I hope he can come to visit you at Malhaven. He's going to be residing with his spinster aunt until he establishes his new business and can afford to rent his own place. It will be good for him to have young company by befriending my cousins and his fellow countryman, Henri. He's a very friendly chap – we met at university," he'd remarked.

Rachel supervised the weighing of sugar, butter, flour and cocoa. Rationing of some ingredients was still in force and they needed to be careful, avoiding waste. Whistling was soon detected outside.

"Uncle Tom," announced Hope, dusting her hands and clambering down from the kitchen chair. "Now we can go for a walk."

"Not until Uncle Tom has finished his drink," Rachel protested, as Tom entered the kitchen.

"We are baking a chocolate cake for Mr Frenchman to eat," Con announced.

"He's a French man not Mr Frenchman," corrected Hope.

Con failed to see the difference.

"I hope he likes chocolate cake," remarked Tom, washing his grubby hands.

"Everybody likes chocolate cake," decided Hope, licking her fingers.

"Wash your hands, little miss," Tom remarked and lifted the young girl over to the sink.

***

"Last one to try," commented Darcy, dejectedly. A full morning touring antique shops in the city of Newcastle had proved useless. Darcy had showed her sketches of the miniatures she was trying to locate, to the proprietors of the various establishments. She used some 'sob story' about them being unintentionally sold during the war, and how her dear uncle wanted to find them again.

"You should be on the stage," Josh remarked after hearing her performance for the sixth time that morning.

Returning to the car she sighed with resignation.

"What now?" asked Josh.

Darcy shrugged. Her assignment had not produced the expected results.

"Plan 'B'. I'll go to see His Nibs at The Guardian next week and ask him to consider running my article with the sketches…on the understanding that if they are found, I will receive some recompense for highlighting the story. At least that way, it shows him I'm serious about my 'freelance' work and it may make him sympathetic towards me in the future."

Josh sensed his sister's disappointment, but at least it would free up his time to begin working on 'Beryl'.

"Have you seen your pretty nurse again?" Darcy enquired, as they travelled home.

"She's not my nurse, Darcy…but she is pretty. No, I doubt if I will see her. It felt like a dead end."

Darcy pulled a face. "*Faint heart never won fair lady*, Josh…don't let obstacles get in your way. If you want to befriend her, then look for a way to achieve your goal. Be determined."

Josh nodded. He wanted to get to the bottom of this mystery, but more than that… he wanted to get to know Judy Dempster. He'd never felt like this about a girl before… it was different.

Although frustrating, Darcy had found the adventure enjoyable, and she had re-kindled her desire to pursue investigative journalism. She would relish writing up the article to accompany the sketches. At the end of the day, without this hare-brained notion, she wouldn't have turned up at Brian Simpson's house and been offered the delightful little puppy who was filling the maternal longing in her being.

***

A delicious aroma of home baking greeted the siblings as they entered the kitchen on their return.

"Oh, Mother, what delights are awaiting us for tea?" murmured Darcy, bending down to lift the sleeping puppy from her basket in the corner. Lady yawned as Darcy snuggled her face into her silky coat.

"Bread and butter pudding," announced Rachel.

"We put *ants* in it, declared Hope, sitting at the kitchen table.

Josh burst out laughing. "I'm not too happy about that, Hope. I think you mean *curr ants*...is that the word?" he corrected his young cousin, spying a few stray black currants about to be squashed into Hope's pretend pastry pie.

Hope was in her element helping Aunt Ray, as she called Rachel, with her pastry scraps.

"Where's Con?" asked Josh.

"With Tom, in the greenhouse," replied his mother. "He's more at home with soil than flour," she grinned, wiping her hands on her frilly pinny. Even up to her eyes in domesticity, Rachel Smallwood retained her pristine appearance.

"Any success?" Rachel asked, as Josh walked into the pantry in search of food.

Darcy shook her head, and the puppy licked her hand. "No, it was as I suspected. It's too long since the cameos went missing...but at least I tried. So, now I'll write a report and include my sketches. If The Guardian will print my account – somebody, somewhere might know where they ended up. If they do, I hope I receive some monetary gain for the part I played."

Voices approached and the back door opened. Darcy let Lady scamper off to greet the new arrivals. Henri entered, followed by Tom giving Con a piggyback.

Ma chérie," declared Henri, sweeping Darcy into his arms for a big hug.

Josh emerged from the pantry, holding a teacake. "Why the food preparations, Mother? Are we having guests?"

Rachel coughed loudly. "You were all so busy this morning, I forgot to mention this news. We are having a French guest for Sunday lunch tomorrow."

Josh smirked. "I prefer your lamb dinner, Mother," he giggled, and was rewarded with one of his mother's stern faces.

"Less of your frivolity, young man," she admonished.

Darcy sniggered. "Oh, yes...is this Jonty's friend from university?"

"That's right. He's called Marcel Duval. He lives in Calais in France but is moving to live with his aunt in Durham. He arrived a few days ago and telephoned to ask if he could visit us sometime. Your father invited him for lunch tomorrow, so he could meet all the family."

Tom took up the story.

"Please make him welcome. Jonty expects you youngsters to show him some Meckleridge hospitality. He's a stranger to the area, so please be friendly. He should feel at home with two French speakers around the place!" He looked pointedly at Henri and Darcy.

"Why is he moving to Durham?" asked Darcy.

"Something to do with setting up a new business apparently." replied Tom. "I'm not sure of the details, but I got the impression he's a private investigator."

Darcy's face lit up. "Wow…I wonder if he needs an assistant?" she exclaimed excitedly.

Henri and Rachel stared at her.

Chapter 8

Darcy descended the stairs and walked into the conservatory. Her eyes scanned the room, searching for her husband.

"Where's Henri?" she asked, to no one in particular.

"Your lounge, I think," responded Sam, looking up from reading the newspaper.

It was a typical evening at Meckleridge House. The large conservatory, heated by a roaring log fire, was the usual resting place for the extended family after supper – but each family group possessed their own private lounge space.

In its former life, Meckleridge House Hotel provided, in addition to the conservatory, a main lounge, a spacious dining room, a rear lounge and a former library. The latter had been redesigned to become a tasteful lounge for Henri and Darcy's use.

Sam, Chantal and the twins used the main lounge; and Tom, Rachel and Josh used the conservatory, or the rear lounge, situated off the kitchen.

Darcy skipped across to the small former library, Lady at her heels. It was a cosy room, decorated in a light patterned wallpaper. A large Axminster carpet sat on the oak parquet flooring. A small fireplace housed a coal fire, sending a mesmerising glow into the room. A two-seater settee and one armchair were upholstered in floral patterned loose covers. A bookcase, small writing bureau and two small, round, mahogany lamp tables with Queen Anne legs and lamps with rose-coloured shades, completed the furnishings. The only window in the room was tall and thin, the drapes matching the loose covers.

"What's up?" Darcy enquired, as she landed heavily in the space beside Henri on the settee. A painful expression spread across his face. Her eyes sensed his pain before he could verbalise his response.

"Oh, dear, I shouldn't ask, should I? Is it bad?" She reached over and clasped her husband's hand.

"It's bearable," he whispered.

Henri Dukas suffered from a debilitating condition known as *osteonecrosis*. It was caused by a lack of blood supply to his hip joint. He'd been diagnosed two years before he and Darcy married. For a time, it was a barrier, causing Henri to doubt the wisdom of inflicting his unknown physical limitations on an active, outgoing young woman like Darcy. But love prevailed and the young couple cherished a strong hope that one day a medical intervention would be available, to relieve his pain and improve his hip function.

His condition was managed by regular physiotherapy and daily pain relief. Over the years, Henri had learned to limit weight bearing on his joint, but occasionally a fall resulted in a period of bed rest.

Darcy sat gazing into the firelight as the puppy snuggled on her lap. The pink lamps provided a cosy glow and added to the peaceful ambience of the room.

"I just wanted some time…alone…with you, ma chérie," Henri said adoringly, placing his arm around her.

She laid her head against his broad shoulder. Each family unit was under no obligation to meet collectively. Rachel and Tom insisted "we may all live under the same roof, but we are distinct family units".

The only stipulation was if one family group were to be absent from supper, Rachel or Tom were to be informed after breakfast. It rarely happened and everyone was happy to pay their way in the budgeting and household tasks. The system worked well – no doubt a heritage from the hotel days.

Henri stroked Darcy's hand.

"You are so beautiful, I love you so much, Darcy. I can't believe you want to spend your life with me. You are my 'raison d'être' – I couldn't live without you…but…" Henri's voice caught in his throat.

Darcy lifted her head and Henri bent forward to express his devotion in a long, lingering, passionate kiss.

It was Darcy who broke the spell. "I heard a 'but', Henri?"

He swallowed and lay his head back against the settee, shifting his seating position with a groan of discomfort.

"I want you to make me a promise, ma petite fille," he announced. "Promise me you will pursue your dream, to become a freelance journalist. The passing of our little one… was so heartbreaking…but who knows…perhaps it was for the better? What use would I be as a father?"

Darcy shook her head and placed her hands over her ears.

"I refuse to listen, Henri Dukas – you promised me before we were married you would not engage in 'pity parties' over your ailment – so don't go breaking that promise. You will be a perfect father – when the right time comes…it's just going to be delayed, that's all. Sam is convinced the possibility of surgery for your condition is not too far distant …we will continue to hope and trust and maybe our next baby will have a fit, able daddy."

Darcy flung her arms around Henri, and they hugged tightly.

"But Darcy, I meant what I said. You must begin your career – look for opportunities and seek them out. I'm sure Josh will help you."

Darcy looked thoughtful. "I won't need Josh when I can drive myself around again. But I'm grateful for your support…we'll see what turns up."

Henri reached out and enveloped Darcy in a loving embrace.

***

"Busy, busy," instructed Darcy, hoping the puppy would perform. She was idling along the grass verge, opposite the house, after returning from church, supposedly exercising the puppy. At least training the little dog gave her an opportunity to escape her mother's lunch preparations. Yet everything was underway for Sunday lunch…their guest should arrive soon.

A crunching noise on the driveway drew Darcy's attention…what on earth was that? Darcy watched as a strange grey vehicle chugged up the driveway. It was a car… yes… but it looked primitive and well, ugly. It was a strange shape – very rounded, unlike anything she'd seen before, and it… rattled.

CHAPTER 8

As the car halted, Darcy's attention was drawn to the figure emerging from what she could only describe as a *tin can on wheels.* Its occupant was tall, well-built and extremely handsome. He was dressed smartly in beige slacks, brown jacket and white open necked shirt.

The new arrival was stunning; Darcy jumped to attention and called out. "Bonjour, Monsieur!"

There was little doubt this dark haired, attractive specimen of masculinity was their expected French guest. She tugged on Lady's leash and approached the car.

"Madame Dukas, I assume. Your cousin, Jonty, described your beauty *par excellence."* As he spoke, his bright eyes surveyed Darcy's face.

"It is a pleasure to meet you 'in the flesh'. Jonty has often talked of your beauty and brains, and I admit I have been looking forward to making your acquaintance."

Darcy felt herself blushing as he reached out and lifted Darcy's free hand, bringing it to his lips and kissing it. Lady skittered at his feet.

"*Enchante, madame,* I am Marcel Duval," he added, then bending down patted the excited little spaniel.

"*Hello, bebe chien, comment tu t'appelles?*"

"This is our new puppy, Lady," Darcy responded.

The front door opened, and Darcy's parents stepped outside, and introductions and greetings ensued.

Within minutes, Marcel had been given a welcome 'Meckleridge style'.

Soon Sunday lunch was underway and being enjoyed by all. Marcel Duval felt quite at home amongst two native, French citizens – Henri and Chantal.

"How is Jonty?" asked Josh, immediately warming to the French visitor.

"He is well and sends his love. He's hoping to visit next summer. He has praised you all. He talks frequently about his English family. I am excited to get to know each of you."

"I'm surprised he hasn't found himself a bride yet." Josh smirked, knowing his cousin possessed a 'roving eye'.

"No, he's still a free man and dare I say it 'enjoying himself'!" Marcel grinned.

"Do you have a special woman, Marcel?" asked Darcy in her blunt, curious way.

"Darcy!" gasped her mother in rebuke.

Marcel was momentarily stunned by Darcy's query.

"Non, Madame…I am single. I enjoy female companionship, but my work is not conducive to family life."

Darcy thought he looked sad at the thought.

"Why have you decided to move to Durham, Marcel?" enquired Henri.

The French guest looked thoughtful.

"Well, it is my birthplace. I was born in Durham and lived there as a young child. My mother is English. She and my aunt travelled to France years before my birth. My aunt was a lady's companion, like your sister, Tom."

Tom smiled. Jonty's mother Peg had worked in France before marrying.

"My parents met when my father was a young medical student. His family disapproved of their proposed marriage, so my mother returned to her family home, which was why I was born in northeast England. They were married two years before the war, when he became the doctor in a little village near to Calais. I have lived there ever since and have dual nationality. But I am keen to return to Durham and find work." Marcel put a spoonful of food in his mouth.

"We have something in common, Marcel," commented Henri, "I also moved to northeast England from France, initially to work…but then I met my dear wife and settled here. I hope things work out for you."

"What do you do for a living, Marcel?" asked Chantal, curious to know the reason behind his return to northeast England. Marcel took a drink of his water, then using his napkin, wiped his mouth, before replying.

"I am a private investigator."

Darcy's ears pricked up. "What do you investigate?" she asked with curiosity.

Marcel smiled at Darcy. "Anything I can undertake, without the situation requiring wider resources, as I work on my own."

"Oh, are you a Sherlock Holmes type of detective?"

Marcel swallowed a mouthful of food. "In a way…yes, I guess that's a good description…although I have yet to find my 'Watson'." He chuckled and Darcy lifted her eyebrows.

"I think we need to have further discussion, Monsieur Duval. I am also an investigator, from a journalistic viewpoint."

Marcel stared wide-eyed at Darcy.

"Really…that's most intriguing. Yes, we must share notes sometime."

A silence fell over the assembled group. A seed had been sown…two like-minded people…Marcel Duval and Darcy Dukas.

In the distance Rachel thought she heard a cockerel crowing…

"Let Marcel eat his lunch, everyone," said Tom.

***

After lunch Josh, Darcy and Henri suggested showing Marcel around the Meckleridge estate, while the others attended to the dishes. Sam and the twins took the dog for a walk.

"Jonty has told me about the summer holidays he spent here in these grounds – camping and playing games. It is just as he described it. I have little memory of England. My aunt returned to live in Durham last year, and I saw an opportunity to come back. My work is flexible. I have been involved in divorce cases which pay well... but I long for more exciting work."

Henri looked at Darcy. "You need to talk to my wife... she also longs for challenging assignments."

Josh was the first to spot Marcel's car.

"Wow, Marcel ...a Citroën 2 CV. How fascinating. Often referred to as the 'deux chevaux' ...two horses...am I correct?" As he was commenting, he walked around the visitor's car.

"Yes, also known as *an umbrella on wheels*. Whatever the name, it's a great little car and economical. It's unobtrusive, which is necessary in my line of work," replied Marcel.

Darcy looked on and shook her head. "I don't think you'll manage to disguise yourself around Durham, driving that car, Marcel...it kind of stands out...it's unusual. I haven't seen one before."

Marcel smiled broadly. "Mimi and I are good pals. We've had all sorts of adventures together. She's here with me for the foreseeable future."

Darcy began to laugh.

"Oh, you two should get on well together," she nodded towards her brother. "That chump over there has just acquired an old jalopy and named her 'Beryl'. What is it with men and cars and giving them names?"

Marcel looked interested. "You have a car called 'Beryl'?" he asked.

Josh smirked as his sister chortled. "I certainly do, Marcel. Would you like to see her?"

"My cue for an exit. Henri ...are you coming with me, or joining the boys and their cars?" asked Darcy.

"Silly question, ma chérie," Henri replied, winking at his wife.

Josh and Marcel headed for the outhouse where Josh kept his car.

***

As Darcy and Henri returned to the house, someone was standing on the doorstep, ringing the bell.

"Chrissie!" yelled Darcy, enveloping her friend in a big hug. "It's great to see you. Henri, you remember Chrissie, my old school friend, she's been living in Yorkshire but has recently returned to Malsett."

"Of course, I remember," remarked Henri, kissing Chrissie on both cheeks.

Darcy led the way into their lounge.

"I'll make you girls a cup of tea so you can have a chat. Then perhaps I will join the car appreciation party." He smiled, as Chrissie looked on puzzled.

"Don't ask," commented Darcy.

Chrissie looked around the delightful lounge. "This used to be the library, as I recall," she said.

Darcy nodded. "Yes, my parents kindly converted it into a private lounge for Henri and I."

"It's tasteful," remarked Chrissie.

"I see your handsome husband has retained his particular French charm," she commented, recalling his greeting.

Darcy grinned. Chrissie always admired Henri and his 'very French ways'.

"Oh, he's such a dear, Chrissie. We are so happy to have found each other. He dotes on me…and well… I dote on him also. I think this 'baby thing' has drawn us closer together."

There was a squeak at the door and Darcy jumped up to open it…allowing Lady to enter.

"Darcy…who's this…where's Jess?"

"Ah, Jess was old, Chrissie. She died a while ago." Lady gave Chrissie a sniffy, waggy welcome. "Meet my new puppy, Lady. I've only had her a week, but already she has stolen a piece of my heart."

She added, "I'm so pleased you've come to visit, Chrissie. We mustn't lose contact again. It was very remiss of me not to keep in touch, but now we have reconnected, we must make a point of meeting regularly." Darcy bent down to pick up the puppy, offering her to Chrissie.

"Here, have a cuddle and get acquainted," she said.

Henri arrived with Chantal carrying a tray of tea and two pieces of chocolate cake. After a brief conversation, Chantal and Henri left the two old friends.

"Now, Chrissie, it's private in here. Do you feel like telling me about the last two years? I won't take offence if you don't want to, mind. But I was so concerned to hear you've had a bad experience."

Chrissie looked thoughtful.

She's changed, thought Darcy. Her once shoulder length, mousey hair, was now short and permed…tidy, but in an aging way. Her former stylish clothes had been replaced with a frumpy twinset and pleated skirt and flat laced shoes. Chrissie was not the attractive, fashionable young woman who'd attended Darcy and Henri's wedding two and a half years earlier.

Yet, one thing had not changed…Chrissie's pretty face. Her cute little nose, long lashes and sparkly white teeth retained the 'natural beauty' she'd always possessed.

Chrissie drank her tea and stroked the dog.

"He used me, Darcy. I was a fool. I'd always liked him. I'm sure you can recall the days I used to drool over him on the bicycle outings."

Yes, Darcy remembered.

"You liked him long before I did, as I recall." Flashbacks pervaded Darcy's mind of the handsome Grady Forrester befriending her on a cycling trip when Chrissie was absent.

"I was gutted when he started making a beeline for you, Darcy. But then I caught the attention of Alisdair Swan, and he was equally good looking. So, somehow, I accepted Grady was meant to be with you. It meant our friendship was unaffected."

Finishing her tea, she replaced her cup on the tray as Lady waddled off to take up residence on her mistress's knee.

"Where did you meet Grady…in Yorkshire…I mean?"

Chrissie lay her head against the back of the settee and sighed.

"I was at a dance in a village outside of York with my cousin Anabelle. I couldn't believe it was him. I'd forgotten he was at university in York. He was all gushing and treated me like a long-lost friend. I thought he'd be engaged or at least in a steady relationship, but he wasn't…at least that is what he wanted me to believe."

Darcy turned her head on the side – this sounded like the Grady she knew…suspicious.

"Did you start courting him?"

Chrissie nodded. "I was infatuated by him. I was desperate to have some freedom. My aunt's little house was so overcrowded with us all living there. So, when he offered to rent me two rooms in the city centre… I jumped at the chance."

Darcy felt she could see where all this was leading.

"I was a 'good girl' for quite some time, Darcy. He was very attentive. Took me out for rides in his car, treated me like a lady…cherished me. I was so elated…but stupid. Mother was furious when she found out he was paying the rent. 'You're a kept woman,' she said… 'it will end in tears,' and it did."

"But when did it turn serious?" Darcy asked.

"When he went to work in London, after finishing university. He would get the train to York on a Friday night and stay until Sunday…that's when it turned serious. I guess he finally wanted his payment.

"Soon, he would only turn up on a Saturday or a Sunday, then skipped some weekends and finally, he didn't show at all." Tears trickled down Chrissie's face. The hurt and humiliation were obvious.

"Eventually, he told me he couldn't afford the rent because he was getting engaged to a girl he'd met at university. I was given a month's notice. It was painful, Darcy. I liked him…very much. But looking back I was just being used. Thankfully, there were no consequences." Chrissie's face was etched with remorse. "I don't know if I will ever be able to trust a man again."

"So, is this recent?"

Chrissie shook her head.

"No, my cousin Annabelle came to the rescue. We decided to share a room in a house in York, so I didn't go back to my aunt's. But after Grandma died, my mother decided to come back here, and I was given the chance to train in the family business. So, here I am …new job… the past is behind me. I only wish I could find a dishy Frenchman like yours, to fall in love with," she giggled.

The door opened and Henri walked in.

"Excuse me, ladies" announced Henri, "Marcel is about to leave… are you coming to wave him goodbye?"

Darcy jumped up. "Coming," she called, and dashed out of the lounge followed by Chrissie and Lacy.

Marcel was thanking Rachel and Tom for their kind hospitality as Darcy and Chrissie arrived. Darcy made a quick introduction, then they watched him climb into his funny car.

"See you again soon, Marcel," Josh shouted, above the engine noise.

They all waved as the 'deux chevaux' chugged off down the driveway.

Chrissie bent forward and whispered in Darcy's ear. "Mmm…who is he?"

Darcy lifted her eyebrows. "A dishy Frenchman, Chrissie… dishy and single."

Chrissie's face was a picture!

Chapter 9

A groan sounded from his room. Josh was heading along the landing when he heard it.

"Good grief, young man. Have you let all your tidiness vanish into thin air? This won't do!" Rachel was scanning her son's bedroom floor, where he'd left scattered items, full of good intentions to sort later.

The pair almost collided as Josh approached his room.

"There you are...get that lot sorted, pronto, young man! It's my day for cleaning the east bedrooms and I can't even bring the vacuum in here!" Rachel was going red in the face with frustration.

Josh towered above his petite mother. He reached out and placed his hands on her shoulders, smiling sweetly. "Mother, I'm sorry, I was on my way to tidy it. Can you start with another bedroom and then it will be ready for your assault," he announced, grinning. He gave her a quick hug as she headed off to the next bedroom.

Josh sighed. His mother was known for her fastidious housekeeping regimes. She'd commented at breakfast she was going to 'prepare' a room and offer Marcel to stay over sometimes.

CHAPTER 9

"He's got a room with his aunt at her house in Durham, but I think he wants companions of his own age. We have a spare room or two, so perhaps he could come over on a Saturday and stay overnight. I think it would be a welcoming gesture and I'm sure Jonty would appreciate us looking out for his friend."

Murmurings around the breakfast table seemed to give assent to Rachel's idea.

True to form, Rachel had decided to act on her plan. Josh was at a loss as to why it needed special preparation. Only six bedrooms were used by the extended family leaving four on standby for guests. Come rain or shine, Rachel had her routines, and it was east-facing bedrooms for their weekly clean today…another day, the west-facing bedrooms would receive their treatment.

Josh retrieved his belongings. He was enjoying the relaxation from strict army routines and kit inspections since his return from the garrison. Perhaps he had engaged in a 'kick back' moment, pulling off his clothes last night and dropping them…did it really matter?

Clothes sorted and bed made, he sat on the chair in the corner of the room.

Try as he may, Josh Smallwood could not eradicate Judy Dempster from his mind. He went to sleep dreaming about her and woke up thinking about her. This 'forbidden' thing was tantalising him…why? There were many beautiful twenty-year-old girls in the surrounding district of Malhaven, so why did one girl feature so highly in his thinking?

As if some unseen hand was working on his behalf, he'd bumped into her at the garage the previous day. After Marcel's visit at the weekend, he'd decided to begin his overhaul of his old jalopy, Beryl. He listed a few items he needed, borrowed his dad's car and headed for the local garage, Robson's in Bronhill.

He was dressed ready for work – scruffy jeans, oiled stained shirt and a cap. He parked the car and entered the office, where a queue had formed. It took Josh a few minutes to register the customer standing directly in front of him… Judy Dempster!

Should he speak? He was unsure…but it was a coincidence. Living in the same town they were bound to meet at some point.

Throwing caution to the wind, he bent forward and whispered over her shoulder. "Fancy meeting you here," he remarked. The light fragrance from her delicate perfume caught his attention.

"Oh, goodness, you startled me," Judy responded, half turning to face him.

"Excuse the outfit." He grinned. "I'm busy working on my car and need supplies," he added.

Judy looked surprised. "A car?" she enquired.

Josh chuckled. "Yes, but she's in a sorry state at present… needs a lot of attention."

The storekeeper called Judy forward, "Next please," and their conversation ended abruptly. After paying for her goods, Judy exited the office. She fluttered her eyelashes and mouthed "Bye" as she'd left. He'd winked and grinned, as his stomach performed a somersault…gosh she was a looker.

That brief encounter had filled his dreams during the night. He'd tried to recall the smell of her perfume, but the greatest impact had been her willingness to speak. If he was 'forbidden'…why speak? Somehow, he felt they'd made a connection – opening the possibility to engage her in further conversation, should the opportunity arise. But would it?

A commotion downstairs caught his attention. He left his room.

"It's here, it's here!" his dad was chirping.

"What's here?" asked Josh, almost colliding with his mother, as they both made their way hurriedly towards the staircase.

"It will be the television set," Rachel announced.

"Oh, yes, I'd forgotten about that," Josh remarked. When he'd returned home, he'd been informed about the order.

Josh and his mother entered the conservatory just as two young men, wearing tan overalls, were positioning a mahogany cabinet in the corner of the room, along from the fireplace. Tom was directing operations, as the delivery men from Pattison's and Sons in Malsett carefully manoeuvred the large item into its new home.

Darcy was already watching the proceedings. After a period of knob turning and twiddling of wires at the rear of the cabinet, some grainy semblance of a grey image appeared on the tiny screen.

At Rachel's insistence the 'newfangled contraption', as she referred to it, had been selected to complement the furnishings in the large conservatory.

"It needs to look stylish and blend in," she'd declared, when viewing the offerings in Pattison's showroom a few weeks earlier.

"This one might suit your requirements, Mrs Smallwood," the proprietor had suggested, thumbing through the catalogue. "But these speciality ones will need to be ordered."

Having carefully selected the chosen article, Rachel had seemed more amenable to the prospect.

She stood at the back of the room as the men went to check on the position of the outside aerial, which had been erected a few days ago.

"We'll make some adjustments on the roof and be back shortly," said one of the men.

"Close the cabinet doors," Rachel instructed; Tom obeyed, and Rachel nodded.

"It will fit in, I suppose, although I still think it will be a short-lived craze, hyped up for the Coronation next year."

Tom shook his head. "I'm not sure I agree with you, Rachel. I've been longing to have one. Apparently, they can't keep up with the demand. Every household will soon be buying one. There are so many interesting things to view – news programmes, quiz programmes, sport, drama…and even special programmes for little ones, like the twins."

Darcy watched on, surveying her family's excitement, a lump forming in her throat. She bent down to pick up her puppy as the delivery men re-entered the room. Why did the mention of little ones enjoying the new gadget fill her with such sorrow?

Quietly, Darcy slid unseen out of the room. She placed the sleepy puppy in her basket in their lounge and set off up the stairs on a mission.

***

It was five weeks since Leon's birth and so far, Darcy had refrained from entering the nursery. Back in the spring, after her pregnancy was confirmed, Tom had engaged the services of a local builder. His task was to create an adjoining doorway between Darcy and Henri's bedroom and the room next door - which would become the nursery for the baby.

A similar alteration had been completed a few years earlier, when Chantal was expecting the twins. It had been a successful renovation, so was readily agreed upon for Darcy and Henri's room.

Until now the room had lain untouched. It wasn't locked, but Rachel was careful to avoid her cleaning regimes when Darcy was in the house. She sensed it would take time for her daughter to set foot in the room she'd so lovingly prepared.

Darcy entered the room from the landing. Had it been in use, this door would have been locked, to ensure privacy. The only locked door now was the one joining the two rooms.

The time had arrived – she would allow herself a few moments of painful reflection.

The drapes at the window were white with tiny yellow and green flowers. Rachel had made them, adding cream linings to add to the weight and limit the degree of light which would show through.

The walls were neutral, adorned with the animal sketches drawn by herself and framed by Henri. The cot was one used by the twins; the other one was in the attic. A large set of drawers, a small wardrobe and two comfortable padded chairs filled the remaining space. A sink in the corner was the only remnant of the hotel days.

A large rug covered most of the wooden floor. Darcy noted the neat pile of bedding positioned on the cot – mostly hand-me-downs from Chantal's twins, but a small eiderdown and pillowcase, made from leftover curtain material, was a new addition.

Darcy tried to stem the flow of tears which threatened, as her eyes surveyed the colourful sketches on the walls.

She sat down heavily in one of the armless chairs, recalling how her mother had referred to it as a 'nursing chair'. She clutched herself – her discomfort had thankfully abated, thanks to Chantal's careful post-birth management.

Clasping her head in her hands she let her feelings go… the tears erupted… the trickle became a flow…the flow becoming a gush. She gulped as the grief swept through her being. Her shoulders heaved in remorse. Why, why was her little one taken?

Her dad had said it was God's will for her life.

Chantal had explained it was nothing she had done wrong – just one of those things – no rational explanation.

Her mother had said it was life…it happened …she was young …there would be more babies.

Nancy had quoted her mother and aunt having stillborn babies, then going on to have healthy ones.

But none of this was helping.

She looked up, wiping the tears on her cardigan sleeve. Her gaze rested on the drawers. Inside she knew was the layette – tiny white cardigans, booties, matinee coats and hats, plus a large pile of white terry towelling nappies. She would not torture herself any further today, by looking at those.

She stood and walked over to the dark green Silver Cross pram in the corner – a gift from her parents. Gently she rocked it and lifted her head…relief seemed to sweep through her.

One day this room will be filled with a newborn's cry, she told herself. One day I will sit in that nursing chair and give sustenance to our offspring. Everything is ready… except for the right time.

She recalled her dad's words after the birth.

'In due season,' he'd said. 'In the fullness of time, Darcy. Trust is a confident expectation of something. There are seasons of life when we are asked to trust…this is one of them.'

***

Two days later, Darcy heard voices in the rear yard. Rachel was busy at the kitchen sink when Darcy peeped over her shoulders.

"What's he doing here?" she asked, noting Marcel Duval talking to Josh.

"He's offered to help your brother fix his car," her mother replied.

Darcy wandered out to join them.

The two young men were deep in conversation, looking at Marcel's Citroën car when she approached.

"Bonjour, Monsieur Duval," she exclaimed.

Marcel looked up. "Hello, Darcy. I do hope we can be on first name terms," he added, grinning. "And what are you up to on this chilly October morning?"

"Oh, I'm trying to keep out of Mother's way by writing an article for the local newspaper," she responded. "If I hang around for too long, she'll give me a job to do. I thought you would be solving some exciting crime in Durham by now."

Marcel locked his car and stood back.

"A bit early yet. I need to rent an office first, print some business cards and advertise in a newspaper. Which newspapers do you suggest?"

Darcy looked thoughtful.

"Well, the Northern Echo. Then there's the local weekly papers like the Malsett Guardian and The Granley Chronicle. There are probably more on the other side of Durham. I could ask at my former place of work if you want."

Marcel looked attentive. "I'd appreciate that, Darcy. I'm aiming to be up and running by the first week in November."

"Darcy…stop talking. Marcel and I have important things to be doing," Josh rebuked his sister.

Marcel stifled a laugh and winked at her.

After lunch Darcy was exercising Lady when Marcel found her on the lawn.

"Has my brother given you a few moments' respite?" Darcy enquired.

Marcel was dressed casually and wearing a large black apron over his clothes, courtesy of Tom.

"I'll catch him up," he replied. "I wanted to see where Henri works." He watched as Darcy threw the ball for Lady.

"She's fast," remarked Marcel, observing the swift spaniel.

"Yes, but she doesn't understand the game yet…she retrieves it, then wanders off across the grass."

"Give her time…reinforce and reward…she's only a puppy."

They followed the dog.

"Tell me about your work, Marcel, it sounds intriguing."

"My work varies, but so far, I have undertaken a considerable amount of matrimonial work – gaining information for couples seeking to divorce each other. It's tiresome, involving long hours of surveillance…but it pays well and has given me a decent income." He bent to pick up the ball and throw it for Lady to retrieve again.

"When my aunt was over in the summer, I asked if she would like a lodger for a few months and she agreed. It will give me a chance to branch out in a different direction. I've finished all my current work and given up my office in Calais. I intend to see where it goes in Durham over the next few months. I'd really like to get into investigating fraud." They ambled across the lawn.

"How did you meet Jonty?"

"University – we both studied law. But as you know, Jonty wanted to become a solicitor, and I'd always wanted to be a detective. I was set on joining the local gendarmerie, like your Uncle Pierre, but I was offered some work on my own and it just developed from there."

"It sounds exciting," Darcy added, genuinely admiring Marcel's determination.

"My objective is to provide tangible evidence in a discreet and legal manner."

"What will it involve?"

"Surveillance and undercover work. With a background in law and a natural curiosity, I hope to build a reputation with both companies and individuals."

"Gosh, it sounds fascinating. I guess from a journalist's standpoint we have similarities, but my end goal is to file a report for a newspaper or magazine," Darcy commented. "I'm intrigued by the idea of undercover work…it sounds just up my street – a bit of cloak and dagger stuff!" she exclaimed, chuckling.

"Yes, I can see the similarities – we are two likeminded people, Darcy."

Lady took off at speed.

"Oh bother, I need to follow her. If you head off in that direction, Marcel, you will find the greenhouses and my hardworking husband," she indicated.

They parted.

Tiredness had overtaken the young puppy and as Darcy caught up with her, she rolled over for a tummy tickle.

"You silly girl, come on, let's go indoors, it's too chilly to stay out here." Autumn was certainly in the air as Darcy headed back to the house, carrying the dog.

Her mind was racing. After her 'release' in the nursery the other day, her 'heart to heart' discussion with Henri, and today's conversation with Marcel, Darcy felt ready to commence her new career…but how?

She liked Marcel Duval and felt they had much in common. Perhaps they could work together in the future – he could do the investigating, and she could do the reporting. How their two worlds could connect she was unsure…but the more she thought about it, the more exciting the idea became.

She left the dog in her basket and slowly climbed the stairs. Another hare-brained idea mulling around in her brain. Her friend Chrissie needed a male companion in her life. After her hurtful experience with Grady Forrester, she was due some love and affection…Marcel appeared to be footloose and fancy free…so maybe… if she could give a little help and encouragement in that direction …a touch of matchmaking might be in order.

Mother's suggestion of accommodating Marcel on a Saturday night could help…mmm…a foursome? Invite

Marcel and Chrissie out for dinner with Henri and herself… yes…possibilities jumped into her mind.

Darcy had a spring in her step. Ideas were one thing… but actions were another!

Chapter 10

"Josh," called Rachel, replacing the telephone receiver, "tidy yourself, young man, you can see the dentist at 10.30 this morning – they've just had a cancellation."

Josh was not amused. He was dressed in his work gear; all set for a morning disgorging the inner workings of Beryl's brakes.

"Aww, Mother …must I?" he moaned, but knew it was useless arguing.

"Your teeth are more important than that heap of nuts and bolts. You need to look after them or you'll end up with dentures, like me," she commented.

That fact was enough to satisfy Josh - he baulked at the thought of false teeth, worn by many of his parents' generation.

Idly thumbing through a National Geographic magazine in the dentist's waiting room, Josh was surprised to hear a vaguely familiar voice.

"Toothache?"

He looked up to see Judy Dempster. He uncrossed his legs and smiled as she sat in the seat opposite.

"Thankfully...not yet, but an inspection is required. You?"

Judy pulled a face. "I need a filling. I hate the thought of that drill."

Josh was intrigued. "I thought nurses were brave souls," he teased.

Judy giggled. "This one isn't. I'm quite happy inflicting discomfort on others in the course of my duties...but when it comes to personal pain, it's a different matter."

"Joshua Smallwood," called the receptionist.

Josh closed his magazine, stood and replaced it on the table in the corner.

"My turn...hope you can cope with the pain," he remarked. "Good to see you again, Judy." He followed the receptionist out of the room.

Once again, his and Judy's paths had crossed...was this just coincidence? When he left the surgery, he decided to loiter on the street – he reasoned Judy was more important than Beryl. His wait was rewarded.

"Do you get the feeling we are meant to keep bumping into each other?" he asked jumping into step beside her.

"I've no idea and I've got an aching mouth. Will you please cross over the road. Malhaven is far too small a place for us to be seen together. As I've already told you, I must not fraternise with you."

This time the previously friendly Judy seemed guarded and unnerved. Josh detected a hint of anger, akin to the day she spoke to him in the hospital. He sighed...his plan had failed.

"As you wish," he replied, shaking his head. Then he crossed the road.

It was another 'dead end'. Her attitude and behaviour bothered him. Their brief encounter in the garage and then in the dentist waiting room had been friendly, giving him hope. But her cutting remark on Front Street in Malhaven troubled him. What was behind it? And more to the point... how could he find out?

***

"Sam, phone call for you," shouted Josh later that evening. He placed his hand over the receiver – he had no idea as to Sam's whereabouts. He spoke to the caller again.

"Can you give me a few minutes please and I'll try to locate him...who shall I say is calling?" he asked.

"It's his daughter, Francesca," came the reply. It was strange, Josh pondered as he went in search of Chantal's partner, to hear a 'live person' giving a name to what for many years had been a secret.

The existence of Sam Carter's daughter only came to the family's notice when a young Josh, Darcy and Henri had travelled to Edinburgh years ago. Since then, her name was hardly ever spoken.

Locating Sam, he directed him to the telephone.

When Sam returned to the conservatory, Chantal looked up.

"That was Francesca – she would like to visit us," he announced.

The occupants of the room were engrossed in a topical programme on the new television, but Rachel overheard.

"Your daughter is most welcome to stay with us, Sam – did she say when?"

"Next weekend, if that is convenient and she would like to bring a friend…a male friend."

"No problem," announced Rachel. "It's beginning to feel like the hotel days again," she added, resuming her interest in the television.

Chantal was watching Sam. "You seem unsure, Sam…I thought you wanted to invite Francesca to meet us."

Sam sat forward in his chair resting his chin in his hands.

"I guess I just wanted things to be tidy. It means I'll be introducing my daughter to the twins, and I'm still not married to their mother."

Chantal stood and walked over to Sam, draping her arms around his neck.

"Sam…let it rest. We will be married soon. Young people today are broadminded. Let's enjoy this family occasion. It will be good for Francesca to meet her half-siblings and at least she still thinks that."

Sam tilted his head and gazed into Chantal's face. "I'm tired of all this subterfuge. I've a good mind to tell Francesca the truth and to pot with Evelyn's feelings. Why is life so complicated?"

Chantal pecked Sam on the cheek and sat down. Yes…it was complicated. But Sam was Francesca's legal father – so why upset the apple cart? Chantal felt for her partner. He wanted to 'come clean'…but what good purpose would it serve?

***

Marcel was delighted at the prospect of staying overnight at Meckleridge House and readily accepted Rachel and Tom's offer. He arrived early on Saturday to help Josh with his work on the old car.

It was too soon for Darcy to organise any matchmaking with Chrissie, so she settled for a weekend of getting to know Marcel Duval. She learned he had lived in France since he was ten years old.

"You speak English so well, no one would ever guess," she remarked.

"That's because my mother insists we speak English in our home. When Jonty and I became friends, he was also an English speaker, so we could use both languages."

The young people seemed to be at ease in each other's company and over supper they were laughing and joking.

"Now, Darcy, I have something to ask you," said Marcel. "Officially, my investigation business has yet to start, but my aunt has offered me some work which seems too good not to accept. It may indirectly help me in the future...but I need some assistance. Can we have a private chat, with your husband, of course."

Darcy was filled with curiosity and after supper they went into Henri and Darcy's lounge.

After Henri poked the fire and added some logs, Marcel began.

"My Aunt Bertha, with whom I live, has a job as a housekeeper for a retired bank manager called Reginald Coleman. She works six days a week from nine in the morning until mid-afternoon. His house is within walking distance from where we live."

Darcy listened with interest.

"Over the time she has been in his employment, she has noticed a deterioration in his abilities; however, he is reluctant to admit it. He thinks he's sharp minded...but sadly he isn't. His nephew turned up a few weeks ago and started poking around in Reggie's office. Bertha noticed things had been moved...as if he was searching for something. All she does, is tidy up." Marcel cleared his throat.

"When Reggie started asking where she had put various things, she was taken aback, and feared he was going to accuse her of something. Then some money went missing."

Darcy stared at Marcel. "Does he know about his nephew's visits?"

"Yes, I get the impression the nephew has a bit of a grievance with the older man."

"Is he at home when the nephew visits?"

Marcel shook his head. "No, that's what bothers Aunt Bertha. You see, Reggie belongs to some charitable trust and spends every afternoon at this house they own. The nephew deliberately visits when Reggie's out."

Darcy was intrigued but was failing to see how she could be connected to this situation.

"I suggested doing some undercover work to help, as Reggie refuses to contact the police with the nephew being his sister's son."

The light was beginning to dawn on Darcy. She sat forward in her seat.

"Do you want me to help with this undercover work?" she asked eagerly.

Marcel smiled. "In a word, yes! It would involve you becoming a temporary secretary – a role more suited to a woman than a man."

Darcy rubbed her hands with glee, anticipation rising...a real, investigative role.

"I would of course be on hand to guide you, but I would remain unseen. I could show you how to lay a trap for this supposed thief."

"When do you want me to start?" asked Darcy.

Marcel raised his eyebrows. "Well, firstly Bertha needs to convince her employer he needs to engage a temporary secretary. Then I need to meet him and suggest how this could work for his benefit. I can't give you a date yet, but in the meantime, you could be thinking up your 'cover story' and Henri…do you approve of your wife being involved in work of this nature?"

Henri looked into Darcy's eyes …how could he refuse?

"As long as you are sure she will be in no danger, I have no objections," Henri replied.

Marcel paused. "Undercover work always carries an element of risk, Henri. People do not like to be deceived, but I do not expect any danger."

Concluding their discussion, they joined the rest of the family, but Darcy was already planning her role as an undercover secretary for Reginald Coleman.

***

Darcy sought out Marcel at every opportunity she could find over the weekend. She needed to have a clear picture of the scenario in which she might be required to work.

"Why, if this Mr Coleman was a bank manager, would he leave amounts of money lying around?" she asked.

"I haven't a clue, Darcy, but if his focus wasn't on his office, he may have become careless."

CHAPTER 10

"So, my role would be to organise his office initially, is that the plan? But surely the nephew will become suspicious if things start to look tidy?" Marcel looked thoughtful.

"Until we visit the premises we won't know for sure, Darcy."

Even after the weekend was over Darcy couldn't let the subject drop.

"It will be an adventure," she commented to Henri. "A chance for me to undertake some real investigative work. I'm going to use a fake name – just in case Reggie's nephew tries to trace me. I will call myself Rose Caudwell. I will be a plain, dumb-looking young woman who wants to be a secretary. I will have a quiet persona, only speaking when spoken to…I know what to do, Henri…just trust me."

"Ma petite fille, you are full of ingenuity, but you must be cautious, don't drop your guard – or you could put yourself in danger."

Marcel telephoned his friend Jonty and told him about the plan.

Jonty listened, then commented. "My cousin Darcy may not realise the potential danger she is placing herself in. She has led a sheltered life, Marcel, marrying when she was young. I'm concerned she may not have the ability to handle things if she were to meet Mr Coleman's nephew."

Marcel did not agree. "I think you underestimate your cousin, Jonty. From what I can deduce, she could be ideal for this kind of work."

"Promise me you will keep a keen eye on her, Marcel – any hint of danger please get her out of there," he urged.

Marcel was aware of the close bond between the cousins and appreciated Jonty's protectiveness, although he felt Darcy Dukas was more than capable of looking after herself.

Jonty's concern caused him to telephone Darcy, the same evening.

After conducting pleasantries, Jonty jumped straight into the issue with his feisty young cousin.

"Marcel has told me about this plan to help with some undercover work."

"Yes, I'm so excited, Jonty, it's the kind of work I relish undertaking."

"Be careful, Darcy. You are too impulsive and can be thoughtless and insensitive to those around you…your ambition fuels you," he warned. "Darcy, you sometimes become frustrated and bored. You have a short fuse and are prone to flying off the handle. Please think before you act." Jonty did not mince his words. He knew his cousin's temperament and felt he was the only one to try to give her advice.

Darcy, however, was not about to be sidetracked.

"Jonty, thank you for your interest and concern. It's a good job I don't take offence… I hear what you are saying and will think carefully about how to conduct myself… but as I said to my dear husband…you need to trust me!"

Jonty spoke to Henri, reiterating his concerns to his French cousin. Henri listened and agreed.

"Yes, Jonty, everything you say is true, but Darcy will be Darcy, and we can only advise her." He shook his head in resignation.

"She's your wife, Henri, surely you have some sway with her," commented Jonty.

"Yes, but she is also my best friend…and more than that – I trust her."

Jonty Thibault had done all he could do …he only hoped his cousin would exercise caution.

***

Marcel made contact early the next week to say his aunt had arranged for Darcy to attend an informal interview with her employer, Reginald Coleman. Marcel would come over on Wednesday morning to collect her.

Josh did a double take when he saw his sister waiting in the lounge for Marcel.

"Good grief…who are you?" he asked looking her up and down. He noted her tartan pleated tweed skirt, high necked cream blouse and Fair Isle knit, beige cardigan and flat lace shoes. Her hair was styled in a tight bun at the base of her neck.

"Keep this to yourself, Josh Smallwood, but I am Rose Caudwell, the daughter of Marcel's Aunt Bertha's friend." She did a twirl for her brother's benefit.

"I have an interview today for a role as a temporary secretary. I am about to do some undercover work to aid Marcel," she explained with glee.

Josh let out a low whistle. "Why the weird outfit? You look like someone from the 1930s."

"Excellent," replied Darcy. "That's the desired effect." Then reaching into her bag she picked out some tortoiseshell-rimmed spectacles and proceeded to place them on the end of her nose. Josh almost erupted as his sister stood pigeon toed and looking gormless.

"Ten out of ten for the disguise, Darcy – you don't look as if you possess the brains to boil an egg, let alone succeed in an interview."

A noise in the hallway beckoned the arrival of Henri, closely followed by Marcel who observed Darcy's attire.

"Well done, Darcy, your disguise is amazing," he declared. "You have an inventive wife, Henri."

Henri placed his arm around Darcy and hugged her. "My little star…your disguise is perfect. Now off you go and don't forget to look dim."

Darcy pouted and put on a 'dim looking' face, which sent the menfolk into peals of laughter.

If Marcel's aunt, Bertha Remington, was surprised at Rose Caudwell's appearance, she showed no hint. She was a spinster lady in her late fifties. She had worked in France and Switzerland for many years, as a lady's companion. She'd returned to live in her family home in Durham, after her mother died. The house was small and terraced, close to the city centre.

Marcel introduced Darcy to his aunt.

"This is Rose Caudwell, Aunt Bertha. She is 'in role' ready for the interview…you two can become properly acquainted later."

Bertha gave a knowing smile. "Pleased to meet you, Rose – now, you are my friend's daughter. I understand your Aunt Peg was a lady's companion before her marriage."

Darcy smiled…such subterfuge!

"It's only a fifteen-minute walk across town to my employer's house, so I suggest we set off…Mr Coleman is expecting us."

Marcel and Darcy listened as Bertha chatted about her role as a housekeeper.

"Housekeeping makes a change from correspondence, packing and unpacking suitcases, travelling and attending endless tea parties, which were my main tasks as a companion. I enjoyed my career, and I've seen many lovely places. But all good things must come to an end."

Darcy enquired about Mr Coleman.

"He's a retired bank manager and a widower. His wife's death was sudden. I went to work for him soon after she died. The poor man isn't coping well, and I hate to think he is being cheated by his obnoxious nephew. The chap just turned up one afternoon a few months ago and started rummaging around in Mr Coleman's office. I was alarmed, but Reggie said he was trying to locate a document relating to some land his mother supposedly owned."

The streets were busy, Marcel and Darcy found Bertha was an agile woman for her age.

"It felt a bit awkward alerting Reggie to my suspicions – family business is private – but when he asked me about some money going missing, I knew I had to speak up. That's when I decided to ask Marcel for his help."

"How does Mr Coleman spend his days?" asked Darcy, remembering to stay in her role.

"He's a trustee for an old house in Durham. It's a historical place and needs sorting. He works on a voluntary basis, cataloguing antiquities and such like. He's passionate about it. He's a real gentleman – I think you'll like him."

Darcy could have been made for the stage. Bertha introduced Marcel, explaining his line of work. Then she introduced Rose, as her friend's daughter, looking to secure some secretarial work. Darcy was shown Mr Coleman's office and given a rough idea of the layout. To say it was a mess was an understatement.

An hour later, the newly appointed secretary for Reginald Coleman was sitting in Bertha's living room. Marcel had an amused grin on his face.

"You can drop the dramatics now, Darcy," he exclaimed. "You passed with flying colours. Your new job begins next week."

"Would you like to stay over some nights, Darcy? It will be easier than travelling backwards and forwards each day," Bertha asked.

Darcy looked thoughtful. "Thank you for your kind offer, Bertha. I'll see what my husband says."

After enjoying a cup of tea, Marcel drove Darcy home.

"That outfit was very convincing, Darcy...where did you source the clothes?"

"Oh, that was easy. Nancy, our farm manager's wife, has a huge trunk of old clothing, shoes and bags from her mother's house – she let me raid it."

"You need to expand your cover story, in case the nephew becomes curious and turns up asking questions," Marcel commented.

Darcy hesitated.

"Okay. I live in Durham and I'm an only child. I have been away at a girl's boarding school. I am naive and have little experience of the wider world. I'm a bookworm and a history fanatic. My idea of a day out is visiting Durham Cathedral...how does that sound?"

Marcel grinned. "Brilliant – that should be enough to avert the nephew's idea of befriending Rose Caudwell.

Careful with the history bit, though… he might trick you."
Marcel concentrated on his driving, then asked, "So, what really interests Darcy Dukas?"

Darcy chuckled. "Well, I am an avid reader, and I did take a secretarial course before taking up my position with the Malsett Guardian. My ambition is to be an investigative journalist. But as for my real interests…mmm….all things French, I suppose… in particular …French men."

Marcel almost drove his car off the road!

Chapter 11

Blood spurted from Josh's arm as he grabbed the oily rag. He gritted his teeth, stifling the urge to cry out in pain. The rag was inadequate at stemming the sticky red liquid pouring from the gash in his arm. He scanned the garage for something to soak up the blood but drew a blank, so leveraging his other arm out of his shirt, he managed to wind it around the wound. He headed up to the house, shivering.

Rachel was in the kitchen as Josh almost fell through the back door.

"What on earth?" she shrieked.

"It's a deep gash, Mother – can you help?"

Rachel peeled back the sodden shirt. "Hospital, Josh – that needs cleaning and stitching." She grabbed a towel, at the same time shouting for Tom.

"Where's your father when we need him?" Rachel shouted again, but her cries were met with silence. Josh was looking pale. She guided him to a chair then quickly reached up to a top cupboard, lifted down a bottle of brandy and passed it to her son.

"Take a gulp and hold that towel tightly over the wound," she instructed. "I'll have to drive you myself. First, I need to get you a jacket. This is unbelievable – a doctor and a nurse live in this house and neither of them are here when you need them." She assumed Tom was out on the estate and Chantal had gone to the library. Returning with the clothing and her coat she heard yapping.

"Oh crumbs, the dog! I'll have to lock you in the kitchen, Lady."

Rachel moved with speed, hastily scribbling a note to say where they'd gone. A few minutes later they were pulling up outside the casualty department of Malhaven hospital.

"Go in there," she pointed to some double doors. "I'll find somewhere to park the car."

Josh stumbled out of the car, feeling extremely lightheaded. The towel his mother had wrapped around his arm was turning red. The receptionist at the desk looked up and shouted, "Nurse, can you help please?"

Josh turned and the last thing he remembered was staring into an attractive face, before everything went blank.

"Josh, Josh…wake up," urged a familiar voice.

Josh blinked and slowly opened his eyes. Someone was patting the sides of his face.

"Ju…Ju…dy!" he exclaimed.

"Here, drink this and bend forwards," the nurse instructed, handing him a glass of water.

His memory began to click into place.

"What happened?" he asked, bewildered. His head was throbbing, and his arm was hurting…big time.

"I don't know what happened to cause this, but when you turned to face me at the desk, you collapsed in a heap at my feet," she chuckled. "I know you've been trying to attract my attention, Josh Smallwood, but this is a bit extreme. Now, I need to get you into a cubicle and clean you up, before the doctor arrives."

Over the next twenty minutes Josh was treated to first class treatment by student nurse Judy Dempster. She guided him into a cubicle, removed his jacket and blood-stained shirt, helped him onto a trolley and proceeded to clean his deep wound. When Rachel arrived, she was told to take a seat in the waiting room.

"What were you doing to cause this?" Judy asked, removing her surgical gloves and picking up a board containing a form.

Josh sighed. "I was working on Beryl. I reached out to grab a tool and felt this rip on my arm."

Judy stared in alarm at Josh. Suddenly, he realised how his words sounded and tried to stem the laugh emerging from his throat.

"Beryl is my car, my old jalopy," he explained.

Judy hesitated. "Okay, injury sustained while mending a part on a motorcar...will that suffice?" She jotted down her notes. Their eyes met and lingered for a few moments, just as the curtain opened and a young male doctor stepped into the cubicle.

"Right, nurse, what's the problem here?" he asked.

"This is Joshua Smallwood. He sustained a deep gash to his arm while working on his motor vehicle. I have cleaned the wound."

Josh watched as the medical duo attended to his needs with professionalism. Once the stitches were in place, Judy gave him an injection. He glanced sideways to see her face which showed no reaction. The doctor instructed Judy as to the medication required, which she wrote on the sheet… then he left.

"Why are you working in casualty? I thought you were on the maternity ward," Josh asked Judy, as she was retrieving some tablets from a cupboard.

"It's the last part of my training before I qualify. I've already taken my exams. We do three months on different wards to gain overall experience. When I attended to your sister, I was in my last two weeks on the maternity unit." She placed the tablets in an envelope and sealed it.

"Take two of these at night and two in a morning, until you return for your check-up, Mr Smallwood. Now, do you think you can stand up?" Judy placed her arm around Josh's shoulder as he swung his legs off the trolley. They paused.

"One, two, three," said Judy, but a wave of dizziness halted the process. "Sit for a couple of minutes," Judy suggested.

"Could you just check my eye, nurse," Josh murmured. Judy bent forward and quick as a flash Josh gave Judy a peck on the cheek, then chuckled. Judy pulled back, a look of annoyance on her face.

"I've met your type before, Mr Smallwood, I think you are perfectly able to get to your feet." Josh felt chastised … but gleeful.

"Can't blame me for trying, nurse…am I still 'off limits'?" Josh searched her face, making no attempt to stand up. He detected a warmth in her expression.

"Officially...yes."

Josh tilted his head to one side. "Unofficially?" he ventured. "As in ...maybe?"

Voices could be heard outside the cubicle as Josh's mother was shown through the curtain.

"Oh, Josh, how are you?"

Josh stared at his mother. "I'm okay...a bit sore, but I've received excellent care from Nurse Dempster." He grinned.

Judy proceeded to help Josh to his feet and led him out into the waiting area, followed by Rachel.

"Just sit here, Mr Smallwood, and I'll get your follow-up appointment. The wound will need to be checked and dressed in three days' time."

Josh and Rachel sat in the busy waiting area. Judy walked up holding an appointment card.

"Monday morning at 11am, Mr Smallwood," she announced. "Keep it dry and elevated. No messing about with your old car – do you understand?"

"Perfectly," Josh replied, taking the card.

Rachel placed the jacket around his shoulders. Josh attempted to stand but fell back into his seat.

"Careful," admonished Nurse Dempster. "Do it slowly." At the second attempt he felt steadier.

"Thank you for your assistance, Nurse...will you be around when I return for my appointment?"

Judy twisted her lips. "Possibly," she added.

Josh winked at her...somehow, he felt like he'd broken down a barrier.

***

"Darcy, I could do with some help," announced Rachel, as her daughter flitted across the hallway towards the stairs. "I'm way behind with my chores after spending time at the hospital with Josh."

Reluctantly, Darcy agreed. "Oh crumbs, I'd totally forgotten we have Scottish guests staying for the weekend, haven't we?" Sam's daughter, Francesca, and her boyfriend were due to arrive on Friday evening.

"Chantal is taking the day off tomorrow to assist with the housework, but I would welcome your contribution in the baking department."

Darcy wasn't averse to baking, in fact she quite liked it, but her mother was so organised her skills were rarely called upon. Scones were Darcy's speciality – fruit and cheese scones. Like her cousin Hope, Darcy had played with the scraps of dough, squishing stray currants and mixed peel into her pretend scones. It was a natural transfer in adult years to produce the real thing.

"No problem, give me ten minutes and I'll be down to make some scones." She disappeared up the stairs.

Darcy's scones were a delight to eat – soft and fluffy. But the space around her when baking, tended to resemble a war zone. Darcy was an untidy baker, which irritated her mother, but the result more than justified the mess. She was sending clouds of flour across the kitchen table as she weighed out her ingredients.

"Francesca's not much older than me…is she?" she enquired.

Rachel paused. "Er…three years older, I think. Sam is very proud of her. She's just finished her studies to be a GP, qualifying a few months ago. I think this visit is rather premature for Sam and Chantal – they were hoping to be married before Francesca and the twins met."

Darcy shrugged, rolling out her dough.

"Mother, times have changed – young people are more open to situations like Sam and Chantal's – I don't think it matters at all; anyway, who's judging?"

Rachel continued with her task. Yes, it was a different world now, especially since the war. Divorce used to be looked upon with such disdain…but now?

Josh meandered through to the kitchen and sat down at the kitchen table.

"You look glum," commented Darcy, observing her brother's arm in a sling. "Is it painful?"

Josh nodded. "Nagging a bit." He turned to his mother. "Marcel is coming over early on Saturday morning to assist with Beryl, and he's going to stay over again."

Rachel lifted her hands and smiled. "The more the merrier – it will be like one of our house parties from the hotel days."

Darcy looked up from forming her scones with a cutter.

"Mother, would you mind if I asked Chrissie to join us on Saturday evening? I think she's a bit lonely, having just come back to Malsett from York."

Rachel agreed. Darcy smiled to herself. Perhaps Marcel and Chrissie might get to know each other.

***

Francesca Carter and her boyfriend, Jack, were given the traditional Meckleridge House welcome. By the time they arrived, the twins were tucked up in bed.

CHAPTER 11

"Better to meet the children in the morning," Sam explained, after introducing Chantal.

Francesca gripped Chantal's hand and drew her into an unexpected hug. Chantal had doubted herself in the run up to the introduction... would Francesca accept her?

"I look forward to getting to know you, Francesca," she announced.

"We already have two things in common, Chantal," she replied.

Chantal looked lost.

"Love for this gorgeous father of mine," she explained, placing her arm in Sam's. "And a medical background."

"Indeed." Chantal smiled. "But I am only a humble midwife."

Sam looked at his partner and beamed. "She is a highly talented midwife and a tower of strength, Francesca ...and is soon to be my wife."

Chantal felt herself blushing.

"I hear there are several names on the viewing list for Matthison Hall, already. How are the moving out plans progressing?" he asked; but before Francesca could reply, Tom called everyone into the dining room for their meal.

Over dinner, the youngsters made the Scottish guests welcome and by the end of the meal, it seemed hard to remember they'd been strangers only a few hours ago.

Darcy warmed to Francesca immediately, and later in the evening, Francesca spoke to her.

"So, Darcy...you are Tom and Rachel's married daughter...is that correct?"

Darcy smiled at the young Scottish woman, whose brown wavy hair framed a pretty face with fine features. Francesca was tall and slim and tastefully dressed.

"Yes, I'm the oldest. Josh, my brother, will be twenty-one next spring."

"How long have you been married?"

"Almost three years," explained Darcy. "Henri came over from France to assist my father in his horticultural business, we fell in love and married on my twentieth birthday."

Francesca smiled broadly. "He's very handsome, Darcy, I can see how you were attracted to his French charm."

Darcy blushed and dropped her eyes.

"Do you have an occupation or does your gallant husband provide for you?"

Darcy sat up straight in her chair. "I was…am…an investigative journalist. Until recently I was employed by a local newspaper, but since…" Darcy's voice trailed off and Francesca noticed the sad countenance on the young woman's face, as she looked off into the distance.

"Has something happened?" she asked, reaching out and touching Darcy's arm.

Darcy blinked…why hide behind her personal tragedy? She decided to explain.

"Yes, I recently gave birth to a stillborn baby boy."

Francesca clasped a hand to her mouth. "Oh, my dear…I am so sorry for you and Henri. Was it a full-term birth?"

Darcy felt at ease with Sam's daughter. "Eight months…he was perfect…except he failed to breathe.

Chantal was my midwife. She told us it is more common than people think – but it tends to be hushed up, as if it didn't happen."

Francesca took hold of the young woman's hand. "It's a situation which needs to change, Darcy. Did you hold your baby after the birth?"

Darcy nodded. "Yes, I was fortunate. Chantal, as my aunt and midwife, insisted Henri and I were allowed to spend some time with our little boy. I've since talked to other mothers in a similar situation, who were denied holding their baby. It was only brief…but at least we managed to say goodbye to him, before he was taken away."

The two young women sat in silence. Francesca squeezed Darcy's hand. And looked into her eyes.

"You are brave talking about it, Darcy."

"I want to do more than talk about it, Francesca. I want to write about it. It's a scandal. Stillborn babies are snatched away and disposed of – we have no idea where our Leon is buried. After he was taken, I was treated as if nothing had happened. It was mental cruelty. Something must change…I don't know what…but I intend to write an article, and have it published, hopefully in a national newspaper. The whole process was cold and clinical."

Francesca could feel the hurt, the sadness…the deep emotional distress tormenting Darcy.

"I agree with you, Darcy. If it will help, I could ask some of the young mothers at my surgery, who trod a similar path, if they would be willing to share their experiences. Perhaps you could put together a questionnaire, and I will approach the women I feel could assist you."

Darcy was amazed. This was the first time she had found someone who seemed to be sympathetic to what she and Henri had suffered.

"Thank you, Francesca. Investigative journalism is the public's way of learning the truth about concealed issues."

Francesca nodded.

***

The following day Con and Hope were introduced to their big sister. The concept was beyond the young children's understanding, but Francesca won their admiration by focusing on their individual interests. Hope wanted 'Fran' to play 'schools', which she did… allowing Hope to be the teacher, while she acted as the naughty girl in the class. Con took delight in explaining to Francesca's boyfriend the importance of nurturing a young seedling. Jack was amazed at the young boy's knowledge.

An outing to the playpark rounded off the morning, including a game of 'hide and seek'.

"They are delightful," exclaimed Francesca as they made their way back to Meckleridge for lunch.

"Any update on the house hunting?" Sam asked, tentatively, knowing it was crucial to the house and contents sale.

Francesca stopped walking and smiled at her father. "A definite yes, Dad. Mither has decided to lease an apartment, in Abbeyfield on Dalton Road."

Sam looked perplexed until Francesca reminded him of some landmarks in the city suburbs.

"Oh, yes, I can picture them now. Quite spacious as I recall."

"Yes, it ticks her boxes – still in an upmarket location, close to her Bridge Group and two of her 'set' live nearby. I'm going to move in with her in the short term, until my house sale is completed. My house is closer to where I work, but only a short bus journey from Mither's apartment."

"Fran," interrupted Hope. "I think you are pronouncing the word mother wrong – it's mother, not mither." Francesca and Sam laughed.

"Little ears, Francesca – better tell me the rest later."

While Con and Hope were becoming acquainted with Francesca, Marcel arrived to help Josh with his jalopy. After listening to the details of Josh's injury, the pair walked down to the outhouse where Beryl resided.

"I was making great strides until this happened," Josh moaned. "It's set me back at least a week. I'm so grateful for your assistance today, Marcel."

"You tell me what to do and I'll tackle it as best I can, with your overseeing eye, of course."

The two young men worked intensely until lunchtime.

"I sense an urgency to have Beryl up and running soon, Josh…am I correct?"

Josh pulled a face. "Sort of, Marcel. I've got my eye on a girl and I'm hoping I can wear her down and get her to accept a date very soon, hence I need my wheels ready."

Marcel looked intrigued. "Why do you need to wear her down…is there some kind of problem with just asking her for a date?"

"It's complicated, Marcel. I've known Judy since school. She was the nurse on Darcy's ward when she lost the baby and when I spoke to her, she rebuffed me. A week later I saw her at a local dance and asked if we could be friends…that ended the following day with a puzzling comment about her family forbidding us to be friends. I don't know what I've done, Marcel." He paused, pointing at a bolt which needed tightening.

"However, something is working in our favour, because I have met her on three separate occasions since then… the garage, the dentist's and would you believe it …she was the nurse who attended to me, when I had this accident! I think there has been a slight shift in her attitude towards me, so next time I see her, I'm going to ask if we can meet properly."

Josh felt relieved to have shared his tale of woe with Marcel. He liked him and felt they could become friendly.

"Sounds a tricky one, Josh. But remember my kind of work…I'm good at digging into mysterious things. Let me know if I can help in any way."

Later that evening, the walls of Meckleridge House resounded to lively chatter, peals of laughter and high-pitched voices, as the crowd of youngsters enjoyed Rachel's cooking and some dancing, courtesy of Tom's gramophone.

Chrissie had accepted Darcy's invitation to the house party and for the first time in many months she 'let her hair down' and enjoyed the company of young people, including a young Frenchman by the name of Marcel Duval.

Chapter 12

Rose Caudwell arrived at the terraced house in Durham at 8.30 on Monday morning. It was cold but bright for early November. Henri drove her in his sports car. After discussing the situation with her husband, Darcy had packed a small suitcase and decided to accept Bertha's offer of hospitality.

"I'm only a phone call away," she'd commented to Henri. "And you could pop over one evening."

Henri was reluctant to be separated from his young wife but accepted that it made sense for her to stay in Durham whilst fulfilling her investigation assignment.

After a rattle on the door knocker, Bertha Remington opened the door. Stepping into the hallway, Darcy introduced Henri.

"Put your suitcase in the room at the back, overlooking the yard," Bertha indicated, as Darcy climbed the stairs.

Marcel appeared from his bedroom. "Good morning, you two. Are you all set? That was a great night on Saturday. Your parents certainly know how to entertain," he remarked, smiling.

Henri followed Darcy into the bedroom where she would be staying. It was small and functional.

Bertha called from downstairs. "We need to be on our way, Rose."

Quickly, Henri and Darcy said their goodbyes and returned downstairs.

Bertha was fastening her coat and checking her hat in the hall stand mirror. Marcel was standing in the hallway.

"I'm not coming with you – I've got things to see to, but you know what to do, Rose – hopefully there will be no problems. We'll have a good chat later, when you return."

And just like that, Darcy Dukas in her alias as Rose Caudwell, was launched into her first undercover assignment.

"What time does Mr Coleman expect you?" Darcy asked, as they left the house.

"Reggie's not bothered about time keeping. I set my own hours – but I try to be there before half past nine."

Their walk took them down North Road and across Framwellgate Bridge. Rose stopped and stared up at the cathedral which dominated the city.

"I love Durham Cathedral," she commented to Bertha, while peering over the bridge into the River Wear. The cathedral was on a hill almost surrounded by the river – an advantageous position when it was built nine hundred years ago.

Momentarily, she recalled the day she and Henri had visited the towering building, before their romance began. It was the day the 'ice broke' between them – she always looked on that occasion as the beginning of their love story.

CHAPTER 12

"We need to hurry, Rose, or we will be late," Bertha urged.

The presence of the solid cathedral gave Darcy a comforting feeling.

They continued up Silver Street, across the marketplace onto Claypath. Eventually, they turned into Providence Row where Reginald Coleman's house was situated. The walk had taken twenty minutes, and Rose was pleased they had arrived, as her toes felt pinched in her borrowed shoes.

"Right, Bertha – remember I'm Rose, and I'm not the brightest button in the box."

Bertha smiled – she liked this young woman.

Rose placed her glasses on her nose, her mental prompt to act 'dim'.

Mr Coleman's study was at the front of the house just off the hallway. It was dark and smelt musty. Heavy drapes were drawn across the windows.

"Welcome to my study, Miss Caudwell," Mr Coleman announced, rising from his desk to shake Rose's hand. She guessed he was in his mid-seventies.

"As I indicated last week, I'm not keeping on top of things these days, but a couple of weeks should restore the place to order."

Rose glanced around the room…there were piles of papers everywhere – on the desk, on chairs, on top of filing cabinets and on the floor. The room was in chaos.

"I'll do my best, Mr Coleman," she responded, flatly.

"I'm involved in a restoration project for a historical house in the city. I'm a history fanatic and the society to which I belong recently purchased the house. Sadly, it is in disrepair, but we have a dedicated group of volunteers who are keen to restore the place. Because of my background in banking, I was given the task of overseeing the finances, but I underestimated how much paperwork would be involved. Thankfully everything is kept at the house. I love being there looking through the many artefacts and the fabulous library."

Rose dreaded to think how disorganised that office would be – sorting this room would be a formidable task.

"May I open the curtains please – my eyes aren't too good," she lied. A desk lamp did little to brighten the room. "What do you expect me to do, Mr Coleman?" she asked.

"Sort the place, young lady, that's your job. I gather from Bertha you can organise and file things, so I think I'll leave you to get on with it. If you come across any cash, put it in the black box, which you'll find in that bottom drawer. I tend to leave money lying around in various places and I must get into the habit of keeping it in here instead."

He made to leave the room.

"My nephew Gordon may visit. He's my late sister's son. We are not on the best of terms. I intend to leave my assets to the historical society when I 'pop my clogs'. Gordon is furious about this. His mother was left a piece of land but the documentation for this is missing. My nephew is convinced it is in this office. He visits when I am at the house and rummages around. I think he helps himself to any cash he finds in the process. If he finds the document, he can happily have it. I just wish he wasn't so sneaky about it." Rose nodded, trying to look glum.

"Well, I'll leave you to begin, Miss Caudwell," he concluded and left the room.

***

Josh had prepared himself for disappointment. He felt sure reflecting on their recent encounter in the hospital casualty department that Judy Dempster would be cautious. He knew he'd caught her 'off guard'. Their brief connection, although overshadowed by pain, discomfort and embarrassment on his behalf, had shone as a beacon of hope. As the weeks had passed since their encounter in the park, he'd found himself drawn to the young woman. The knowledge that any liaison between them was forbidden only fuelled his fondness for her. The proximity afforded during his medical care was a bonus opportunity. He only hoped he hadn't 'blown it' by giving her that peck on the cheek.

After checking in at the desk he took a seat in the waiting area, his eyes scanning the room for any signs of Judy, but she was nowhere to be seen. He watched and listened. The staff were so busy, darting here and there. It was a relentless flow of injuries and concerns, some more apparent than others. The medical staff worked carefully, affording each patient the same concern and care, no matter what ailed them. This all helped to sharpen his admiration for Judy Dempster.

Suddenly, his heart quickened as he heard her voice calling his name from behind.

"Come this way, please," she instructed. He followed along another corridor this time to a separate waiting area where Judy pointed to a chair without making any comment – professionalism, he assumed. Another lengthy wait ensued. Judy passed in front of him numerous times but made no acknowledgement of his presence.

He possessed no plan of action other than to speak to Judy… if an opportunity afforded itself. His turn came. He was shown into the treatment room by a different nurse, and his heart sank. The nurse removed his sling and bandages. She was efficient. The doctor arrived. Josh was surprised at the size of his wound – it looked raw and angry with the stitches, but the doctor gave grunts of satisfaction over his findings. He asked Josh to perform various movements with his fingers, wrists and arms.

"Good, Mr Smallwood, the damage seems to be limited to the wound itself, which will heal in time. Nurse will dress it again and make a further appointment for you. In the meantime, try to engage in gentle arm, finger and wrist movements." The doctor left the small room. Just as the nurse was putting together the clean dressings, the door opened, and Judy stepped inside.

"Sister wants you," she said to the nurse. "I'll see to the patient." The nurses swapped places. Unbelievable…now was his chance!

"How've you been?" he asked, by way of introduction.

Not a flicker on her face as she worked efficiently. She gave a curt reply. "Well, thanks." She wasn't making this easy.

"Did you think any more about that 'maybe'?" He dared to ask.

Momentarily, she looked up and their eyes met… something was there. His heart fluttered. She shrugged and continued to wind bandage around the wound. He placed his head on the side.

"Come on, Judy…you want to, don't you?" he whispered. "Somewhere out of town – away from busy bodies and gossip mongers." No response. Time was running out.

A tap on the door signalled the entry of the sister.

"Hurry up, Nurse Dempster, there's a long queue out there." His chance was gone.

The sister left and Judy moved away from Josh, buying herself time with her instruments.

One last attempt... "Name a place, date and time and I'll meet you. I can get a car," he whispered. A minute later she handed him his appointment card along with a scrap of paper. He glanced at it. It read:

'Granley bus station, next Saturday 3pm – might not turn up.'

"It's a date," he said, walking on air.

"No, it's not," she added. Josh turned and left the hospital.

***

Rose Caudwell set about her new job in a business-like fashion. Each evening, she reported to Marcel.

"Day after day, Marcel, all I find is total disorganisation. There is no system whatsoever. Honestly, you'd think he had deliberately tried to confuse any semblance of order in the place," she sighed.

"Are you sure this isn't too tiring for you?" Marcel enquired. Both Henri and Jonty had told Marcel how Darcy was recovering from a traumatic experience and needed to be careful.

"Of course it's not too tiring. You've been listening to my husband and cousin – they are so protective. I'm made of strong stuff, Marcel, so don't worry about me."

Marcel smiled at Darcy. When she came back from Mr Coleman's house she unclipped her bun, releasing her curly locks and changed into a shirt and slacks ..she was so attractive.

"So how long do you think it will take to reorganise Mr Coleman's study?" he asked, dismissing the inappropriate thoughts going through his mind.

"Oh, at least another week." She grinned. "Then, we can set out our plans to trap the nephew. What have you been up to this week?"

Marcel raised his eyebrows. "I'm making progress. I have viewed three potential offices. One seems to tick the boxes. It's above a public house, with its own side entrance, close to the city centre. I need to place a down payment of six months' rent to secure it." He looked thoughtful, then resumed. "Then I must source a desk, some chairs, filing cabinets and cupboards. I hope to visit a saleroom to purchase these – I'm not buying new items."

Darcy's face was a picture, Marcel noticed.

"What's so amusing?" he asked, grinning. Gosh, her humour was infectious.

The cogs were whirring in Darcy's mind…dare she express her idea?

Marcel waited, he could tell she was up to something.

"I've got a suggestion…but I doubt if you will agree," she teased.

"Out with it, madame…don't leave me in suspense."

Darcy paused.

"Well," she hesitated, "I won't be offended if you think it's ridiculous."

She was certainly a wily character, thought Marcel.

"Has the door got a half glass window?"

Marcel was totally perplexed. "Er, yes…it was previously rented by a tutor."

CHAPTER 12

"Excellent," came the response. "Then it should be straightforward to have your agency name embellished onto a new opaque glass panel."

"Yes," coaxed Marcel. "And the agency name will be?"

Darcy stood up, her eyes were on fire, her gesticulations were wild. "I can see it…oh, Marcel, I'm so excited. It's going to be …" She rattled her hands on the table, signifying a drum roll… "*DD's INVESTIGATION AGENCY*…what do you think?"

Marcel was flummoxed.

"*DD*'s?" he queried.

Darcy's eyes nearly popped out of their sockets in excitement.

"*DD*'s as in *Duval and Dukas*, of course. It has a ring to it, don't you think? A mysterious French-sounding ring. Of course, I will be a sleeping partner… I mean thing…not a partner…just a thing…a background person…someone who occasionally helps…someone with whom you can confide in… a human sounding board…what do you think, monsieur?"

Marcel was flabbergasted. Where had this idea of helping him after this first case, come from? But that was Darcy…give her an inch and she'd take a mile. He was being drawn into Darcy's web – like a fly with a spider. Oh, she was so tantalising.

She sat down and instantly looked defeated.

"You've got reservations, haven't you?" she voiced.

Marcel rubbed his head – what could he say?

"Yes and no, Darcy. I'm interested…it's intriguing! I agree it has a certain ring to it. I was thinking along the lines of *Duval*

Investigations … but the word 'agency' gives a professional feel. The *DDs* adds an air of mystery. But what will your husband say? It implies I have talked you into something."

Darcy was shaking her head. "Of course it doesn't. Listen, look at it this way. It's my gift to you. I don't want a penny from you for this assignment I'm on. I'll do it for free and gift my name – an inauguration gift to the agency. I might never be needed again…but I was here at the beginning…it feels significant, somehow. Please think about it."

Marcel stood up and walked over to Darcy's seat. He held out his hand, which she took. Then after a firm handshake, he added: "I like it, but it needs to have Henri's approval. If it gets it, then next week, I'll have my business cards and headed notepaper printed. I'll also order a new door panel and place an advert in the local newspapers. "Welcome aboard, partner," he announced.

***

Darcy was eagerly anticipating her reunion with Henri on Friday. Four nights away from him had been torture. She longed to feel the strength of his arms around her and fall into his loving embraces.

She donned her Rose Caudwell persona as she entered the house on Providence Row. Henri was coming over to collect her from Bertha's at 4 pm. Six hours of sorting, organising and filing. Was she making any headway? She must remain positive. She still couldn't understand how bank statements from before the war were placed beside estimates for roof repairs done last year. What did he do … think about the most random place to file them?

CHAPTER 12

Reginald was at the historical house and Bertha had gone into town to do some shopping. The house was quiet when the doorknocker reverberated through the hallway. An interruption was the last thing she needed. Should she ignore it? It could be Marcel.

"Bother," she muttered to herself as she made her way to the front door, remembering to put on her glasses.

Her jaw dropped, as she looked at the face of a stranger. Instinctively, she knew who he was and screwing up her eyes, she stared in a vacant fashion at the visitor.

"Oh, my, who are you?" the stranger exclaimed. "I was expecting Miss Remington to answer."

Rose stood frozen to the spot. He was not the slightest bit as she had imagined him.

"Excuse me," she retorted loudly, as he attempted to step over the door threshold. "Neither Mr Coleman nor Miss Remington are here. Can I take a message please?" she asked.

The short young man removed his trilby hat. His hair was light brown and wavy, matching his small moustache.

"Good day to you, whoever you may be. There is no message to give. I'm Mr Coleman's nephew, Gordon Sinclair. More to the point...who are you?" he asked with a definite northern accent.

Darcy retained her composure, screwing up her eyes. "I'm Rose Caudwell, Mr Coleman's secretary. I was not aware any visitors were expected today. I will let them know you called. My instructions are to allow no one into the house in Mr Coleman's or Miss Remington's absence." Rose twisted her face, trying to look dumb.

Gordon Sinclair was obviously annoyed.

"This won't do, I've travelled ten miles to visit my uncle's home and now I am being refused entry by some stuck-up, thick-headed, secretary."

Rose scowled at the man. "I'm only obeying orders," she commented, inwardly trembling.

Suddenly, without any warning, he pushed past Rose, strode into the hallway and headed for the study door.

"Hey, you can't do that," she shrieked. "You're not allowed in there."

"Oh, yes, I am, Miss Dumbface, I have every right to be here."

Stepping into the study, he let out a low whistle. "Is this your doing?"

"I have been employed by Mr Coleman to keep this office tidy," Rose responded.

Gordon Sinclair guffawed.

"Well, good luck to you on that score, Miss Dumbface. I've been trying to locate a document in old Reggie's possession for months without success…I think the old geezer has stashed it away somewhere deliberately. I suspect he's going a bit…you know." He pointed his finger at his head making circular movements. "But I intend to find it and claim what is rightfully mine, plus anything else I find which takes my fancy," he added, winking at her.

Rose could feel her skin creeping. The man was sleazy and insulting.

"I'll leave you to your task…but I'll be back next week, so try to…er…prepare yourself for my visit. Good day, Miss Dumbface." He swung out of the room and slammed the front door as he left.

Rose was shaking. That was awful. She felt intimidated.

Yet, she knew she mustn't complain, or Marcel and Henri would remove her instantly. No, she would mention his visit, but say she prevented him from searching the study, which effectively was the truth. She would also ensure she was not left alone in the house again.

Chapter 13

Darcy was waxing lyrical about her first week in her undercover role at breakfast. As usual, the family were enthralled by her dramatic accounts. But Josh's mind was elsewhere...his maybe date. Devouring his breakfast, he excused himself and set off to apply the finishing touches to Beryl, his old jalopy.

He stood back to admire his handiwork. After his accident last week, he thought it would set him back on the time front, but Marcel's help last weekend had been invaluable. After his follow-up appointment at the commencement of the week, he was energised to spend every spare minute on the old girl to make her roadworthy.

Here she was...his pride and joy. Sadly, she needed attention to the bodywork, but that was a task to be tackled another time. He was sure Judy would appreciate the effort he had made. He could have asked to use his dad's car...but somehow it didn't seem appropriate.

He was pleased his arm was healing. Under his shirt and jacket sleeve, his wound was invisible. His task this morning was to tidy up the interior. He set about cleaning and polishing the windows, inside and out. He wiped and polished the dashboard and door handles. Mother had supplied some rugs and cushions, which hid the tatty leather work.

Completed, he revved up the engine and reversed out of the outhouse, to take the newly revamped Beryl on her maiden voyage. As he was driving past the back door, his dad was exiting the house.

"Well done, young man. May I have a lift?" Tom climbed into the passenger seat. "Where are you headed?" he asked his son.

"Just up to the garage for some petrol. But I'm taking her for a spin later," he remarked, careful not to indicate he was going on a 'maybe date'.

Tom was complimentary about the renovation work, saying how good the engine sounded. "When I get back home, I'll look out some rubber mats for the floor well," he offered.

The hours seemed to drag. He pressed his trousers and shirt and polished his shoes – habits formed during his army days. Thankfully, Saturday was an 'out and about' day for the family, so no one was paying attention to Josh's activities. He'd told Marcel he was going to be out today, which suited the Frenchman, as he was busy with his agency plans. However, Marcel still intended to keep his Saturday evening rendezvous at Meckleridge House.

Slicking back his neatly trimmed hair, Josh admired his clean-shaven face, another inheritance from his time doing National Service. He was ready, surprising himself how nervous he felt. He'd dated many girls…but somehow this felt different.

He was aware of the thin strand linking him to Judy – almost as if at the blink of an eye she would change her mind and not show up.

He surmised the chosen meeting place was to avoid any prying eyes. Granley was five miles from Malhaven – a coal mining town. He'd only visited it on a few occasions with his dad, and in the farm truck with Bennie. These visits had involved collecting items, so they were brief.

He guessed Judy had chosen the location, the bus station – so she could take a direct bus from Malsett. What a palaver. He was travelling from Malhaven to Granley to meet Judy… who must take a bus up to Malsett from Malhaven, then another bus to Granley! All because of what? Some stupid family thing. He hoped his time with Judy today would enable him to solve this mystery. It felt deceptive…but he was grateful she had agreed to meet him.

He set off with plenty time to spare. He drove down the main street in Granley …what a dejected looking place. There were people dashing about, attending to shopping chores. He noted the various buildings one would expect in a small town – bank, churches, post office, shops of various types, a couple of public houses and a café. He noted the location of the latter. It was a cold November day, and Beryl did not possess any heat, so maybe they could benefit from the warmth in the café.

He located the bus station – he was freezing. He decided to park and walk around to keep his body moving. First problem – should he wait at the top entrance, or the bottom exit? Where did the bus from Malsett drop its passengers? He selected a position from which to watch the residents of Granley stepping on and off the buses.

CHAPTER 13

Why were people always in a hurry when travelling? Without exception the folk he observed were focused – their faces set, their stride purposeful. Rails separated the vehicles from the queues.

He stamped up and down, trying to generate some heat into his freezing bones. He was thankful for his scarf and gloves. Glancing at his watch he realised it was five minutes past the appointed time.

He'd prepared himself for disappointment, just as he'd done on his hospital appointment…but that produced a positive outcome – so he was hopeful. Five minutes grew to ten minutes, and Josh sighed. Had she led him on another wild goose chase? She was probably at home, sitting cosy in front of a roaring fire, laughing at his stupidity.

Suddenly, he heard a noise from behind. He turned and saw her figure standing three yards away beside the ladies' toilets entrance.

"Psst," she called.

He began to walk towards her.

"Walk to your car. I'll follow," she instructed. Memories of the run around in the park a few weeks earlier, flashed before his eyes.

A few minutes later he was unlocking his car. Although it was only three o'clock, the daylight was poor. Judy arrived and he opened the passenger door. Once inside she pulled off her headscarf and shook her hair. Josh climbed in and removed his gloves.

"Wretched things, headscarves, but it was a necessary part of my plan."

Josh shook his head and smiled. His heart was thumping. She was beautiful and here he was, sharing a small place with her, in the intimacy of his own car. Despite the cold – he felt triumphant!

"Come on…get moving," she urged.

Josh started the engine and put Beryl into gear.

"Where to?" he asked.

Judy shrugged. "Anywhere, apart from Malhaven and Malsett."

"Fine," muttered Josh, driving his old jalopy out of Granley.

"You do realise it's far too cold to sit in the car…unless you want to snuggle under a rug?" he chuckled. Why couldn't it have been a balmy summer's day, instead of a cold, damp, November afternoon?

"We could go for a walk…or find a snack bar. I think I spotted one on Front Street in Granley."

Judy looked at her watch which did little to encourage Josh…this was turning out to be harder than he'd anticipated.

"I don't know Granley. I just plucked it from thin air remembering a bus showing the name."

Josh was astounded. "Oh, I thought it held some significance for you." He found somewhere to reverse the car, and they headed back towards Granley to find a carpark.

Ten minutes later they were sitting in Fimambro's – an ice cream parlour in Granley. It was a moderate size with dark red bench seats and tables. In the corner was a juke box – a craze amongst the young people in the town. Several were standing around tapping their feet to the beat of the music. It was busy, but Josh spotted a couple vacating a booth in the corner and hurried towards it.

"Phew, that was jammy," he commented, as they took their seats. It was basic but cosy even if the windows were steamed up.

"What would you like to drink?" he asked, looking at the stained handwritten menu.

"Hot chocolate, please," Judy responded, without even glancing to see what was on offer.

Josh placed their order at the counter and when he returned, he noticed Judy had removed her gloves and shrugged off her coat.

"So, if Granley was a random choice, where else would you have picked?"

She looked at him and lifted her shoulders.

"No, idea. We live in such an out of the way place in Malhaven. If asked, I could invent a nurse I was friendly with…it might get me out of a tight corner."

Josh studied her face. A thought struck him. "Would you do that…for me… considering we are practically strangers?"

A slow smile spread across her face, which caused ripples of delight in Josh's stomach. "Of course…and we are not strangers, Josh. I can remember you way back in the second form – you were all pimply."

He felt himself blushing as he recalled those early teenage days. "A sight to forget, Judy. I hope I've improved," he chuckled.

"Well, I wouldn't be sitting opposite you now if you hadn't improved," she added.

"I'll take that as a compliment. I remember you in fifth form on that geography field trip, but you only had eyes for Fred Butler."

Their drinks arrived and they each wrapped their hands around the hot mugs.

"Yuck! Don't remind me. I haven't a clue why I was attracted to him, he was so full of himself, unlike you…you were different."

He tilted his head on the side and asked, "Different… in what way?"

Judy paused, as if seeking an appropriate answer. "Strong, silent, moody, mysterious. I suspect there are hidden layers to you, Josh Smallwood."

He wasn't sure how to take this. He watched as Judy looked at her watch, so decided to divert the conversation. "Am I permitted to drive you home?" he asked, tentatively.

Judy looked horrified. "Goodness me…no way. I need to be on the five o'clock bus or there will be trouble brewing with my dad."

They chatted about the music playing on the juke box. Josh asked if she'd been to many dances since the one where they met.

"Only two, Dad doesn't approve. I get to go occasionally, so I can keep my friends."

Josh paid for their drinks and buttoning up, they left the snack bar. Quite naturally Judy linked Josh's arm…he felt elated.

Back in the car Josh turned to face Judy.

"I enjoyed that…can we repeat it sometime?" For the briefest of moments, he feared he had overstepped the mark, then her eyes lit up.

"Yes, Josh, it's been good and yes, I would like to meet you again sometime, but it is so risky. It's got to be away from

Malsett and Malhaven…if Dad ever found out, he'd…" Her words drifted away.

Josh bent forward and cupped her chin. He could see fear in her eyes.

"You're frightened of your dad, aren't you?"

She remained motionless. He moved in closer and kissed her gently on the lips. Pulling back, she grabbed his wounded arm. He winced.

"Oh, I'm sorry I forgot…how is your arm?"

"Healing," he replied, annoyed the mention of his accident had disrupted the flow in their discourse. She reached out and took hold of his hand.

"My dad is all eaten up over this thing about your family, Josh, but I must dash. Same place next week?"

Josh agreed and watched as she put on her headscarf again. He jumped out of Beryl, intending to walk Judy back around to the bus station, but she shook her head.

"Best not, Josh. I'm scared someone recognises us. Goodbye, see you next week." He watched as she walked away, then returned to his car.

All the way home Josh replayed the look of fear evident in Judy's eyes. Two things had been achieved today. Firstly, Judy was happy to meet him again…that was a positive. Secondly, Judy's father had something against his family… that was a mystery.

***

Marcel was just parking his 2CV car in the rear yard as Josh drove past to return Beryl to the outhouse. Marcel walked down the slope to meet him.

"That was good timing," Marcel remarked, then noticing Josh's smart appearance, asked, "Have you been somewhere special this afternoon?"

Josh closed the out-house door and joined Marcel. "Success, my friend. Remember me telling you about that 'maybe date', last week? Well, good news… it happened this afternoon."

Marcel slapped Josh on the back. "Great. How did it go?"

"It wasn't a conventional sort of date, but it went well, and… we're repeating it next week. However, I'm no nearer discovering why our friendship is forbidden. All I could glean is that her dad holds something against our family. I'm not sure she even knows what it is, Marcel."

Slowly, the two young men walked up the slope towards the house.

"Sounds like the kind of thing I could look into for you, Josh."

"Really?" Josh asked. "Is that the sort of stuff you do?"

"Mysteries are my speciality, Mr Smallwood," he chuckled. "I'm serious, Josh. And I'm not looking for payment – your family have been so kind to me. If I can unearth some helpful information, then I will. I'll get some details from you later."

An idea had begun, and Josh felt hopeful.

Rachel was in her element. Organising house parties back in the hotel days had been her speciality. The objective was always to let the guests have a great time. Delicious home cooked food, lively entertainment, discussions and debates and a relaxing atmosphere were the required ingredients.

CHAPTER 13

"You're enjoying all this entertaining again, aren't you," observed Tom, as she was laying the table in the dining room.

"Yes, it's so good to see the next generation enjoying themselves. It's only what you make it, Tom. It would be so easy to eat, then all drift off to our rooms or sit in front of that contraption in the corner of the lounge. Young people need fun, and I hope my organisation will provide that."

Tom listened and reflected. Since the arrival of the television, he'd noticed how conversation seemed to cease when everyone was focused on the programme.

Saturday evenings were usually 'do it yourself' but Rachel had upturned that idea since Marcel had been visiting.

"Who's coming tonight apart from the family and Marcel?"

"Just Darcy's friend Chrissie. But Tom, I was thinking about asking Sam to invite Francesca to stay over Christmas. She seemed to enjoy herself when she was here."

"No problem with me. Don't they make more fuss of New Year in Scotland, than they do about Christmas?"

"Yes, that's true. We celebrate both. It will be a big one for us next year, Tom…our silver wedding anniversary."

Tom walked over to his wife and gave her a hug. "Where have the years gone, Rachel? We must plan a big family event for then …see if Peg and family can make it."

"Yes, well… to the here and now. Can you sort the drinks, Tom?"

Darcy had briefly mentioned her suggestion of the name for Marcel's agency, on her return from Durham.

Henri listened and looked thoughtful. "I understand your enthusiasm, Darcy, but we barely know Marcel – aren't you in danger of linking yourself with him, if you do this? Your undercover assignment is surely just a temporary thing. Adding your name into the agency gives it a more permanent feel. Don't be hasty."

Darcy was not impressed with Henri's reaction.

"No, it doesn't. I told him that. I may never do any work for him again. I'm not financially involved in any way. I regard it as a friendly gesture…a support. Please consider it, Henri…he needs to get his stationery sorted and the door thingy done this next week."

Henri agreed to 'sleep on it'.

Marcel stood in his room. He'd only known this family for a few weeks, but already they'd become a big part of his life. They were so welcoming. He thought back to his own family home in Calais. He loved his parents, and they supported him, but they lived their own lives. They were always attending functions which did not include him. As an only child he'd often felt left out. He held fond memories of living in that little house in Durham, before his parents married. Once he'd moved to France things changed. Family occasions were limited to a routine chat over their evening meal.

Meeting Jonty at university had opened a whole new lifestyle for him and he'd enjoyed visiting Jonty's family home in Lyon. He could see the similarities between Tom and Jonty's mother, Peg. He was enjoying lodging with his Aunt Bertha, but he looked forward to these weekend stays at Meckleridge House.

The meal was in full swing, when the telephone rang. It was Francesca. Hearing her name prompted Rachel to propose her suggestion. She'd already mentioned the idea to Chantal and Sam, who seemed open to the prospect. She went out into the hallway as Sam was listening to his daughter.

"Ask her about Christmas," she mouthed.

Sam nodded.

When Sam rejoined the others, Chantal gave him a questioning look.

"Great news, Evelyn and Francesa are moving out of Matthison Hall at the end of November. I hope the house contents sale can take place early in the new year."

"Rachel," he called across the table, "Francesca would be delighted to join us for Christmas."

Whoops of joy sounded from the youngsters. Francesca had made an impression on them all.

Yet, one guest around the table looked on quietly. Chrissie Leveridge was feeling out of place. She'd known Darcy since school days. They'd shared their teenage struggles together – likes, dislikes and boyfriend crushes. But now Darcy had moved on. Here she was happily married, living in a supportive extended family home and embarking on her dream job, to become an investigative journalist.

Whereas she was living with her widowed mother and working in the family business. There were no problems at home, but it was her past which saddened her – she was tainted. Who would want to relate to her? She'd been a fool and now she would live to regret it. Grady Forrester had taken something precious from her.

She watched on, noticing the Frenchman Marcel Duval, he was so handsome, and single...how could she ever attract him? He had eyes for only one person – her friend Darcy Dukas.

Chapter 14

Darcy was apprehensive, as Henri drove her to Durham. A bleak, cold November day heralded the second week of her undercover work. She'd played down any hint of the intimidation she'd felt during Gordon Sinclair's visit, when talking about it to Marcel and Henri… but now her bravado seemed to have vanished.

Henri talked about the agency name on the journey over and he'd seemed to have warmed to the notion. Trying to stay light-hearted, Darcy chuckled, "There's another name beginning with 'D' which could be added."

Henri glanced at her.

"Dumbface," she announced with glee. "Mr Coleman's nephew called me Miss Dumbface on his visit…so, 'DD's' could stand for Duval, Dukas and Dumbface Agency."

At times like this, Henri realised how innocent and playful his young wife could be. Did she realise the dangers this kind of work could produce?

"Darcy, I would not be sharing that with anyone, it's not exactly professional," he rebuked.

Darcy pouted. "No, perhaps not…but it's fun."

Marcel accompanied Bertha and Darcy to the house in Providence Row on Monday morning.

"I want to discuss the next stage of our investigation with Mr Coleman," he explained.

Rose donned her glasses and adopted her role, as they sat in the parlour with Reggie Coleman. The elderly man praised Rose's efforts during the previous week.

"That's good to hear," remarked Marcel. "Now, Mr Coleman, your nephew visited on Friday afternoon. I understand he is prone to making these unannounced visits and Rose did a splendid job of explaining her presence."

Reggie rubbed his chin. "He is convinced I have a document in my possession, relating to a piece of land his mother was supposed to own. I handled my sister's estate when she died. Gordon was just a youngster – his father was never on the scene. Quite frankly, I have no idea about this document, but he is convinced I'm hiding it. However, it's this money business which rankles me. I don't like the idea he is stealing from me."

"I have found money, Mr Coleman," interjected Rose. "I put it in that cash box, as you instructed," she explained. Rose had found amounts of money, stashed away, some in envelopes, in small amounts, hidden amongst files. Once again Reggie applauded Rose's work.

"So, Mr Coleman, I take it you are still in agreement for Rose to entrap your nephew?"

Reggie sighed. "I want to teach him a lesson – let him know I'm on to him. I want to give him a fright. I have no intention of going to the police though."

Marcel understood. If the work were to become a police matter, it would be out of his hands. This way, he could create a situation where the culprit could be caught… hopefully 'red handed'.

"We have no idea when Mr Sinclair will return, but I will show Rose the procedure. She will then lay the trap. I intend to be on the premises, hidden of course, to confront the culprit when Rose gives the signal."

It all sounded surreal to Darcy. She was working at the heart of an active situation. Yet, her excitement was overshadowed by fear – Gordon Sinclair had unnerved her.

During the conversation, Rose learned Gordon's visits were usually made towards the end of the week.

"He knows when I go out shopping. Invariably, he shows up before I leave the house on a Thursday or a Friday morning. He's such a smarmy character, offering to make me a cup of tea when I return," remarked Bertha, with obvious distaste.

"Well, I'm taking no chances," added Marcel. "I have things requiring my attention on Monday and Tuesday, but we will put our plan into action for the end of the week."

Reggie was more than happy to leave this young investigator and the temporary secretary to carry out their work, and was soon off to his usual haunt.

Before he left, Rose showed Marcel the remaining cabinets and a cupboard, yet to be sorted. They decided on four areas of the study where Rose would leave the trap.

"What was Henri's decision regarding 'DD's'?" asked Marcel, as he was about to depart.

"He's okay about it, Marcel. He had reservations at first but eventually came around to the idea. How about you? Have you had any further thoughts?"

Marcel grinned, watching Rose sorting a pile of papers which had been living on the floor, in a corner.

"I like it. It hints at more than a one-man band. Today, I am signing the lease on the office space, I'm going to order my business cards and hopefully 'DD's Investigation Agency' will be up and running very soon."

On Wednesday morning, Marcel handed Rose a pair of rubber gloves. Then retrieving a jar and a brush from his briefcase placed the items on an old newspaper on Reggie's desk. The office did not resemble the dark, untidy, musty room it had been ten days ago. With Rose's careful handiwork, piles of unsorted documents were reorganised and filed in some semblance of order. The drapes and windows were opened each day, allowing light and fresh air to pervade the room.

Under Marcel's direction, Rose carefully dusted some £1, and 10-shilling notes. These were placed in a dusted envelope and put in a file. The amounts were small, and the files were made to look haphazard, as if they were unsorted. Four areas were selected.

"Surely, one of these will attract Mr Sinclair's attention. Once his fingers touch this, he will be marked. It can only be removed with a particular substance, or repeated washing."

But Gordon Sinclair made no appearance on Wednesday.

Returning to their lodgings, Darcy made to go upstairs, as was her habit, to rid herself of her disguise.

"Do you enjoy dancing, Darcy?" Marcel asked from the hallway, as she reached the stair head.

"Of course, Marcel, surely you gathered that the other week at Mecklerigde, when Francesca visited. Why do you ask?"

"I love dancing and have discovered a venue in town, where a dance band plays each Wednesday and Saturday evening. So far, I have not attended, but by way of a change, would you like to go there tonight for a couple of hours after our evening meal?"

Darcy was stunned. Should she? Dancing was something she missed. Henri's condition made dancing impossible and to avoid aggravating the issue, the young couple rarely frequented any such establishment. Dancing at Meckleridge House was limited to guest occasions.

Marcel sensed her hesitancy. "Give Henri a call and ask for his permission, Darcy. I'm not trying to be underhand. All this undercover work is wearying for you. I only wanted to offer you a moment of escapism."

Put that way, it seemed a possibility…why trouble Henri… he was such a dear… he would probably tell her to go and enjoy herself.

"I'll have a think, Marcel, but I doubt if my 'Rose wardrobe' will turn up anything suitable to wear," she commented.

"You'll be fine, Darcy. I'll be going in any case, but I thought it only polite to invite you."

Darcy went to her room and changed into a dress. Something about Marcel's phraseology rankled her…why did she need Henri's permission?

After supper, Darcy looked at Marcel. "I'll join you," she said and started to clear the table.

Bertha reached out her hand. "Leave those, I'll see to them," she instructed. "Have yourself a change of scenery, it will do you good."

Grabbing her coat Darcy joined Marcel.

CHAPTER 14

The Alambra was a dance hall in Durham. Since his move to the city, Marcel had ventured out a few times, visiting various public houses and the cinema. He'd been eager to attend the dance hall and now was his opportunity.

Darcy adored dancing and having an agile dance partner was such a bonus. As Marcel had said… it was true escapism. The dance band played, and Marcel whirled and twirled his partner, as the pair released some pent-up energy. The time flew by. Walking back, Darcy thanked Marcel.

"That was just what I needed, thanks for suggesting it, Marcel. It was a good venue. Maybe we could do it again sometime and ask Josh, Henri and Chrissie to join us."

Just after eleven the next morning, there was a rattle on the doorknocker at the house in Providence Row. Bertha was in the kitchen and Marcel was upstairs. Rose answered the door.

The smarmy Gordon Sinclair stood on the doorstep grinning smugly.

"Good morning, Miss Dumbface. As promised, I am back to continue my search." He walked into the hallway before Darcy could reply.

Bertha appeared from the kitchen.

"Are you going out shopping today, Miss Remmington?" he asked. "I'm already acquainted with my uncle's new secretary. I don't envy her job trying to sort that office." He prattled on and as planned, Bertha put on her coat and hat to supposedly go into town.

"I'm sure Miss Secretary, here, can make me a nice cup of tea in your absence," he commented.

"My name is Miss Caudwell," announced Rose indignantly.

Gordon ignored her and made his way to the study. The muscles in Rose's stomach clenched...was this it? She followed Mr Sinclair into the room.

"What's your system?" he asked. "Do you have one?"

Ignoring his derisory comment, she explained her system.

"Receipts are in this drawer – under year headings: invoices are kept in the top drawer, in separate files – paid and unpaid. Information pamphlets are kept in the filing cabinet over there. Bank statements are in the drawer underneath. I haven't started on that cabinet or the small cupboard in the corner yet," she remarked.

Gordon listened.

"Then I'll look in there today," he commented. "You get on with your business and I'll attend to mine. I'm after an old planning document...don't suppose you've come across one of those?"

Rose pursed her lips and put on her 'dim' face. Gordon shook his head.

"Er...I might have found something like that. I put it in a tray in that cupboard over there," she replied.

Gordon followed her directions. Time to act, thought Rose.

"I'll go and make some tea," she announced, and opening the door coughed loudly – the signal for Marcel, who was loitering on the landing. She closed the door and walked through to the kitchen to make a pot of tea.

Marcel descended the stairs surreptitiously and paused outside the study door. He could hear doors and drawers being opened and closed... fingers crossed; their act of trickery was working. He went in search of Rose.

"So far, so good. Give him a few minutes and go back into the study," he whispered. Rose was returning to the study with the tea tray when she heard Gordon speaking to himself.

"What the blazes is this…?" he remarked.

Marcel signalled for her to go into the study. She put the tray down on the hall table and opened the door. Gordon was standing by the window rubbing a pink stained handkerchief over his hands.

"Oh dear, Mr Sinclair, whatever is the matter?" Quickly, Gordon stuffed his hand and handkerchief into his pocket.

"I think I'll leave my search for another day, Miss Caudwell," he grimaced, just as Marcel stepped inside the room.

"Who are you?" asked Gordon, with a look of suspicion.

"I'm Marcel, Bertha's nephew," he replied, offering his hand. Without thinking Gordon responded…too late…a pink tinged hand was in evidence. Marcel gripped Gordon's hand and held it tightly.

"Miss Caudwell, could you check those areas, please," Marcel instructed.

Darcy put on her rubber gloves and proceeded to examine the four areas. Gordon wrenched his hand from Marcel's grip and made for the door, just as the key was turned from the other side by Bertha, who had only walked around the block and returned to play her part.

"Do you have anything to say, Mr Sinclair?" asked Marcel, as Gordon tried the knob.

"I might have guessed that stuck up little tart was up to no good," he snarled. "Who did you say you were?"

"I'm a private investigator and I have reason to believe you have availed yourself of some money belonging to Mr Coleman."

Gordon pulled himself up straight and reaching into his inside pocket, slammed the money onto the desk.

"There, have it and tell old Coleman I don't take kindly to being tricked. I deserve every bit of that cash I find lying around in here. He's leaving all his dosh to that wretched house project when he goes. By rights it should come to me. I'll find that document one day," he growled.

Rose completed her search and placed the four empty envelopes on the desk.

"Your uncle hired me to unveil your suspected thievery, Mr Sinclair. He wished to take no action if we were successful, so take this as a warning. You have got off lightly today but give your uncle the respect he deserves. Everyone is entitled to leave their possessions to whoever, or whatever cause they want." Marcel tapped on the door, which Bertha unlocked.

Then Gordon beat a speedy retreat, slamming the front door.

"Phew," remarked Bertha – "I hope that's the last we see of him."

"Let's hope... now, team, a cup of tea would be in order."

Bertha picked up the tea tray.

***

Darcy relayed the climax of her undercover work to the family over supper on Friday evening.

CHAPTER 14

"How much longer will you be working in Durham?" Tom enquired, when Darcy returned home on Friday teatime.

"Probably a couple of days' work left at the house, then Marcel is getting the keys for his new office on Wednesday, so I've offered to help him sort things. I imagine I'll be back by the end of next week."

"You were very brave, Darcy," remarked Chantal.

Darcy grinned at her aunt. "It must run in the family," she responded.

Her aunt's bravery during WW2 was a close family secret. Chantal had worked with the French Resistance but pledged to keep the details confidential, other than to her closest relatives.

"How are things progressing with the house sale, Sam?" Darcy enquired. "I feel as if I've been away for months, instead of a couple of weeks."

"Francesca and her mother are moving into a new apartment at the end of the month. This will enable me to sort through the items for the house sale, to be held early in the new year. Then the property can be put on the market. There's already a list of interested parties."

Rachel looked thoughtful. "I suggest you go up with Sam, Chantal. There may be items of furniture you would like to keep. Furnishing a house from scratch is expensive. We'll look after the twins."

"Thanks, Rachel, that's a great idea," remarked Sam. "I would like Chantal to see the inside of the house before it sells."

Chantal smiled. Yes, she would enjoy that, having only seen the house by peering through the gates years ago.

Darcy turned to her brother. "Any further developments with you, Josh?"

"Nothing to report," he added, hoping to sound nonchalant, annoyed with his sister for raising the subject of his personal life.

"So…the roof didn't collapse during my absence …did it?"

"I missed you." Henri grinned. "And so did Lady." The little spaniel jumped up at the mention of her name.

Darcy went in search of Josh after supper.

"Come on, Josh Smallwood…I want details. Marcel said you had a date, and he's offered to help you uncover a mystery."

Josh sighed. His sister was like a dog with a bone.

"I met Judy in a roundabout way, but I'm none the wiser as to her problem with me. However, she has agreed to meet me again. I get the feeling she's frightened of her father and dreads anyone seeing us together. We met in Granley, of all places. I'm grateful to Marcel for his offer, but I may need to see her a few times to get anything for him to work on."

Unknown to Josh, his mother overheard the last part of his conversation.

"Josh…what's all this about?" she asked with curiosity.

Josh gave his sister a stern look.

"Nothing, mother," he remarked, annoyed at his mother's prying.

"Don't you keep secrets from me, young man, I need to know."

Josh was annoyed. Nothing was private in this house. "Mother, it's my business…not yours…or Darcy's…it's personal and private. I'm going to my room." He stormed out of the kitchen.

Rachel looked at Darcy in amazement.

"He's turned quite cheeky since his stint in the army. Do you know what it's all about?" Rachel asked.

"Oh, let him be, Mother. He's almost twenty-one…a grown man. He's entitled to live his own life."

Rachel stood with her hands on her hips. "If he's living under this roof and we're keeping him fed and watered …then I reckon I deserve to know what's going on in my son's life."

Darcy rolled her eyes and left the kitchen.

Chapter 15

DECEMBER 1952

It was almost four months since Josh's return to civilian life, and he was still unemployed in his mother's eyes. Technically, he was working as a farmhand, receiving a nominal wage for helping on the farm, as and when his services were required. Bennie, the farm manager, was attending medical appointments frequently, and Josh volunteered to step in and cover for him, so Tom decided to employ him.

He'd also taken over some regular delivery slots from the market garden to various outlying places. In between, he seemed to be the family chauffeur – ferrying his mother around and frequently collecting the twins from school.

Amid all this, his restoration work on Beryl continued to vie for his attention and Josh was struggling to see how he could ever maintain a full-time job.

Yet financially it bothered him. He would soon be twenty-one and he needed to start saving for his future.

CHAPTER 15

"All set for tonight?" asked Darcy, as he popped into the kitchen for a drink.

"Yep," he responded. "Plans are made – we're meeting Marcel at his aunt's house and leaving the car there."

Josh's friendship with Judy was progressing since their 'maybe' date in November. They'd repeated the same routine each Saturday, visiting the café in Granley. It wasn't ideal, but it provided a way for them to become acquainted, without the fear of being seen by someone who would inform Judy's family. They were quite relaxed in each other's company now and enjoying their new friendship. But Josh was keen to take their friendship a step further.

"Let's be adventurous," Josh announced to Judy the previous week. "My friend Marcel visits a dance hall in Durham and is keen for Darcy, Henri, you and I to join him. I think Darcy is going to ask her friend Chrissie to join us. Think about it, Judy – we could spend quality time, dancing… might that be possible?"

Judy was reluctant. "I'd love to do that, Josh, but I would need help… perhaps I could ask Joan, my nurse friend, if I could stay at her house next Saturday? Leave it with me and I'll let you know."

Josh had reservations as to Judy's hopes, but on Tuesday evening there was an unexpected phone call for him.

"Hello Josh… I've got some good news. I'm invited to stay at Joan's house next Saturday night, and dad says I can go. Can you meet me at the usual place, but at six o'clock. I'll go down like I usually do in the afternoon, then get ready at her place. I can direct you to her house when we return."

Since their first rendezvous in Granley, Judy had become acquainted with a nurse who lived in the town. They'd met on the bus and become friendly – it provided a perfect cover for Judy's secret meetings with Josh.

The young people met at Marcel's lodgings. Introductions were made and they walked to the venue. Darcy was excited, but apprehensive – she'd decided to keep quiet about her previous visit to the establishment– she wasn't sure why, but now it was troubling her. She'd suggested the visit to Marcel, who made it sound like his idea. Tonight, she wanted to see if she could do some matchmaking with Marcel and Chrissie.

The group were in high spirits. The dance hall was decorated for Christmas. Within a short time, they were dancing, laughing and chatting like a group of old friends.

"What's the problem with your brother-in-law?" Judy asked Josh, as they walked onto the dance floor.

"He's got a medical problem with his hip…it's called *osteone*…something…it ends with an '*is*'."

"*Osteonecrosis?*" queried Judy.

"Yes, that's it. He was diagnosed before they were married. He's hoping for an operation someday."

Josh swirled Judy around the dance floor. "Hey, you're a good dancer," he remarked, holding her hand and stepping from left to right. The music was lively, as Carl Cochcrane and his band performed their repertoire of popular music. Judy was breathless as the energetic dance ended.

"A drink," she declared.

Holding hands, they sauntered back to the table to join the others.

"Got you some lemonade," Henri indicated. "Those dance routines certainly put you through your paces," he teased.

"Where do you usually go dancing?" Darcy asked Judy.

"The Youth Club dances and occasionally up at The Mason's – but they are mild compared to this."

"Yes, this place is in a different league. I love watching the interaction between the couples – I bet there's some matchmaking goes on in here," Darcy commented, wishing Marcel would ask Chrissie to dance.

"My father would have a fit if he could see me," added Judy.

Josh put his glass down. "Why, because of me?"

Judy's eyes nearly popped out of her head. "Oh, gosh, he'd be furious if he saw me in here and even more furious if he saw me with you!" she exclaimed. "He's so against dance halls in general. He calls them 'dens of iniquity' – he considers them to be places of vice. He reckons girls come to ruination if they frequent dance halls."

"Your father sounds like a lot of fun, Judy. Is there a reason why he thinks this way?" asked Josh.

Judy shrugged. "He's so straitlaced and religious. Come on, Josh, let's dance," she added, pulling Josh to his feet "May as well dance, when I've got the chance."

Soon, the young couple were performing lively footwork, kicks and flicks, as Josh spun his partner around in time to the heady beat of the band.

"She's friendly," commented Darcy to Henri and Chrissie. "I like her – do you know her, Chrissie?"

She shook her head. "No, but I think I know who she is – her father owns one of the funeral places in Malsett."

Darcy was observing Josh and his girlfriend. "I think my brother is enjoying himself," she commented, her eyes twinkling.

Henri put his arm around Darcy and pulled her close, kissing her cheek. "Why don't you dance with Marcel, Darcy," he whispered.

Darcy stiffened. "Would you mind?" She looked deeply into her husband's eyes.

"Not at all, ma chérie …you were made to dance," he replied.

Should she? She was itching to be on the dancefloor… but what about Chrissie?

Five minutes later, Marcel and Darcy were jiving in the middle of the dancefloor. Henri watched on. It was a hard burden to bear, but he could not deny his young wife the pleasure she found in dancing. He'd decided years ago, he must encourage Darcy to enjoy herself. He could not put restraints upon her because of his own physical limitations. One day, he told himself, one day I will dance again…he allowed himself to dream.

He was aware of Chrissie sitting watching the others.

"Do you like dancing, Chrissie?" he asked.

She smiled…such a pretty smile, Henri observed.

"I love dancing, Henri – but you need a partner."

Henri tapped his leg. "I feel so useless, but it doesn't stop me from enjoying watching the others."

"Do you still hope for surgery?" Chrissie asked. She was aware of Henri's hip problem.

Henri nodded. "Sam, Chantal's partner, is an orthopaedic surgeon. He keeps me informed about articles he's been reading. He reckons a hip replacement will become routine for conditions like mine in the future. Darcy and I remain hopeful."

The tempo of the music slowed. Darcy felt embarrassed at the thoughts of swaying in Marcel's arms, so she tapped him on the shoulder.

"I'm going to sit down, Marcel, but would you do me a favour please?"

His eyes widened.

"Would you ask Chrissie to dance later? She's had a few problems recently and I'm trying to encourage her to get out and about and meet people again."

Marcel nodded in agreement. Darcy hoped she'd sounded vague enough. She genuinely wanted to see her friend become happy again.

To avoid looking too obvious, Marcel went to replenish their drinks. A while later, Josh and Judy were still dancing.

"He's got it bad…I do believe my little brother is in love," Darcy declared.

The band changed to an upbeat number. Marcel looked over at Chrissie.

"Would you like to dance?" he asked. Chrissie agreed and Marcel led her onto the dance floor. The tempo was lively and soon Marcel and Chrissie were showing their moves. Darcy watched on with delight.

"That's more like it. She always was a good dancer. I'm pleased she hasn't lost her touch."

Henri grinned. "What mischief are you up to, Madame Dukas?"

Darcy pretended to look startled. "Mischief? Whatever do you mean, monsieur. I see two lovely young people enjoying themselves. I think dancing is wonderful. Many young people find their life partner on a dance floor…did you know that, Henri? You do realise we are helping two young couples tonight?"

Henri looked perplexed.

"Well, Marcel and Chrissie would not be here if it wasn't for us…and I doubt if my brother would have thought of visiting a dance hall in Durham, if it hadn't been for my suggestion," she explained. Then to herself she thought… and if it hadn't been for Marcel bringing me here a few weeks ago, then the whole idea would not have entered my head! Somehow this form of reasoning made her little secret from Henri, sound acceptable.

Henri just shook his head at his wife's comment. Darcy's brain worked in wonderful ways. It was one of her many endearing attributes. She was happy in her own little world…and if Darcy was happy, then Henri was not complaining.

As Marcel and Chrissie left the dance floor, another couple welcomed the slower pace of the music. Josh and Judy swayed along to the slow rhythm, their faces touching.

"Mmm…this has been a great night, Judy," Josh murmured in his partner's ear. "Let's come here again… is that a possibility?" He pulled back and stared into Judy's brown eyes.

"I'd love to, Josh; it beats the café any day. But I'm not sure how I can manage it. However, I've got an idea I'm working on."

Josh was attentive.

"It's only a slim chance and it will need my father's approval…but I'm thinking of applying for a nursing job in Durham. I finish my training at the end of this month, and I was looking at the list of vacancies – the hospital in Durham is advertising."

"How would that help us?" he asked.

Judy smiled. "If I'm successful, then I would need to get lodgings in Durham – which would mean being free from my father's watchful eyes."

A slow smile spread across Josh's face. He squeezed her gently. "That would be terrific," he responded.

The band began to play a song with a smooth, catchy tune and the lyrics tickled the ears of Josh Smallwood.

Later that evening, Josh walked Judy to her friend's doorway at a house in Granley. They loitered on the doorstep. He took Judy in his arms and held her close. It was the first time that evening they'd enjoyed a measure of privacy. They embraced. The night was bitterly cold, but the fire in Josh Smallwood's heart was providing enough warmth for both.

"Oh, Judy, I'm so pleased you relented and allowed our friendship to develop into something. Did you hear the lyrics of that song before we left the dancefloor tonight?"

Judy looked puzzled. "Which words?" she asked.

"*The ones about thinking of you does things to me!*" he replied.

"Josh Smallwood...are you flirting with me?" she giggled.

"Yes, Judy Dempster, I am. The title of that song speaks volumes... I will never, ever, forget you, my darling." He hummed the tune in her ear then sang the lyrics softly.

Judy held onto Josh, as he kissed her with an intensity leaving her in no doubt as to his feelings for her.

***

Darcy had enjoyed her undercover work helping to expose Gordon Sinclair's skullduggery. It hadn't been a journalistic opportunity, but it had given her an insight into its potential. Since her time in Durham, she'd been working on her article about stillbirth. The three months' lapse since her own experience was helping her to heal mentally. Last week, she'd received some completed questionnaires from Francesca – Darcy had formulated a simple array of questions, born out of her and Henri's own experiences.

Recently, she had used her journalistic skills to trace other women who'd travelled a similar path. Chantal had proved helpful, approaching previous patients, some of whom were only too pleased to give their experiences anonymously. Others were willing to talk firsthand to Darcy, but some remained apprehensive and not willing to participate.

Darcy now felt much more informed, and one message was loud and clear – the treatment of the parents of stillborn babies must change. Darcy was compiling her article entitled '*The Birth of New Thinking*'. It was a gripping, heart wrenching read. She'd spent hours perfecting its literary impact.

She had drawn the reader's attention to the time of great emotional distress and the guilt experienced, by what in essence, was an unavoidable outcome. The need for support and tangible information was stressed as a necessity, and a cessation of this 'stiff upper lip' approach to treat the stillbirth as if it had not happened.

Time was needed for the parents to grieve with their baby, if requested, not having it whisked away. The need for knowledge as to the whereabouts of the stillborn infant was required, so that parents could visit the burial site to grieve.

In many cases, women were nursed on maternity wards – which was so insensitive. Provision must be made for facilities away from newborn babies. The overall approach was archaic, cold and clinical.

Henri, as usual, was the first to read it.

"Darcy, this is profound. You've caught the true feelings of our experience. I hope it receives due credit."

Rachel and Tom added their views. "It comes across as intense and heartfelt. It could pave the way for improvement in this area."

Chantal also read the account. "You've tackled a subject dear to my heart, Darcy. I've seen so much suffering and heartache in my midwifery experiences. In one short article you have given an accurate account of basic facts."

Sam added his praise. "They say *the pen is mightier than the sword*, Darcy. Your words could cause ripples leading to waves on this topic."

Finally, Darcy sent a copy to Francesca, who telephoned after receiving it.

"Darcy, you are so gifted. This is excellent. A piece of writing which deserves exposure. It could be a catalyst for change. You must send it to Scottish newspapers, as well as national newspapers."

Buoyed on by the approval and encouragement, Darcy set about finding the appropriate addresses.

***

Christmas was approaching and Josh wanted to buy Judy a gift. After wandering around the shops in Malsett, he made his choice – a neat, gold, heart-shaped locket. After their special night dancing in Durham, it was back to the café in Granley.

"Tell me about your Christmas, Judy – what will you be doing?" he enquired.

"I've volunteered to work on Christmas Day," she informed him, as they sipped their hot chocolate. "Our usual Christmas routine involves going to church on the morning. We have visitors for lunch – usually strangers – some less fortunate souls Dad has found in need of a Christmas lunch. Afterwards, we go around the area delivering parcels to some of the congregation, who are ill or unable to get out and about."

Josh considered Judy's answer. "Is all this your dad's idea?"

Judy nodded. "Yes, deep down he has a good heart… but doesn't show it to his loved ones. It doesn't add up. On one hand he is a good, compassionate church goer…but on the other hand he is a strict, stern father. I find it hard to reconcile the two personalities. It may be my last Christmas at Malhaven Hospital, so I thought I would offer my services. Sister was delighted. What will you be doing?"

"Well, Mother goes into overdrive. Francesca is coming to stay for two days. Marcel was invited to stay but he's having lunch with his aunt then they are both coming over from Durham for tea and supper. I haven't been around for the last couple of Christmases, with doing my National Service, but I expect the twins will be creating an uproar," he chuckled.

Then looking serious, he added. "I wish I could see you on Christmas Day. Which way do you walk home?"

Judy stared at Josh, questioningly. "I walk down Oakdale Road, along St Cuthbert's Avenue and down Church Bank."

Josh mentally walked her route, seeing a glimmer of an opportunity. "What time does your shift end?"

Judy began to smile. "Sister said I could leave at five o'clock."

Josh beamed. "Make sure you pass the church, Judy. It will be quiet around there, at that time, I will listen for a sneeze." He winked.

On Christmas Day afternoon, after enjoying his first Christmas at home for three years, Josh slipped away. He drove Beryl to the top of Church Bank and parked her a distance from the top. Then putting on his coat, scarf and gloves, he locked the car and walked down the hill to stand in the shadow of the large church gateposts to wait.

The area was deserted, Christmas festivities keeping people occupied. He had attended the church that morning, along with his family. He looked across at the vicarage next door. It had been his dad's home as a youngster, when Josh's grandfather had been the vicar.

Right on cue he heard a noise… muffled footsteps. It was so cold his breath was forming a haze. He held his breath then heard "Achoo". He looked out of his hiding place…and there she was…his Christmas present!

He pulled her into the shadow of the gatepost. She was wrapped up against the bitter chill.

"Merry Christmas, my darling," he uttered Before Judy could respond, his lips found hers and they embraced with intensity and longing. "I've bought you a gift, but open it in private," he remarked, then handed her a small package.

"Thank you," she whispered, "but I didn't get anything for you."

"This is my gift," he responded, finding her lips again.

After a further embrace, they could linger no longer. Josh watched as she continued her way home from work... what would 1953 hold for them?

Chapter 16

MARCH 1953

"Twenty-one, Josh Smallwood. You've got the key to the door," beamed Rachel, hugging her son as he entered the kitchen. It was a bright spring morning.

"A bit pointless, Mother, seeing as the door to Meckleridge is rarely locked – apart from that day I returned after completing my National Service," he chuckled.

Darcy looked up from her breakfast.

"Stupid phrase," she mimicked and sang the lyrics…

'Twenty-one today. Twenty-one today

He's got the key to the door

Never been twenty-one before.'

"Shut it, Darcy!" Josh eyeballed her, sitting down to enjoy his bowl of porridge.

"It's a shame none of our French relatives can be with us this evening," moaned Rachel. "So, it will just be a small affair - the family, plus Marcel, your pal Sid and his girl, and Chrissie."

Josh was quite relieved. His mother was famous for putting on a 'do' for special anniversaries. He didn't mind when it was for someone else – but Josh didn't like being the centre of attention.

"Is Judy coming?" asked Darcy.

"Oh, yes she is," announced Rachel, triumphantly.

Josh looked at his mother.

"This will be the first time we've had a chance to meet the young lady who has captured my son's affections. Honestly, I was beginning to think she was a figment of your imagination, Josh. The number of times I've asked you to bring her to meet us…I've lost count."

Josh sighed. He'd wanted to bring Judy to meet his parents since Christmas, but she'd always shied away, saying it was too risky.

Judy was living in Durham now, not far from Baxter Street where Bertha and Marcel lived. She was enjoying her freedom away from her strict parental home. Josh was also relishing the opportunities her new living arrangements afforded. The days of meeting in the café in Granley were a thing of the past.

Following her successful job application, she'd commenced working in the hospital in Durham at the end of January. At least four nights a week Josh would drive his old jalopy, Beryl, across to Durham. Sometimes, they visited the cinema, sometimes a café, but each week on Wednesdays and Saturdays they went dancing. The pair were fanatical about dancing.

Whenever the band played 'their song' – *Unforgettable* – they would swoon around the dance floor, lost in the lyrics and tones of the song. Josh was sure he was in love. Judy was on his mind morning, noon and night and he ached to see her during the days of the week they were unable to meet. She visited her family home on a Sunday and it grieved Josh that she was in Malhaven on those days – so near and yet so far.

Judy would be twenty-one in August...free from her father's control. In Josh's mind, he was determined to pluck up the courage to propose to her on that occasion. His problem, however, was his occupation – he was still a general dogsbody around the place. How could he ask a young woman to become his wife when he wasn't properly employed? He was listed on the estate's books as a farm labourer, with a small weekly wage – which helped to pay his petrol for Beryl.

As well as that, Josh was still in the dark as to the reason why Judy's father, Bernie Dempster, would not tolerate his family. He suspected Judy was unaware of the reason. According to Judy, her father was a man of strict principles. He was a local methodist preacher – on 'The Plan'. He didn't smoke; he had taken the pledge and didn't drink alcohol; he was a well-regarded, compassionate man in their church community. But it seemed to Josh the man had no 'fun' in his life.

Judy, unlike her younger sister Patricia, was a rebel and as her friendship with Josh had progressed, she'd been eager to break through the barriers – having an occasional cigarette, attending dances and tasting alcohol. Patricia obeyed the family rules.

Marcel had asked Josh if he wanted him to investigate the issue, the previous week.

"No, Marcel, not yet. We're enjoying our newfound freedom, and I would hate for anything to upset the situation. If I need help, I know where you are."

Marcel was making headway with his Investigation Agency. Having advertised his services in the local newspaper, he'd been successful in acquiring a few clients, including divorce work.

"I thought you moved to Durham to do different work?" remarked Darcy.

"Yes, I know, but it provides a steady income. Any day, a new client could walk through the door with something more challenging – then my agency will be motoring. I've got itchy feet to solve your brother's and Judy's mystery, but he's not bothered."

Darcy was also getting itchy feet – on two scores.

Firstly, her matchmaking with Marcel and Chrissie was not proving successful. Chrissie was taken with Marcel, and under Darcy's suggestion she'd restyled her hair and bought some new clothes. However, Marcel, although pleasant and sociable towards Chrissie, had not invited her on a date.

Secondly, after sending her article to various newspapers she almost grabbed the hand off the postie each day in her anxiousness to receive a reply.

Her first response was disappointing. She was given credit for raising an important issue, but the London newspaper suggested it would be more suited to a women's magazine than a daily broadsheet. This infuriated Darcy.

"Try a Sunday newspaper," Tom suggested. Tom had been an avid newspaper reader for as long as he could remember. "The News of the World is a popular Sunday paper, although some regard their articles as sensationalist."

Darcy looked thoughtful. "Good idea, Dad, people have more time to read articles like mine on a weekend."

CHAPTER 16

The telephone rang. It was Francesca. She'd kept in regular contact with Darcy regarding the newspaper article. "Any reply from the newspapers?"

"Yes, I've sent it to some Sunday newspapers – two nationals, The News of the World and The Sunday Post. I've also tried our local Sunday paper, The Sunday Sun. I'm awaiting news of my submissions," Darcy informed her.

Sam came to the phone.

"Good news, Dad. The last collections from the contents' sale have been made, so the house sale can proceed. When are you coming up? I can't wait to show you and Chantal my new house. I can accommodate you all."

"That's splendid, Francesca. I'll check my work rota and consult Chantal. Maybe next weekend – I'll be in touch."

At last things were moving with Matthison Hall. Sam rejoined Chantal in their lounge. They were relishing a couple of hours' break from their boisterous offspring. When Nancy had delivered the eggs earlier that morning, she told the twins about some newly hatched chicks. They begged their parents to take them over to the farm.

"Listen, I've got an idea," Nancy had suggested. "I think your mammy and daddy need a little rest, so put your coats and boots on and come back to the farm with me." The children raced off to collect their belongings. "I'll keep them out of mischief until lunchtime," she informed Sam and Chantal.

Nancy adored the twins – they were the grandchildren she and Bennie had longed for.

"That was Francesca," Sam informed Chantal, sitting beside her. "Finally, the last of the contents' sale items have been removed – now I can inform the estate agent to commence the viewings. Francesca wants us to go up to Edinburgh as soon as we can and stay with her."

"Oh, Sam, that would be great. I was beginning to think I would never see the place."

Sam nodded. The arrangements for Sam and Chantal to visit prior to Christmas had gone astray when the chosen date clashed with the twins' Christmas concert. Then when they'd rearranged the date for early in January, Con contracted chickenpox, followed a few days later by Hope. Chantal would not leave Rachel to look after two sick children, so Sam went on his own and oversaw the preparations for the sale, selecting a few items to retain. It was no surprise to discover that Evelyn had chosen the better pieces of furniture, but he was past caring. This visit would give Sam a chance to meet the solicitor and receive a divorce update – it was six months since the proceedings had begun.

Sam picked up Chantal's left hand and stroked her 'fake' wedding band which was her mother's wedding ring.

"One day soon, Chantal, you will wear your engagement ring and your own wedding band." Chantal kissed Sam on the cheek, visualising the beautiful diamond solitaire ring Sam had given to her after his father's funeral. Among his father's possessions, safely stored away at the bank, were some items of jewellery. John Carter had purposefully not left these at home, anticipating that Evelyn could avail herself of them. Sam appreciated his father's foresight and, returning home, had given the ring to Chantal. She loved it and treasured it – but would not wear it until Sam was a 'free' man. Perhaps that day was approaching.

***

CHAPTER 16

The preparations for the twenty-first birthday party were in full swing when Chantal went into the kitchen. Rachel was applying the finishing touches to the birthday cake. It was a rectangular chocolate sponge cake with chocolate buttercream icing. Rachel had piped 'Happy 21st birthday' on the top. In the middle was a layer of green icing plus an iced cricket bat and ball – a tribute to Josh's cricket involvement.

"He'll eat all that by himself," remarked Darcy, watching her mother. "I think since his stint in the army, he's more into football than cricket…but he'll eat it whatever it says!"

Twelve people were expected at the party. Marcel and Judy were the first to arrive. Marcel had offered to transport Judy to save Josh wasting petrol when he was coming over in any case. Judy was still scared of being seen in the locality. "I'll show Marcel the back roads," she'd commented.

"Darcy insists you stay overnight – we have plenty of spare rooms. I think I told you the house was a hotel before the war. It will mean we don't have to watch the clock."

Judy had been vague about visiting her family that Sunday, indicating she had been asked to do some weekend shifts.

Josh was waiting on the driveway for Marcel's car. He wanted to speak to Judy before she went in to meet the family. She stepped out of the car and Marcel indicated he would park his vehicle in the rear yard.

Judy was wearing a camel coat covering what Josh suspected was a beautiful dress. As usual, his heart did a little flip as she walked towards him. She had a particular eye for fashion. Her brown hair was loose, its waves framing her pretty face. He reached out and took her hand, leading her into the hallway and across to the dining room.

"I wanted to say a quick word before you meet the family," he explained.

"Tonight, Judy, marks a milestone for me – my twenty-first birthday. I'm not big on birthday celebrations, but I knew Mother would want to fuss over this one." He coughed.

"I hope you won't feel overwhelmed by them. I appreciate the effort you have made to be here – I know it's a risk for you, being so close to your family home." He paused and swallowed...this was harder than he'd expected.

"I want to say something important." He took hold of both of her hands. "You are very special to me and...I think...think I'm in love with you. No that's not right...I know I'm in love with you, Judy."

She shivered and looked up into his eyes.

"You're cold, I'm an idiot, I should have picked a better time to say this to you."

Judy reached up to touch Josh's cheek. "Stop apologising, Josh. I'm fine. Thank you for those lovely words...you are special to me, also."

Josh cupped Judy's face with his hands and sealed his words with a loving kiss. The intensity of the moment sparked a deep connection.

"Judy, you make me so happy I want to shout it from the rooftops – I wish our friendship could be open. Come on let's meet the family." Josh took Judy's coat and small vanity case. "I'll leave these downstairs... you can collect them later."

Judy looked elegant in a straight, close-fitting jade green dress. The sleeves were long, and the neck was v-shaped.

She was wearing the gold locket Josh had given her as a Christmas gift. "You look beautiful," he commented as he opened the door.

"I'm nervous," she replied, picking up her black patent handbag which perfectly matched her high heeled shoes.

He took her hand. "Don't be, they're a friendly bunch," he said with a tight squeeze.

Just as they were about to open the conservatory door, Rachel stepped out.

"There you are, Josh…and this must be Judy."

Judy extended her hand.

"Pleased to meet you, Mrs Smallwood," Judy said, trembling.

Rachel grasped the outstretched hand.

"Mother, this is Judy Dempster," interjected Josh.

The two women shook hands.

"Welcome to Meckleridge, Judy, I've been longing to meet you properly – we did meet at the hospital."

Judy smiled sweetly.

"Tom!" she called. Josh's father appeared, and introductions were made.

"I'm Tom and this is Rachel – none of this formal Mr and Mrs stuff, Judy – welcome to our home."

Judy stepped into the conservatory to be greeted by a sea of faces. Josh was still holding Judy's hand.

"Everyone, this is my friend Judy, you can introduce yourselves later."

Judy looked at the assembled guests, recognising Darcy, Henri, Marcel and Chrissie. Two other young people were strangers. Immediately she tensed.

"What's wrong?" whispered Josh.

"Who are they, Josh?" she asked, beckoning to the young couple.

"That's Sid, my old pal from school...don't you recognise him? His girl comes from Newcastle." Josh walked over and made the introductions...but it did little to calm Judy's apprehensiveness.

Drinks were served and within half an hour, Judy had spoken to Darcy, Henri and Chrissie and had met Sam and Chantal.

"Josh often talks about your twins – they sound quite delightful," remarked Judy to Chantal.

"Yes, they've recently started school and are keeping us right on a few things," she chuckled. Chantal asked Judy about her new job at the Durham hospital and in a short time they were chatting freely.

Eventually, the guests were invited to partake of the celebration buffet and were shown into the dining room where Judy had spied the banquet earlier. The table was laden with goodies – beef, pork and ham sandwiches, meat pies, sausage rolls, sausages on cocktail sticks and cubed cheese. The dessert offerings were trifle, meringues, chocolate eclairs, madeleines and iced buns. In the centre of the table, the birthday cake presided.

After everyone had indulged in the food, Tom rattled on the table. "Now everyone, please take a glass of champagne." He paused while Chantal and Darcy handed out the flutes.

"Now, Josh, your mother has gone to great lengths to produce this masterpiece despite the rationing, which still plagues us. There are twenty-one candles on this cake, one for every year of your life. It gives me great pleasure to reflect on those years and to stand here today and wish my son 'many happy returns'. He's a great lad, so unassuming and easy going. I wish him all the best as he steps forward into the future. Now, Rachel, light those candles."

Rachel struck a match and after three attempts the candles were lit. Tom led the guests in singing the chorus of 'Happy Birthday' and Josh blew out the candles to lots of hoots and cheers, as the toast was made.

"Speech," called Sam.

Josh had been dreading this part. He cleared his throat. "Er…I…er…I just want to say a big thank you to Mother and Dad for providing this party and to everyone for coming here tonight to celebrate my special birthday."

Darcy cheered and clapped furiously, knowing it was all her brother would say.

After the cake was cut and eaten, the guests returned to the conservatory, where the rugs had been rolled to the side of the room and Henri oversaw the gramophone.

"Let the dancing begin," he announced.

Darcy walked up behind him and placed her hands on his shoulders.

"Dance, ma chérie, I have pleasure in watching you," he whispered.

Darcy reached up and gave him a peck on the cheek. She smiled as she noticed Marcel leading Chrissie onto the dance floor. At least they both seemed to enjoy dancing and were friendly… but sadly, there was no spark there. Darcy, however, was determined to prevail.

Soon, the area in the large conservatory was being utilised as it had been many, many times in the past. The dance music was varied to suit the tastes of the group. From lively jive dances, big band quick steps, sedate waltzes, foxtrots and even some Charleston moves from Tom and Rachel, Sam and Chantal.

Marcel danced with Darcy, Chrissie, Chantal and Rachel. Josh and Judy were perfectly at ease, gazing lovingly at each other.

"My, my, what a beautiful pair they make," remarked Rachel to Tom, as she observed Josh swirling and twisting Judy around the floor.

The time ticked by. The guests enjoyed further drinks. Then the beat became more subdued and active kicks were swapped for a slower pace. Josh hugged Judy tightly – they had been inseparable all evening.

Suddenly, there was a loud banging on the front door. Rachel looked at Tom in surprise.

"I'll go," he indicated.

The hallway was lit with dim lamps.

Tom opened the front door. A tall, bulky man wearing a suit and trilby hat was outlined against the moonlight.

"Good evening," Tom began.

"Never mind the niceties, Smallwood. I've come for my daughter, Judy."

Tom's initial shock turned to recognition.

"Bernie Dempster!" he exclaimed, standing back to allow the angry man to step into the hallway.

Chapter 17

Without invitation, the new arrival pushed his way past Tom and strode into the conservatory. The dancers froze to the spot as the music continued. The uninvited guest grabbed Judy roughly by the arm. Henri lifted the needle on the gramophone as the man shouted.

"Out of here now, Judy. Collect your belongings and come with me. Let's leave this house with its Sodom and Gomorrah morals."

Sam stepped forward. "Excuse me, sir, that is an uncalled-for comment," he exclaimed.

"Out of my way, you sassenach," he growled at Sam.

Judy was yanked across the room towards the door. Josh stood in bewilderment at the sight of his beautiful girlfriend being snatched from his arms. He quickly leapt across to bar Bernie Dempster's exit through the door.

Judy began to screech.

"Dad, Dad, stop it…I can explain." Her voice was high pitched, and tears were streaming down her face.

"You'll explain it, my girl, but not until we are away from this house of low repute."

Tom was standing in the hallway. He signalled for Josh to step aside.

"Mr Dempster, we can explain," Josh begged.

"Shut up, young Smallwood, and fetch her coat. She'll pay for this defiance."

Tom stood in the man's path. "Mr Dempster," he said calmly. "Surely, we can talk civilly about this misunderstanding. Your daughter is a guest in our home at our son's coming of age birthday celebration."

"Don't you try to gloss over the facts, Tom Smallwood. You're just a chip off the old block, thinking you can talk your way out of this situation. This is my daughter, and she has disobeyed me."

Rachel passed Judy her coat as Darcy retrieved her handbag and small case.

The family watched on helpless, as Bernie Dempster flung open the front door and marched his twenty-year old daughter towards his car, bundling her inside.

It was an abrupt end to what five minutes ago had been a splendid evening.

The guests felt uncomfortable, but Tom insisted everyone stay put, while Chrissie and Chantal offered to make tea for everyone.

"How on earth did Judy's father know she was here tonight?" asked Josh. He looked lost, in despair. "I'm frightened for her…he was an angry man…what will he do to her?"

Sid walked over towards his pal standing in front of the fireplace.

"I think I may be the one to blame," confessed Sid.

All eyes glowered at him.

"My grandma was at our house, as I was leaving. She asked where I was going. She remembered your family and asked if you had a girlfriend. I might have told her you were courting Judy Dempster – I didn't realise there was a problem."

Josh looked gobsmacked but then his pal didn't know about Judy's dad's attitude.

Tom interjected. "Don't blame yourself, Sid, you weren't to know Judy's dad would react that way."

Sid thanked Tom for his understanding but felt so guilty to have inadvertently caused this situation.

"Now, everyone, drink up and try to remember the good things about tonight, not this last episode. I am sure this is a misunderstanding. I will try my best to find out what's behind it. Josh and Judy need our support. I'm sure things will be sorted soon."

***

Unfortunately, Tom's prediction was not easily resolved. Initially he had an embarrassed and greatly aggrieved son to handle. Josh retreated to his room as soon as the other guests departed. Tom gave Josh half an hour, then knocked on his bedroom door.

"Josh, can I come in? It's better to talk about it."

But Josh refused.

Marcel was staying overnight.

"Let me try tomorrow, Tom," he suggested, when Tom returned downstairs. "We've become friendly, and I know a little bit about the relationship. Josh might be more inclined to talk to someone of his own age about his friendship with Judy."

Tom looked pensive. "From the comments passed by Mr Dempster, it seems to have some history behind it. I'm clueless as to what that may be. I remember him being a year or two above me at school and then more recently as one of the funeral directors in the town – but other than that, I don't know the man."

"I feel so sorry for Josh," commented Darcy. "It would seem Judy's father has a problem with our family which is quite puzzling."

Tom stared at his daughter, aghast. "And why am I only hearing about this now? How long has this friendship been going on?"

Darcy shrugged. "Not really sure…before Christmas?" she suggested. "I know Judy took a lot of persuasion to accept a date with Josh. They've always had to meet in secret."

Tom sighed. "I guess that's why he's been disappearing off in his old car night after night."

Tom looked dejected. "We need to get to the bottom of it. I don't take kindly to my home being referred to in such a derogatory tone. The man may well be upset, but I deserve an apology for the comments he passed tonight."

Darcy turned to Henri. "Fat chance of that happening," she concluded, receiving a stern look from her father.

"I think Josh is dotty about Judy," Darcy added.

Rachel smiled. "I'd go as far as saying he's in love with the girl. He's showing all the signs. But what on earth is that man's problem? It was an awful end to a splendid evening." She looked across at her husband. "Think, Tom, you must have crossed Mr Dempster in some way."

Tom sat down and shook his head. "I think he's a Methodist lay preacher, but that's not much help."

Darcy perked up, "I think Judy has a sister, I remember her at school, and recall her being quite sullen and a loner."

So far, Henri had remained quiet. "Sounds like a case for DD's Investigation Agency," he suggested, grinning.

Marcel looked up. "I'm willing, but only with Josh's agreement."

Marcel approached Josh the next day when he sat down to eat his breakfast, looking as if he hadn't slept.

"I'm willing to dig around for you, Josh. It sounds like a family issue to me. Did you hear Mr Dempster refer to your dad being 'a chip off the old block'?"

Josh shook his head. "What's that supposed to mean?" he asked, with a look of despair.

"Well, if someone is referred to as a chip off the old block – it usually refers to an older relative like a mother or father."

"I'd welcome your help, Marcel. I care deeply for Judy, and I think it's mutual. I'm not giving up without a fight – but I can't afford to pay you."

"Don't worry about that. Your family have been kind to me – it's a way I can repay you. I want to help."

***

ONE WEEK LATER

Lady bounded towards Darcy as she opened the door to the rear lounge. She was surprised to see Marcel and her mother sitting by the fireside, enjoying a cup of tea.

"Hello, Marcel, what are you doing here?"

Rachel was embarrassed by her daughter's direct tone.

"Darcy, just welcome our guest without interrogating him. Marcel is welcome in our home without a specified reason to visit."

Darcy shrugged and dropped her shopping bags in the middle of the floor. Taking off her coat, she flung it across the back of a chair.

"Darcy!" her mother reprimanded her. "Honestly, Marcel I dread to think what Henri and Darcy's house would be like, if they ever moved into their own home. She's so used to me tidying up after her. One day, Darcy, you'll discover what it's like to 'keep house'."

Marcel sniggered.

"Oh, shush, Mother. You'd be lost if you didn't have my mess to clean up. Now, do I get a cup of tea or is this a private party?" Darcy retaliated, pulling a chair up to the fireside. She reached out to warm her hands in front of the glowing coal fire.

"It's still cold out there. The calendar may say it's spring, but the wind blowing down Front Street in Malsett this morning was biting – I wished I'd taken my scarf and gloves."

Marcel was relishing watching Darcy's antics and listening to her chatter.

"In answer to your question, Darcy, I've come over to have a chat with your brother to see how he's coping after the shocking events last weekend."

Rachel and Darcy looked at each other.

"Not too good, I'm afraid," replied Rachel. "Our Josh tends to bottle things up – he's always been like that. It will take a while for him to talk about it and recover from it."

Darcy stared at her mother. "I don't think he's about to get over it, Mother. Josh is in love with Judy – she could well be 'the one'. I think he'll be doing all he can to win her."

Marcel nodded. "Well, I'm hoping to be able to help him. I've spent a couple of days sorting some assignments I was busy with, so now I can concentrate on investigating why Judy's family are so against this association. I'm going to be poking around for information, over the coming days."

"Do you want another drink, Marcel? I'll get you one as well, Darcy," Rachel said, jumping up.

"No thanks, Rachel," said Marcel. "I'll head off to find Josh – any idea where he'll be?"

"Try Beryl's shed…or the farm," replied Darcy. "If you need any help with your investigation, Marcel, just ask – I'm waiting for word back about my newspaper submissions, so I could lend a hand if needed."

Marcel stood and turned to Darcy. He'd enjoyed working with this captivating, young woman and hoped it was something they could do again sometime.

"That's kind of you to offer, Darcy. My first task is to assemble as much information as I can from your family."

Rachel arrived with Darcy's tea. "I don't know if we will be of much help, Marcel. I didn't belong around here before I met Tom. All I know is Judy's father owns one of the funeral businesses in Malsett."

Darcy smirked. "He's well suited to his occupation, if you ask me. What a grump of a man. He's so miserable. I doubt if he can remember the last time he cracked a smile!"

Rachel and Marcel started to laugh as the door opened, and Tom walked in.

"I guess you'll be wanting a brew as well. Marcel has come over to ask us what we know about Judy's father," Rachel told him.

"Nice to see you again, Marcel," Tom remarked.

Tom walked into the hallway to hang up his outdoor wear. Then rubbing his hands together joined the others.

"I'm looking for any detail you can recall – no matter how insignificant it seems," commented Marcel. "You'd be surprised how one small snippet of information can open a line of inquiry."

Tom was looking thoughtful.

"Do you want some notepaper?" Darcy asked Marcel, who tapped the side of his nose and reached into his inside jacket pocket, retrieving a notebook.

"Always prepared, Darcy," he answered, winking at her. All eyes looked at Tom.

"Bernard Dempster was a year above me at elementary school. That makes him fifty-four years old. My brother and I went off to boarding school, so I don't remember him during his teenage years. He had a presence about him – not someone to argue with, a surly character. I don't remember anything else, until my father died. Now, there are two funeral directors in Malsett and because I vaguely knew him, I asked if he would handle the funeral arrangements." Tom took a sip of his tea.

"I was a bit miffed when he refused, saying it clashed with other business. The other firm were only too happy to oblige."

"Was that all he said?" asked Marcel.

"I think so…but now I think about it, when I told my mother about his refusal, she nearly went up in a blue light! Said she wasn't surprised. I thought nothing of it at the time."

Marcel was scribbling in his notebook.

"So, your mother was annoyed you'd asked Mr Dempster – did she say why?"

Tom shook his head. "When mother died, I went straight back to Barclay Funeral Directors. They had attended to my brother's funeral, but I'd forgotten."

Darcy looked at Marcel. "That's fascinating, I do love a bit of intrigue – but how can it help?" she asked.

"It's a detail, Darcy, but as I said before, it may hold some significance."

***

Marcel walked back up to the house with Josh. He'd spent well over an hour with the heartbroken young man.

"I'm sorry I can't tell you more, Marcel. Judy is a very private person and she's loyal to her folks. All I've learned is that Mr Dempster is very stern. He's always had strict rules and expects his wife and daughters to obey them. She was told she must not befriend anyone in our family."

Marcel had then listened to Josh lamenting the loss of his girlfriend.

"We were becoming close, Marcel. I was travelling over to Durham to see her four times a week. It was such a relief when she took that job in Durham. She was amazed her dad allowed it. I went down to her lodgings on Monday…but her landlady informed me she'd left, leaving a month's rent. On Tuesday, I went to the hospital. I knew she was working on Ward 9. I asked if it was possible for them to pass a letter on to her, but they informed me she was on leave. That can't be right. She told me last week she wasn't due any leave until the summer."

"Is there any way you could write to her – get Darcy to type it, so it looks like a business letter?" Josh shook his head.

"I wouldn't put it past the man intercepting it, Marcel. No, I can't risk writing, my only hope of communication is if she writes to me."

Rachel spotted the two young men chatting in the rear yard and went outside, followed by Darcy.

"Not sure if this will be any help, Marcel, but Bernie Dempster is a Methodist lay preacher. He probably goes to the Primitive Methodists at the bottom of Malsett bank. Don't mix it up with the Wesleyan Chapel. Perhaps someone who attends the church might be helpful."

Marcel looked confused.

"Two different church groups, Marcel. I can show you the buildings, if you want," added Darcy.

Marcel smiled. "Thanks, Darcy, that would be helpful – I'll let you know."

Marcel bid them all goodbye and climbed into his car.

Rachel and Darcy returned to the kitchen.

"A word in your ear, Darcy," remarked Rachel. "Be cautious where Marcel is concerned."

Darcy stared at her mother, in amazement. "Mother, what a thing to say! Surely you don't think he has other things on his mind?"

Rachel raised her eyebrows. "I think, Darcy, Marcel is an attractive young man, and you are an attractive young woman. I have watched the way he observes you…his eyes follow you around the room. All I'm saying is… be cautious."

Darcy shook her head. "Mother, you are being ridiculous…I am married to the most adorable man – why would I ever look at another one? I'm merely interested in helping Josh."

Josh was untying his work boots and removing his oil-stained overalls, when Rachel passed him in the kitchen.

"I took the liberty of leaving a letter addressed to you, on your bed, Josh. I didn't think you would want other eyes to notice it."

"Really?" asked Josh in surprise. He rarely received post. He dashed up to his bedroom and lifted the white envelope bearing his name. His heart quickened…Judy!

He looked at the postmark – just able to make out the word *Northumberland.*

He sat down on his bed, his hands shaking as he opened the envelope.

Carefully, he unfolded a large sheet of foolscap paper, which had been folded many times to fit inside the small envelope.

2, Seaview Cottages
Bamburgh,
Northumberland.

Dear Josh,

I can't begin to imagine how angry you must be with my father for the incident at your party. His actions last Saturday night were so rude. To barge into someone's home and speak in that way to your family is unforgiveable.

Josh, I am helpless to do anything. You will see from the top of this letter I am in Bamburgh in Northumberland, staying with my aunt. Her cottage is on the road between Seahouses and Bamburgh – there is no telephone. On Sunday afternoon Dad took me to my lodgings in Durham and ordered me to pack my belongings. He paid the landlady a month's rent and said I wouldn't be returning. Then on Monday he took me to the hospital and demanded I ask for leave with immediate effect, saying it was a family crisis… which I suppose, is true.

Then he drove me to the seaside village of Bamburgh to his sister's house. My aunt Edie is as bad as my dad. She has been a widow for years and lives on her own. Josh, she is like a jailer and such a grumpy person. The place is pleasant but so far, we haven't left the house – I'm not allowed out by myself.

Today, we are going shopping in the village. I am writing this, hoping I can find a post-box. Josh, I need your help – how I have no idea. It's pointless for you to write, as she would destroy it. I'm so afraid. My dad is determined to end our friendship. This is not how I wanted to say this… but I love you, Josh, Judy xxx.

Josh lifted the paper to the crosses and kissed them. She loved him…he loved her…they would find a way to be together…but how?

Chapter 18

Darcy called for Lady and fastened her leash. She wandered around the grounds giving the almost grown puppy her morning exercise. Darcy was restless. Waiting was something she hated – she was made for action. These long days of anticipation of an acceptance letter from the newspaper, seemed endless. Really, she should be seeking other assignments.

Her mind drifted to her brother's predicament. Josh was such an 'internal' personality – her total opposite. It was ten days since the twenty-first birthday party, and he remained tight lipped about it all. Surely, he had tried to speak to Judy. She turned and headed back to the house.

"Where's Josh?" she asked her mother.

"At the farm – Bennie's got a hospital appointment this morning."

Darcy left the dog in the kitchen and made her way along the track leading to the farm. Bennie was the farm manager. He was a similar age to her dad, but recently he'd been unwell. Josh seemed to be spending more time working on the farm in the last few months, helping when Bennie had these appointments. Nancy, his wife, was a kindly soul.

Darcy tapped on the door and walked straight into the cosy kitchen.

"Good morning, Nancy, how are you?"

Nancy was baking bread; her hands covered in flour, kneading the dough on the bench.

"Hello, Darcy – good to see you. I was going to say I'm fine …but I'm not. Give me a couple of minutes to put this dough to rise and we'll have a cuppa."

"I'll make it," responded Darcy, moving over to the range cooker, grabbing the large teapot on her way.

Within minutes, the two women were sitting at the large farmhouse table enjoying a pot of freshly brewed tea. Nancy glanced at the clock.

"Your brother will be in soon. He does like his mid-morning brew and a biscuit," she chuckled.

"I guess that should be plural, Nancy…biscuits. My brother has an enormous appetite." They laughed.

"Eeh, Darcy, you've grown into a fine young woman. Will you be trying for another littlun?" she enquired. Nancy was forthright and Darcy was not embarrassed.

"Eventually, Nancy, we hope to have another baby. But you know I think nature knows best. I'm not ready for all that maternal stuff. I want to do things. I mean, don't get me wrong, I'd be delighted if it happens but, in the meantime, I'm trying to become a freelance investigative journalist."

"Oh, my, that sounds fancy," declared the older lady.

Darcy shrugged. "Not really – I've just conducted some research about stillbirth and how the parents are treated. It's shocking, Nancy. We don't know where our beautiful Leon is buried. Things must change. I've written an article on the subject and submitted it to two newspapers – I'm waiting to hear if they will print it."

Nancy stared wide-eyed at Darcy. "Go for it, girl – I hope you are successful."

After a pause, Darcy enquired about Bennie. The look on the farmer's wife's face was grave.

"It's not good, Darcy. We haven't said much about it, so keep it to yourself, but it's looking as if my Bennie will need a big operation, which of course means he'll be out of action for a few months. Today he's seeing the doctor at the hospital about some results which will decide if he needs the op."

"Oh, Nancy, I'm sorry to hear that. It's a good job Josh is around – does he know the possible implications?"

Nancy shook her head. "Not yet," she remarked. "It doesn't do to look too far ahead. My Bennie is a private person – he'll talk when he's ready."

The door opened and Josh walked in.

"Hi, Darc…what brings you here?"

"I've come to speak to you, Mr Invisible – have your cuppa then I'll tag along with you, wherever you're going."

Half an hour later, Darcy was walking into the farmyard with her brother, having said goodbye to Nancy with a reassuring hug.

"Okay, what's wrong? Why do you want to speak to me?" asked Josh.

"It's you," Darcy declared. "Ever since the debacle at your party you've clamped up, keeping it all to yourself. We're your family, Josh – we want to help."

Josh began loading hay onto a trailer.

"I have talked about it…to Marcel. He's going to do some poking around but that's not going to help the situation with Judy and I."

Darcy looked thoughtful. "Not immediately, but it might help in the future. Back to the here and now…have you tried to contact Judy?"

Josh sighed, heaving a fork load onto the trailer. "Of course I have, stupid, I'm not dim," he huffed. "I tried her lodgings in Durham – she's left, totally. I enquired at the hospital – she's on annual leave, which is a load of codswallop – she told me the other week, she wasn't entitled to any leave until the summer." Darcy listened, pleased her brother had been proactive.

"Then yesterday a letter arrived…Judy's in Bamburgh, staying with her aunt, but it sounds like she's a prisoner."

Darcy stared wide-eyed, watching her brother walk backwards and forwards in his task.

"That's on the Northumberland coast, isn't it?" she asked.

Josh nodded. "Yes, it's about a two-to-three-hour trip, doable in a day and I have the address."

"Are you going to try to see her?" asked Darcy.

"That's my plan, but the way things are with Bennie, I'm not sure I can take a day off."

Darcy pursed her lips. "We'll work on it – don't give up. You can't allow that arrogant man to interfere with your life."

Josh rested his hands on the pitchfork. "But even if I do get to see her...and it's a big 'if'…what can I do? Short of kidnapping her, I haven't got a clue."

"We need to think this through, Josh. Listen, Henri and I could take you up there… on a day's outing. I doubt if Beryl would be up to that kind of trip. It would need to be a Saturday. Leave it with me, Josh. Trust me… I'll think of something."

Darcy wandered off, back to Meckleridge House, as Josh jumped into the cab and started up the tractor. It was a glimmer of hope. Thankfully, his sister was known for her ingenuity. Once she latched onto something, she stuck at it… it brought a sliver of comfort into his aching heart.

***

After rearranging their work schedules, Sam and Chantal headed north of the border, to Scotland. The twins were beside themselves with excitement, mostly in anticipation of meeting Francesca again. The family were to stay with her over the weekend. Because of their young age it was decided to keep the family connection low key – so Franny became the name the children used. They just accepted they had a big sister who lived in Scotland.

"Even if it ever comes to light, and Francesca learns the truth of her parentage, you will always be her father, Sam," commented Chantal. "The girl adores you and it's reciprocated. It's the relationship which counts – not a document."

Sam's eyes filled with tears. "For a few wonderful months I thought she was my own flesh and blood. It seemed to make the nightmare of the marriage to Evelyn worth it… until the woman confessed, and my world fell apart."

"Could she have been wrong, Sam? Did you ever query the situation?"

Sam shook his head. "Only Evelyn knows the truth – one day there may be some kind of medical breakthrough where parentage can be proved – until then we make a judgement based on facts and trust the truth is being told. I do believe Evelyn is correct. If there was any doubt she would have thrown it back at me. She achieved her objective. Her baby was given my name and brought up in a beautiful home. Remember, the biological father was married, so he couldn't have provided for her."

"Did you know Francesca's real father?"

"Yes, he was one of our group of friends. I wouldn't be surprised if there were other women – he was quite the 'Lothario' at the time."

"When you put it that way, Sam, I think it would be best if Francesca never finds out," concluded Chantal. "Did she ever query why you worked away from Edinburgh?"

"Not really, remember she was just a young child when I left – she grew up thinking Daddy appeared twice a year, Christmas and summer. And then there was the war and my missing years. We've become much closer since I came 'back to life', so to speak."

Chantal pondered the situation. It was all in the past and a new chapter was about to begin. Maybe some secrets were best kept hidden.

Driving through the gates of Matthison Hall felt odd for Chantal. She recalled the day, years ago, when she, Darcy, Josh and Henri visited the place. Darcy's investigative skills had sourced Sam's family home. At that time, he was 'missing in action', presumed and declared dead. They had peered through the gates. She had felt nothing. Yes, it was Sam's family home, but he had not lived there for many years, so it was just a building. But now approaching it, she was impressed by its appearance coupled with the fact it was her children's inheritance.

"It's a magnificent building, Sam, I can't wait to see inside."

The Carter family entered the house. Although it was large, they were used to Meckleridge House, so to them it seemed normal. They wandered from room to room. Con and Hope, apprehensive at first, soon relaxed and ran around. There were only minimal amounts of furniture left and some floor rugs. Chantal observed Sam as he gave her the grand tour.

"This was my room as a child," he commented showing her his boyhood bedroom, now empty. Continuing along the corridor, he paused.

"Those rooms were Evelyn and Francesca's quarters," he declared, not bothering to enter, but Chantal did. They were gracious and well proportioned, overlooking the pristine gardens at the rear of the house. Again, they were empty and echoed when the children began to squeal and play hide and seek. Chantal was struck by its beauty. It was a house of character.

Returning downstairs, Chantal viewed the reception rooms – four large rooms and a spacious kitchen. The house was in excellent decorative order. She wasn't sure what she'd expected...but it was strange – it possessed a personality, ready to be moulded by its new occupants.

She walked up behind Sam, as he was staring through the French windows, leading onto the rear lawns. She slid her arms around his waist.

"Any regrets?" she asked.

He swallowed. "Maybe," he commented. "For so long, parting with this house was the only way I could be free from Evelyn. Now she has moved out…it feels different. Coupled with the imminent conclusion to the divorce…I'm seeing it in a different light."

Chantal sensed a sadness in her partner's mood.

"Is it too late to change your mind?" she asked.

Sam turned and looked deeply into her eyes. "What… you mean, stop it going up for sale?"

Chantal nodded. "Put it on hold until the divorce comes through. Then think about it again."

"But our jobs are in northeast England, Chantal."

"Jobs can be found in Edinburgh, Sam. My sister and her family live in Malhaven but remember I lived most of my life in France. It would be a fresh start. Consider it, Sam."

Sam sighed heavily and took Chantal in his arms.

"Oh, Chantal, I love you so much. I don't know what to do…but the prospect interests me. Come on, let's find the children, lock up and go to Francesca's."

***

Marcel looked around the church or chapel as he'd been told to call it. It was unlike the churches he'd visited before. Any kind of religious observance for Marcel Duval was unusual – his parents were not 'church goers'. His French father had turned his back on his Roman Catholic roots as a young man, and his English mother took umbrage at her church's viewpoint when she gave birth to Marcel out of wedlock. So apart from weddings and funerals, attending a place of worship was not a regular event.

His mission this evening, however, was to observe Bernie Dempster in his role as a lay preacher in the Methodist church in Malhaven. It was a mid-week service. Quite by chance, Marcel had seen it advertised and had prepared his 'cover story', if it should be needed. He doubted if Bernie Dempster would remember seeing him at Meckleridge House – he'd been standing at the back of the room.

Unfortunately for Marcel, there were only about twenty people in attendance, and his presence was causing some curiosity. The congregants were a friendly bunch, greeting him with hearty handshakes and beaming smiles.

"Welcome, brother, please feel at home among us" … the message appeared to be universal.

The hymns and prayers were totally alien to Marcel, but the congregation were in good voice. Then the preacher climbed into the pulpit. After reading a portion from the Bible, the man proceeded to preach with power.

After the thirty-minute sermon concluded, Marcel felt extremely uncomfortable. He'd heard of 'fire and brimstone' preaching, but this was his first experience of hearing it. He was, according to Mr Dempster, on 'the broad road which leads to destruction'. Marcel saw no evidence of love in the man, but judging by the 'amens' resounding around the auditorium – it appeared the audience were in total agreement.

He scanned the audience noting two women, sitting at the front, who by their looks he took to be Judy's mother and her sister.

He made to take his leave but was apprehended by a larger-than-life lady in her seventies.

"How lovely to see you, young man, are you a visitor to this town?" After exchanging a few words about the area, he left the building. It was not an experience he desired to repeat.

It had not been his intention to visit the Smallwoods' that evening, but he felt it would be helpful if he could stay with them that night, as he had places to visit in the town the next day. As usual they were delighted to see him. They were intrigued when he told them about his visit to the church.

"Not a man to cross," he warned.

Josh told him about his letter from Judy, and he listened to Darcy's plans to take Josh to Bamburgh to see where Judy was staying.

The next morning, Marcel visited the local town of Malsett. He walked around until he found a florist's shop – Leveridges. He was pleased to see the shop was busy. It gave him the advantage of looking around and listening in to conversations. Without too much effort he learned about a funeral taking place the following week. After the customer left, he approached the counter.

"Perhaps you can assist me," he asked politely. "Can you tell me where I will find a funeral director in Malsett please?"

The shopkeeper looked to be a lady in her fifties.

"Well, we have two funeral directors in the town. It may be wise to make your choice based on the religion of the deceased. If your loved one was a Roman Catholic or Anglican, then try Barclay Funeral Directors. Any other religion then you should be contacting Dempster's Funeral Services."

Marcel reached for his notepad and jotted down the names.

"If it's someone local, perhaps I could advise," responded the shopkeeper.

Marcel attempted to divert the question.

"It's only a preliminary query on behalf of a friend," he explained, bluffing his way through the explanation. "Their relative is gravely ill and they want to be acquainted with the facts before the time comes – I said I would assist with enquiries."

A voice spoke from a table behind the counter. "Barclay's would be my choice. Both are attentive, but Barclay's are friendlier," muttered an elderly lady, absorbed in her work on a flower arrangement she was creating. Marcel looked over as the lady continued to converse.

"In his favour, Bernie Dempster has made a good living out of his funeral parlour – not like his father. He was a waster if ever there was one – gambled his business away." She shook her head in disgust.

Marcel was attentive but the conversation was brought to an abrupt halt.

"Hush, Ada, that's ancient history," remarked the shopkeeper, shaking her head.

Marcel asked for directions to the two Funeral Directors' premises.

"Here's their cards," she said, rummaging in a drawer. "You'll find Dempster's in Taylor Street and Barclay's is at the far end of Victoria Road, just past the bus station."

Marcel thanked the shopkeeper and left.

He smiled. One stray comment from an elderly lady opened a possible line of enquiry. Bernie Dempster's father was a waster…a gambler…and he gambled a business away…interesting!

Marcel headed straight back to Meckleridge House. He found Josh in his garage attending to Beryl.

"Hello, I thought you were busy this morning," Josh commented, looking up from under the bonnet of his car.

"I am, but I came by an interesting piece of information at the florist's shop." He gave Josh a brief version of his conversation.

"I'm beginning to think this 'problem' Bernie Dempster has with your family may go back to a previous generation to your dad, Josh. I need to discover the name of Judy's grandfather. If you are successful in speaking to her, when you go to Bamburgh, see if you can find a name. Alternatively, your pal Sid, who may have been indirectly responsible for the incident at your party…ask him to find out if his relative knows a name."

Josh nodded then asked, "Did you see Chrissie when you went into Leveridges?"

Marcel looked puzzled.

"Chrissie, you know, Darcy's friend. She works in Leveridges – it's her family's business."

Marcel looked wide eyed at his friend.

"Fancy that – no I didn't see her, but that's a useful link, Josh. Chrissie will know the old lady who mentioned that information about Mr Dempster. She might be able to dig up some more tittle tattle, if I ask her."

Marcel left Meckleridge House. He'd hardly paid any attention to Darcy's quiet friend – but suddenly she'd become a person of interest.

Chapter 19

Saturday dawned bright and fair. The day trippers left Malhaven after an early breakfast. Rachel, keen to help, had prepared a picnic basket. Henri was driving Tom's car.

"Take my car," Tom suggested. "There's more room in the back and it's less conspicuous."

It was a fair comment – Henri's sports car could attract unwanted attention.

Josh was sitting in the passenger seat, navigating, and Darcy was in the back seat along with the dog and the picnic hamper. After a halfway break to have a drink, change drivers and exercise Lady, they arrived at their destination before noon.

Leaving the coastal village of Seahouses, they drove along the seafront dotted with sand dunes. There was a stiff sea breeze blowing. Soon, Bamburgh Castle came into view, perched high above the seashore.

"Dad thought there were some cottages before you arrive in Bamburgh, so drive slowly, Josh."

Josh obeyed and sure enough some cottage-style buildings appeared on the left-hand side, as they approached the village. Three pairs of eyes were on the lookout for 'Seaview Cottages' but no names were apparent. They continued until they reached the entrance to the castle.

"Did she definitely say on the Seahouses to Bamburgh road?" Darcy asked.

"Yes," said Josh, despondently. Somehow, he'd expected to find the cottage easily.

"Right, here's the plan," declared Darcy.

"Does it include food?" asked Josh, "I'm ravenous."

Darcy huffed. "I thought being in love was supposed to put you off your food, Mr Smallwood. Never mind... here's the plan. We go back along past those cottages. Find somewhere to park. Have our picnic and take the dog for a walk. We might spot the names of the cottages that way."

"Your mother never ceases to amaze me," declared Henri, as the youngsters devoured the corned beef pie, egg sandwiches and cake that Rachel had packed in the hamper. Darcy fed Lady some scraps. They were parked near to the cottages in a rough, sandy carpark used by visitors to the beach. Darcy was eyeing the area beside the cottages.

"I think there are more buildings behind the front row, maybe even a lane. It needs to be explored on foot."

Eager to begin her task, she climbed out of the car and retrieved her mother's raincoat and a brown hat from the boot. She put them on. Josh burst out laughing.

"What do you look like? A prize idiot – you've just aged twenty years in that get out," he remarked.

Darcy smiled. "That's exactly what I was hoping. I need to create two personas if my little plan has any chance of working."

Henri smiled. He already knew Darcy's plan of action.

"Okay, first you two and the dog stay here… or go for a walk on the beach. Meanwhile, I'm going to go over there to see if I can find number 2 Seaview Cottages. If I am successful, I will walk around the back and see what's behind. Perhaps there is a garden or a yard at the back."

Josh was becoming impatient. The last thing he wanted was to be wandering along a beach while his sister was potentially uncovering the place where Judy was staying.

"Can't I be the one to go exploring?" he objected.

Darcy was definite. "No, you are too involved. Remember Judy's aunt will be wary of any young man hanging around, even though she doesn't know you. Be patient, Josh – one step at a time. That's all you need to know for now." With that Darcy left her frustrated brother and obliging husband and set off across the carpark. She crossed the road to where the cottages were situated.

The buildings were made of wood slats, single storey with slate roofs. There were two units comprising three terraced cottages each, one group was called 'Pleasant View' and the second group was called 'Seaview Cottages'…Darcy's goal.

Number 2 was the central one. Darcy walked slowly, taking in as much detail as possible. Each cottage had its own small garden – lawn and a few shrubs. She bent down, supposedly to remove a stone from her shoe. The woodwork was painted bright blue. There were windows either side of the front door with white lace curtains. Darcy suspected a central hallway…on one side a living room with a kitchenette at the rear, on the other side a front and back bedroom. She doubted if there was a bathroom, which signified there would be an outside toilet and washroom. She stood up again and walked to the end of the cottages.

A rough stone road led to the back. She followed around and as she'd expected, noted each cottage had a small rear garden and an outbuilding presumably an outside toilet and a washroom. There was no back gate, but a low fence ran along the edge of the cottages.

Movement in the garden at the end of the row caused her to be cautious, but the occupant disappeared into the outhouse. Darcy breathed a sigh of relief, then spotted something she could use to her advantage…a broken piece of fence. She continued along the track at the rear of the cottages, making a circuit and returned to the road.

Within minutes, she was sitting in the car, discarding her mother's hat and raincoat.

Josh and Henri stared at her in anticipation.

"Well…did you see her?" asked her anxious brother. Darcy shook her head.

"Of course not, that was just the first stage of my plan… reconnaissance! Now, Henri, drive into the village."

Josh was bamboozled. He'd been instructed to bring writing paper and a pen with him. He fully expected it was to write a note to Judy and try to leave it for her…yet now they were driving away from the cottage.

The village of Bamburgh was small with a triangular shaped area of grass in the centre. There were some trees and seats around the perimeter. Various single storey stone cottages, a public house, a police station, a church and a few shops overlooked the grassed area. At the base of the castle there appeared to be a cricket green and a road leading along to sand dunes. Larger buildings – hotels, Josh guessed – lined this road.

"Drive along there, and find somewhere to park," instructed Darcy.

Once parked, Darcy turned to face her brother.

"Now listen carefully. I want you to write a note to Judy. Make it brief. In one week's time we are going to launch her getaway. Tell her to go to the outhouse at two o'clock next Saturday afternoon and bring minimum stuff, so as not to arouse her aunt's suspicion. I can supply whatever items she has to leave behind. She needs to leave a note on her bed for her aunt, saying she has gone away with a friend and is safe."

Josh stared at his sister in amazement.

"But…what if…" Josh began. His sister scowled at him.

"There are loads of flaws in this plan, Josh…but it might just work…we must trust it will. Now write the note and then I'll explain how we can deliver it into Judy's hands."

Henri and Darcy stepped out of the car.

"So far, so good …are you ready for stage two of the plan, Henri?"

"Yes, ma chérie…you are so clever," he said taking her hand and squeezing it.

"Uh, huh, Henri. I will only be clever if it works. But one stage at a time."

When they returned to the car, Josh had finished his letter. Darcy insisted on seeing it and approved – he had kept to the bare facts.

"Stage two, Josh. This is how it works. I will attire myself with my second disguise – a headscarf, jacket and sunglasses. I am out for a walk with my husband and little dog, who has slipped her leash chasing something. She has followed, through a gap in the fence, into the back garden and refuses to come out. Henri, complete with trilby hat and walking stick, knocks on the front door and explains to whoever answers, presumably Judy's aunt, the predicament. Henri begs her to retrieve the dog and hand her back to his distraught wife over the fence. Stay out of sight until you see Henri enter the garden gate. This is your chance, Josh. It's a tiny house, so Judy will no doubt come out of her room to see what the fuss is over. Give her the note. If she doesn't appear... call for her – the aunt won't hear, as she will be in the garden by now. Scarper as soon as the note is delivered...okay? Lots could go wrong, if it does, just use your common sense. The main objective is that Judy knows about our rendezvous next Saturday."

Secretly, Josh thought the whole plan was crazy...but what was the alternative?

"Something is bound to go wrong, Darcy," Josh exclaimed.

"Shut up and think positively, Josh Smallwood. You want to be with Judy, don't you...then you'll have to take a risk. Henri and I have talked this through, and he is going to make a big fuss about me and the dog being in the garden. Remember she must be at the outhouse at two o'clock next Saturday."

Josh raised his eyebrows, and Henri watched as Darcy donned disguise number two.

Ten minutes later, the group were parked near the entrance to the back lane of Seaview Cottages.

Darcy was nervous but invigorated by her proposed plan. Josh felt sick and Henri was admiring his young wife's ingenuity.

"Don't forget, Josh, if it all goes 'pear shaped', impress upon Judy…the time and place next Saturday." Putting the leash on the dog, Darcy declared, "Right ,troops, let our mission begin." Then she climbed out of the car.

Josh watched as Darcy and Henri walked along the path, Lady wagging her tail and enjoying the impromptu walk. The couple turned into the back lane out of sight. Josh climbed out of the car. He heard his sister's panicked voice, calling for the dog, with a French accent. Henri appeared, moving as quickly as he could manage, and opened the small gate. Josh approached, keeping out of sight. Henri knocked loudly on the door. He couldn't make out the words, but whatever was said, Henri hurried out of the garden. Josh dived through the gate and stared at the open door…Judy was standing in the hallway, looking shocked. She gasped at the sight of Josh!

"Quick, take this… the details are in there," he spoke, thrusting the envelope onto the door mat. He legged it out of the garden, as Judy picked up the envelope and shut the door. He jumped into the car and started the engine. Where were they? He anxiously thrummed his fingers on the steering wheel.

Suddenly, he caught sight of Darcy's headscarf and Henri's trilby hat, bobbing over the hedge of the garden next to their parking space. Darcy was clutching Lady in her arms. He could hear her chastising the little dog, in French.

"*Lady…Je pensais que je t'avais perdue.*"

Henri opened the car door, and they climbed in.

"Drive, Josh," instructed Darcy. Josh engaged the gear and set off steadily along the road away from the cottage.

"Phew, my heart is racing," declared Darcy. "Did you see Judy?" she asked.

"For a split second…literally. She got the letter. How did it go in the back garden?"

Darcy was rummaging in the hamper.

"Splendid! Here's your treat, Lady," she announced, giving the dog some rewarding morsels of food. "Lady played her part to perfection. We walked around into the back lane. I bent down and let Lady off her leash. She was full of curiosity and ran through the gap in the fence, eager to explore. When Judy's aunt opened the back door, I was pleading for Lady to return. The woman looked like a battleaxe, grumbling on about me paying more attention to my dog and keeping her under control. Lady was fussing at her feet. She picked her up and handed her over the fence, just as Henri came around the corner. We thanked her and she went back inside."

"Mission accomplished," declared Henri as the little group travelled back home.

***

Marcel arrived early in Malhaven that afternoon. He knew the Smallwood family were out on their daytrip to the North Sea coastal resort of Bamburgh – but he was on a fact-finding operation. He made his way up the hill to the town of Malsett. The town existed at the top of the hill, because of its deposits of iron ore and westerly winds to fan the furnaces. Like any industrial town, a thriving community had been established around it dating back into the 1800s.

CHAPTER 19

Marcel parked his Citroën car and retracing his steps from earlier in the week, he was soon entering Leveridges, the florist shop. He was hoping to meet Chrissie. As before, one lady was serving a customer, and the older lady was attending to a floral display. Chrissie appeared to be absent.

"Hello, again," said the shopkeeper, recognising Marcel. "Did you find those places the other day?" she enquired.

But before Marcel could reply, Chrissie appeared through the door.

"Marcel, what brings you to town today?" she asked inquisitively, her eyes sparkling. "Are you seeking a bouquet for a special lady?" Marcel was not to be outwitted.

"Indeed, I am," he responded, smiling.

Chrissie turned to the shopkeeper. "I'm acquainted with Monsieur Duval, Auntie May, I'll serve him."

"Give me two minutes, Marcel and I'll be with you," she added, disappearing into the back room.

Marcel stood to the side as another customer entered the shop.

When Chrissie returned, she had removed her coat and attired herself in a dark green overall, bearing an embroidered motif, saying *Leveridges.*

"Now, Marcel how can I assist you?" she asked. Marcel was intrigued. The little wallflower, who hung in the shadows at the Meckleridge House events, seemed to have a new persona. She was every inch the businesswoman, walking him around the vases of flowers, trying to ascertain the recipient's tastes. Marcel listened with fascination, as she guided him through the sizes and costings of the various bouquets and floral arrangements.

"Am I being helpful?" she asked, smiling sweetly.

"Extremely," he replied, noticing her bright green eyes. "Imagine what you would like to receive, Chrissie, and design it for me, please."

Somewhat taken aback, she responded. "Really? Okay. It will take me a few minutes…but give me an idea of your budget."

Marcel shook his head. "Price is no problem," he declared. He observed her selecting the blooms, matching, trimming and arranging. She worked carefully and skilfully, absorbed in her task. The result was a masterpiece, in Marcel's eyes. Having attended to the monetary matters, he enquired, "What time do you finish work?"

Chrissie glanced at the clock.

"I'll be leaving in about half an hour," she replied. "Are you on your way to Darcy's?"

"Yes, they've been away today, so I'm hoping to see them when they get back." He bade farewell and left the shop.

Marcel walked over the road and stood in a shop doorway. There was a cold wind blowing along the street. Remaining vigilant, he was soon rewarded, when Chrissie left the florist's shop. He dashed across the road jumping into step with her.

"Oh, Marcel, what a fright," she exclaimed. "Is something wrong with your bouquet?"

Marcel reached out and touched Chrissie's arm.

"Nothing is wrong, Chrissie. I confess I was not upfront with you. These flowers are for you. Is there somewhere we could go…out of this chilly wind?"

Chrissie was startled. "There's a snack bar in Middle Street," she suggested.

"Perfect, lead the way."

CHAPTER 19

Although not the most salubrious of venues, Fortini's snack bar was clean and warm. Marcel and Chrissie found a booth and ten minutes later, were sipping a warming cup of tea. The flowers lay on the bench seat. Marcel praised her handiwork and asked about her occupation, listening attentively.

"Chrissie, I have a favour to ask you…but please believe me, these flowers are not given with an ulterior motive."

Chrissie eyed the Frenchman suspiciously – she knew it was too good to be true.

"The elderly lady in your shop seemed to know the Dempster family, judging by a comment she passed the other day. I am trying to help Josh uncover a bit of a mystery concerning his and Judy's family. It would seem to be dating back to a previous generation. Is there any way you can ask the lady if she knew the name of Judy's grandfather, please?"

Chrissie was deflated. Here she was being 'used' again, but she was not about to get upset in front of Marcel Duval. She continued to drink her tea, then looked at her companion.

"I think you are perfectly capable of conducting your own enquiries, Marcel. I am not about to interrogate a member of my family on your behalf."

She shuffled along to the edge of the bench seat.

"Thank you for the tea. Now, if you will excuse me, I need to be getting home."

She placed the flowers on the table and stood.

"On behalf of the shop, I thank you for your business today, but I suggest you give them to someone at Meckleridge House… someone you admire…Darcy perhaps? Goodbye." She turned and left the cafe.

Marcel felt 'put in his place'...he had underestimated Chrissie Leveridge.

***

Marcel was waiting for the day trippers when they returned to Meckleridge House. He'd presented Rachel with a beautiful bouquet of flowers as he arrived.

"Thank you, Marcel, they are delightful, but there was no need...you are welcome to visit anytime," she remarked.

Marcel waved away her response saying how appreciative he was of their hospitality.

He was eager to hear how the Bamburgh episode had transpired. Darcy filled in the details, basking in the glory of her devious plan. He watched her antics, but felt a little uncomfortable, as he recalled Chrissie's parting words in the café...were his feelings for Darcy Dukas apparent to others? He quickly dismissed the troubling thoughts.

"Now, if all goes to plan next week, we must find somewhere for Judy to hide – she can't stay here. Old man Dempster will search here first. In fact, the whole plan could backfire on us."

Marcel could almost see her brain working to solve the next problem. "Josh told Judy to leave a note for her aunt saying she was safe and staying with a friend until her twenty-first birthday. She hopes it will be enough to stop her dad from involving the police."

Marcel tried to be helpful. "Perhaps she could stay with my aunt in Durham, but it's not far from where she used to lodge...so I guess that's not ideal," he commented.

Darcy was pacing up and down, clearly agitated. "No… thanks, Marcel, but it needs to be away from here. It's months until Judy turns twenty-one and can make her own choices. Oh, I almost forgot…Judy's grandfather was called Ralph Dempster – Sid asked his grandma. Will it be helpful?"

Marcel frowned – all that fuss at the florist's could have been avoided.

"Yes, Darcy…thank you that's most helpful. Now, we need a date for his death. In the meantime, I have another favour to ask."

Darcy stared at Marcel.

"How do you feel about doing more undercover work for me?"

Chapter 20

Darcy was eager to help. "What's involved?" she asked.

Marcel rubbed his hand across his face. "I've been given an assignment to investigate a suspected fraud at a quarry near to Durham. It requires going undercover as an office secretary, while the real secretary is away. It's due to start after Easter. I was hoping to have time to delve into this problem concerning Judy's family and if I'm stuck in a quarry office – I'm not going to be able to do that."

Darcy looked thoughtful. After Easter…If all went as planned, Judy should be in hiding by then.

"How would it work?" she asked.

"Very similar to the last time. I suggest you resurrect 'Rose Caudwell'. You perfected that role, so why change it? The secretary works three days a week in the quarry office, keeping accounts and sorting the wage packets. However, in addition you would need to work through the books, checking for any discrepancies. The business is losing money, and the owner suspects the problem lies in the bookkeeping. I get the impression he's hopeless when it comes to figures."

"Which days would I be needed to work?" Darcy asked.

"Wednesday to Friday. It would require you staying at Aunt Bertha's again – it's too far to travel from Malhaven every day."

Darcy was hooked.

"I need to talk it over with Henri… but my priority at the moment is to help Judy and Josh," she replied.

***

The Carters arrived back from their trip to Edinburgh. The twins were full of their adventures staying with Francesca.

"What was the house like?" Rachel asked Chantal.

For years Matthison Hall had conjured up all sorts of pictures in her mind.

Chantal reached out and touched her sister's arm. "Rachel…I think Sam is having second thoughts." She looked questioningly into her sister's eyes.

"Second thoughts…what do you mean?" Rachel's voice trembled.

They went into the rear lounge and sat down.

"This is totally unexpected… but exciting, and I want you to be the first to know. I think Sam would like to keep Matthison Hall." Chantal sensed the panicked look on her sister's face.

"It's such a beautiful building, Rachel. It felt so homely – even devoid of furniture. It's always been clouded by Evelyn's presence – but now she has moved out…well… Sam feels it's his family's heritage. It's a similar size to Meckleridge and it's in good repair. I think it would make a delightful home for us…a new beginning. Of course, there's the problem of Sam's job, but in the meantime the divorce would be going through, so it wouldn't be for some time. We could marry, then move to live in Matthison Hall as husband and wife...a new beginning...a heritage for the children...a hope fulfilled, Rachel."

A tear trickled down Rachel's face. She was torn between happiness for her sister and the prospect of losing her, all over again.

"Don't cry, Rachel ...it isn't definite yet."

Rachel dabbed her eyes – she was being selfish. Her sister deserved this happiness after all the difficult years.

"I even have some of Mother's possessions which have been stored away in the attic for years – remember?"

Rachel nodded. After Chantal moved from France some crates had arrived containing their mother's possessions. They'd been stored unopened.

Composing herself, Rachel replied. "It will be a wrench, Chantal - we live together so well. But I agree...it's a fantastic opportunity for you. Ignore me, please – thank you for telling me, I'm sure I'll get used to the idea." Chantal walked over to embrace her sister.

"Keep quiet about it for now, Rachel. Things could change."

The sisters hugged tightly.

***

A rattle sounded on the front door. "I'll get it," shouted Darcy, racing down the stairs. She opened the door.

"Morning, Terry, how are you today?" she greeted the postman.

Lady bounded through the hallway.

"Just look at this bundle of fur, my hasn't she grown," he commented, bending down to stroke the little dog.

Darcy exchanged a few words, thanking the postie, then sorted the pile of letters, according to her mother's housekeeping rules.

An envelope with a Newcastle postmark caught Darcy's attention. It was brown, typewritten and bore her name. Quickly she ripped it open.

"Dear Miss Smallwood,

We are in receipt of your article 'The Birth of Change' and are delighted to inform you we will be willing to publish it in our newspaper on the first Sunday in May. We will be in touch regarding your remuneration in due course."

Darcy could hardly contain her delight. It was Monday morning, and the house was deserted, apart from her mother working in the kitchen.

"Ta-dah," she announced, thrusting the letter in front of Rachel.

"Calm down, Darcy…what is it?"

"Read it. I've just had my article accepted for publication in the Sunday Sun newspaper."

Rachel dried her hands on her apron and took the letter from her excited daughter. She scanned the contents.

"Congratulations – you will soon be famous," she remarked. "I see you have used your maiden name," she added.

"Yes, it links to my other writings. But this article feels more important than my others, it's on a serious subject and may get me somewhere. I must let Francesca know. She was such a help collecting those responses from some of her patients. I'm off to tell Henri," she announced, flying out of the back door.

Rachel watched her retreating figure with pride. Thankfully, her ambitious daughter was turning a negative experience into something positive.

Henri's eyes lit up as his beautiful young wife shared her news.

"Congratulations, ma petite fille, I knew you could do it. Come here." He wiped his hands and stood up. She snuggled into his embrace.

"Are you still annoyed with me?" she asked, muttering into his chest. There was a pause.

During the years of their relationship, the couple had rarely disagreed, but when Darcy had told Henri about Marcel's request for her to go undercover again, he'd spoken sharply.

"I don't want you to go, Darcy. I think Marcel is taking advantage of your abilities."

"It's only for a month," she'd objected, "and I will be receiving payment this time. He's helping Josh, so in a way I'm helping Josh also."

For the first time in their three-year marriage, Henri had turned his back on Darcy as they lay in bed.

The next morning, Henri conceded.

"If it's what you want to do, Darcy, then it's your decision, I won't stand in your way."

It was two days since that conversation, but it was still hanging in the air.

Henri cupped Darcy's chin. "You are my world, Darcy. I cannot imagine a life without you. But you are putting yourself in more danger than you think. Please, please be careful, ma chérie."

Darcy gazed into Henri's eyes. "Please trust me, Henri."

He kissed her lovingly and they pulled apart.

As Darcy returned to the house an idea jumped into her head. Entering the house, she went to the phone to make a call to Francesca in Edinburgh.

***

Rachel looked at her daughter in disbelief. It was two days prior to the planned rescue attempt for Judy, and she had just been given the details.

"This is ludicrous. You could end up being in trouble with the police, Darcy…is there no other way?"

"Mother, there is no other way. Believe me if there were we wouldn't be forced into this hare-brained plan. All I am asking of you, is to find time tomorrow or on Saturday morning to go up to Trespershields and prepare the bungalow for two guests."

"But it's abduction, Darcy!" Rachel exclaimed.

Darcy shook her head. "No, Mother, it isn't. Judy wants to escape from her aunt's home. The only crime being committed here is Judy being kept at her aunt's home against her will. Once Judy has her twenty-first birthday, in August, then she is free to make her own choices."

"Oh, this gets worse…now it's for months, you said it was for a few days." Rachel was exasperated.

Darcy was clattering around the kitchen putting cutlery in a drawer. "It will only be for a few days…the next part of my plan has yet to be finalised."

On Saturday morning, the rescue party left early… this time without the dog. Josh was driving his dad's car. Darcy was wearing her 'Rose Caudwell' disguise but had put a suitcase containing other clothes into the boot of the car.

Josh couldn't resist a laugh. "You look like an idiot," he remarked, looking at his sister's outfit.

Her hair was pulled back in a tight bun; a brown beret was pulled onto her head in an ungainly fashion. She wore a checked coat with a scarf tucked in at the neck, thick brown stockings and flat laced up, brown shoes. She was carrying her spectacles, in her oversized handbag, to put on later. He noticed a clipboard jutting out of the bag.

"What that for?" he asked.

"It's a questionnaire about cleaning products. I am carrying out some market research," she replied.

"What…on a Saturday afternoon?" he asked.

Darcy looked indignant. "Why not? People are off work on a Saturday."

"What if Judy's aunt slams the door in your face?"

"She won't…I will use my charm. Anyway, if Judy follows your instructions she can be away in minutes."

At quarter to two, Judy Dempster laid the two letters she had written on the bed.

The first was addressed to her aunt.

'Dear Aunt Edie,

Thank you for looking after me over the last couple of weeks. I apologise if I have been difficult, but I was brought here against my will. When you read this, I will be gone.

PLEASE DO NOT LOOK FOR ME. I am with friends and am safe. I have left a note for my parents.

Love Judy.'

It wasn't Aunt Edie's fault, and she had been kind in her own way. The second letter was not so polite.

'Father, Mother and Patricia,

When you receive this, I will be well away from Aunt Edie's prison. DO NOT LOOK FOR ME. I am staying with friends and am safe and well. I have probably lost the job I loved, because of your interference in my life. In August, I will be twenty-one and can choose my own friends. I will be in touch after my birthday. You have treated me like a child, but I am an adult and deserve to be treated like one. Mother and Patricia, I hold no ill feelings towards you, but I hope, Father…one day I can forgive you.

Judy'

What more could she say? She concealed her handbag in a bundle of underclothes; took one last look around and left the bedroom, closing the door.

"What are you doing?" asked her aunt, from the living room.

"Just going to rub through a few smalls, Aunt Edie," she replied.

"Can't they wait until wash day on Monday?" the older lady asked in exasperation.

"No, I've run short, they should dry nicely before teatime," responded Judy.

Judy opened the cupboard under the sink and retrieved a bar of household soap. Then putting the plug in the oblong porcelain sink, she partially filled it with warm water. Selecting a garment, she began to rub it with household soap on the wooden draining board. She looked at her watch…nearly two o'clock. She was shaking with anticipation. As she glanced into the back garden, she saw a figure walking up the lane. A surge of excitement gripped her.

A rattle at the front door caused Judy to jump…this was it! Quickly, she opened the back door, as she heard her aunt making her way to the front door.

"Oh, good afternoon, sorry to…" The voice faded as Judy grabbed her smalls, stuffed them into her bag and stepped out into the garden.

She darted across the yard to the outhouse. Josh appeared from behind it and reached out his strong arms to lift Judy over the small fence. He grabbed her hand, and they hurried to the corner of the back lane where Henri was waiting with the engine running. They clambered into the back seat of the car and crouched down, out of sight. Henri edged the car onto the main road.

"Where is she?" called Josh, in agitation.

"She's coming," replied Henri, catching sight of Darcy in his rear mirror, meandering along the footpath.

As she drew alongside the car, Henri flung open the door. Darcy had barely closed it when Henri accelerated, and the car sped away.

Darcy pulled off her glasses and hat and released her hair from its bun.

"I think we did it, folks. Hello Judy... I must say your aunt was an interesting person to interview."

The occupants of the car began to laugh.

"Stay down, you two, until we are a few miles away," instructed Darcy.

So far, the plan had worked.

***

Tom and Rachel arrived back home in Henri's sports car.

"I know it's got style, but give me a sensible car any day," commented Tom, climbing out. They'd spent the morning up at the bungalow at Trespershields. Their small country retreat, a few miles from Malhaven, had been a place of relaxation and solace over the years. It was little more than a shack on stilts, but it had served its purpose. When their home was a hotel, it had afforded them quality family time when the children were young. After falling into disrepair during the war years, Tom and Rachel had restored it.

Sam and Chantal held poignant memories of their reunion at The Bungalow in post-war years and if all went according to plan, once again it would play its part... this time as a hideaway.

Chantal welcomed them with a cuppa, and they sat around the kitchen table.

"What time are you expecting the rescuers to return?" she asked.

Tom consulted his watch.

"If there have been no hitches, they should be at Trespershields by late afternoon. The Bungalow is clean and tidy; the beds are made up and there are food supplies in the cupboard."

"So, is Darcy staying with Judy?"

Rachel took a drink of tea. "Yes…I suspect Henri might have trouble getting Josh away from Judy, but he must get back here in case Mr Dempster comes calling."

Chantal nodded…it was a possibility, and Judy's father might have already contacted the police.

Rachel looked weary and concerned.

"There are potential dangers in the whole arrangement until Judy is away from Trespershields. I can't settle, but Darcy has it all arranged… and we must trust her."

An hour later, Marcel arrived.

"Welcome, Marcel, we can't keep you away from here," Tom commented, answering the door.

"I love visiting your home, Tom, and I'm doing some investigation work for Josh concerning Judy. How's things… today was the rescue day, wasn't it?"

Tom wasn't sure how much Marcel knew – the fewer people who knew, the better, in Tom's opinion.

"Come on through and have a cuppa. We're not 'au fait' with the details – but hopefully the rescue is in progress."

After greeting Rachel and Chantal, Marcel commented, "Your daughter leaves no stone unturned – I trust her ingenuity."

"Well, Darcy can sometimes be economical with the details. Now, have you made any progress with this Dempster business?"

"It's slow, but I visited the local florist's – Leveridges. Quite by chance I discovered Bernie Dempster's father was a gambler and squandered his business away. This comment was made by an elderly lady, doing arrangements, but was quickly quashed by the shopkeeper."

Tom listened with interest and chuckled. "That would be Ada Leveridge – she's a blunt old stick, but a fountain of information. You should try asking Chrissie to help – she works there."

Marcel felt uncomfortable…the least said about Chrissie, the happier he would be.

Tom looked thoughtful. "I expect Bernie would have served in the First World War, because he was older than me. My brother and I were still at boarding school, but my uncle bought the farm around that time, which would have enabled us to work there and be exempt from service."

Marcel stared at Tom.

"Aah, that's interesting. I thought the house and farmlands belonged to the same owner."

Tom shook his head.

"No, not originally. My aunt and uncle lived in Wales. They bought the house just before WW1 began and moved here. It was later, during the war, when my uncle bought the farm."

"What was his name, Tom?"

"Bartholomew Soames, Bart for short – he was a lovely man. He didn't hail from these parts, but when he married my aunt, in later life, she couldn't settle in Wales, so he bought this house and moved here. When he acquired the adjoining farmlands, it became known as the Meckleridge Estate."

Marcel started to make notes.

"This is fascinating, Tom, I just assumed you'd inherited it from your family."

Tom smiled. "Well, I did, but from my aunt not my father."

Rachel interjected. "Tom's father was the local vicar. His aunt and uncle both died soon after Tom left university."

"Do you know who owned the farm before your uncle?"

Tom shook his head. "I've no idea, Marcel. Some old timers like Ada Leveridge or Sid's grandmother might remember."

Marcel nodded. "Well thanks to Sid, we now know Judy's grandfather was called Ralph…does that ring any bells for you?"

Again, Tom was blank. "The name means nothing to me, Marcel," he responded.

***

It was late afternoon when the travellers returned from Bamburgh. Much to Darcy's impatience, Josh had insisted they stopped to buy some fish and chips to satisfy his appetite.

"I hope you realise what a monster my brother is for his food, Judy!" she remarked, laughing, but judging by the look on Judy's face, as she gazed adoringly at Josh Smallwood, he could sprout wings, and she would still love him.

Josh parked the car, having driven for the final stretch of the journey.

"Here we are, Judy, it's not exactly posh – but it's dry and clean and no doubt my mother will have stocked the cupboards."

CHAPTER 20

Judy looked at her surroundings. It was a wooden shack in a field. She followed Josh onto the veranda and stepped inside the wooden structure.

"It's perfect, Josh, so isolated…where are we?"

We are a about seven miles from Malhaven, on the road leading to Blanchland. Is it an area your father has visited to your knowledge? We came here regularly when we were kids – but it's the sort of place you would need to know about to find it." Darcy was bustling around, making some tea.

"It's only for a few days, Judy. I'm keeping the next part of my plan 'hush hush'. Get this tea, then have a bit of time with Josh, before Henri and Josh go back to Meckleridge."

After their refreshment, Josh took Judy over to the river.

"This is a delightful spot," Judy commented, as Josh took her hand. They turned down onto the riverbank just before the bridge.

"Let's sit," he suggested, throwing down his jacket.

Time stood still as the young sweethearts embraced, kissed and wallowed in the luxury of freedom from restraints.

"I love you, Judy," Josh declared, stroking her face. "Though you are quite a challenge," he added.

"Josh, I am so grateful to you and Darcy for getting me away from my aunt's house. It's been a nightmare. My father has probably wrecked my job. I can't go near the place to explain, in case he finds me." Judy looked despondent.

"Can you write to them asking for their understanding?"

"Yes, that's a good idea. Will I see you again before Darcy's next piece of the plan unfolds?"

Josh squeezed her tightly. "Try keeping me away. I'll be back tomorrow, so write the letter and I'll post it."

"All I can hope is that they will accept this 'family crisis' situation and keep my job open until September."

The pull of romance took over, but eventually they returned to The Bungalow.

Something was nagging at the back of Tom's mind, as he was trying to sleep that night. It had been a busy evening. Josh and Henri had returned, leaving Darcy and Judy to sleep at The Bungalow. The family and Marcel had listened in awe to the antics of the 'escape plan' and its execution. Secretly, Tom was proud of his daughter. She was a force of nature, but with a heart to help people. He hoped her attempts to pave the way for Josh and Judy would be rewarded.

Suddenly, he sat up. 'That's it!' he said to himself – Rachel was sound asleep.

The thought nagging at the back of Tom's mind concerned the question Marcel had asked earlier in the day...*who owned the farm before Uncle Bart?*

Tom didn't know, but he'd remembered a box of old documents lurking in a corner of the attic. They dated back to the early days when his aunt and uncle came to live in Malhaven. Perhaps there might be some relevant paperwork in that box...unless the mice had nibbled it! An excursion into the attic was required.

Chapter 21

No-one was going to keep Josh Smallwood from spending quality time with his girlfriend. The next day, he arrived at the hideaway with the remnants of Sunday lunch, but he was careful about his choice of route. Josh had no way of knowing if Bernie Dempster would suspect him of helping Judy, but he was taking no chances. He set off in the opposite direction, then doubled back on himself using country lanes. When he was certain he was not being followed, he took the road to Blanchland, turning off before reaching the village.

Josh wasn't too happy about letting his sister drive Beryl back home, but she indicated she had an important telephone call to make. She also needed to assemble items for Judy to take with her on the next stage of her disappearance.

"Do not drive the normal way home, Darcy," he urged, giving directions for the circuitous route he had taken.

"Good thinking, Josh. Our house could easily be being watched. I'll be careful. Now you two, make the most of this afternoon…dear knows when you will be seeing each other again."

After spending time constructing the letter to the hospital, Josh took Judy in his arms, and they spent an idyllic afternoon together. Throughout their friendship they'd always felt they were looking over their shoulders, fearful of anyone seeing them.

At Trespershields they enjoyed the privacy previously denied to them.

"Judy, you may regard this as totally inappropriate, but I want to ask you something. I don't expect an answer today because you may feel pressured, considering how Darcy and I have helped you."

Judy wrapped her arms around Josh's neck. "I'm listening," she responded.

"I've never felt like this about a girl before. You are special to me...I've already told you I love you. I know I'm young and I don't have a proper job, but I do have prospects. If...and it's a big if...my situation improves... then sometime in the dim and distant future... would you consider becoming my wife?" He was tense and he knew he was rambling.

A slow smile spread across Judy's face. Without speaking she brought her lips to meet Josh's. The intensity of the kiss spoke volumes.

Pulling back, Judy responded. "I hope that gives you my answer...but Josh, we have a problem...an unknown future. I foresee insurmountable obstacles lying ahead of us. We have already taken risks to be here like this. Together, I am sure we will defy my father's boundaries. I love you and will do everything in my power to help us be united. I am prepared to go against my family's wishes...one day I hope we will understand why our friendship has caused so much tension. We need to remain strong and trust each other to overcome the barriers."

The words were spoken with sincerity, but they both knew there was a long, winding road stretching ahead of them.

***

Tom couldn't sleep. He was out of bed before Rachel, which was most unusual.

"What's wrong?" she enquired, sitting up to see Tom hastily putting on his clothes.

"Nothing, it's just a hunch. I need to check something in the attic."

Before Rachel could seek an explanation, he had disappeared.

The attics at Meckleridge House were extensive – it was one thing knowing what he was looking for, but quite another trying to locate it.

In the hotel years the attics were used for family accommodation, but during the war, numerous items were stored in them. When Chantal moved from France, she brought many boxes, which ended up in the attics. When his parents died, items from their house also found a home there. Prior to this his Aunt Dora and Uncle Bart had used the space for storage too.

In essence it was a major task – not one to be achieved quickly.

After searching for an hour, he gave up.

"Did you find what you were looking for?" asked Rachel, as Tom entered the kitchen.

The Carters were just finishing their breakfast. Tom watched Sam and Chantal saying goodbye to their offspring, hastily retreating to avoid sticky kisses. Rachel would be taking them to school.

As quietness fell, he answered Rachel's question. "No, it was a fruitless task. I'm trying to locate a box of documents from Aunt Dora and Uncle Bart's days."

Rachel proceeded to wipe Con's sticky hands.

"That's easy," she replied. "If you'd told me before you went up there, I could have pointed you in the right direction."

Tom stared at his wife in amazement. "Rachel Smallwood, we will have been married for twenty-five years this Christmas, and you never cease to amaze me!" He smiled lovingly at her, as Josh arrived at the breakfast table.

"Have you overslept?" asked his mother.

In between gulps of food, Josh replied. "Yes, I'm running late. I've only got a few hours with Judy before she goes. Is there any food to take up to the Bungalow?"

Tom was becoming impatient. Everyone seemed to need his wife for one thing or another this morning. "Rachel, can you tell me where I can find those documents, please?" he begged.

After showing Josh the basket of food, she had prepared for Darcy and Judy, Rachel sat down.

"Picture the house from above, Tom. All Dora and Bart's boxes are piled up beside the wall which faces the old stable block. One of these days those attics will need a good sorting. That area of the attics contains the oldest stuff."

Tom stood and walked over to stand behind Rachel. He draped his arms around her neck, bent forward and kissed her. Josh smirked.

"My darling...where would I be without you? Your organisation of this house is splendid. Josh my lad, make sure you pick a gem, like your mother, when you choose a wife." He straightened and headed for the door. "If anyone wants me...I'm up in the attics," he called.

Ten minutes later Rachel dashed up the attic stairs. The area where Tom was searching was through two doors so there was little point in calling to him. Josh had left the house, Henri was in the greenhouse, and the twins were playing in the back lounge. She'd locked the dog in Darcy and Henri's lounge, in case of any problems.

She was breathless when she reached the far attic.

"Tom," she called, flinging open the creaky, old door. "Quick, Bennie's being rushed into hospital. Nancy has just telephoned – good job she caught me before I took the twins to school."

Tom left his search. Rachel's face was flushed.

"Calm down, Rachel. Where's Josh?"

Struggling to get her breath, she replied. "He's off up to The Bungalow. Bennie took ill early this morning. The doctor has just visited, and he's sent for the ambulance."

Tom guided his wife through the attics and down the stairs, trying to think through his plan of action.

"First of all, you, my dear, need to sit down," he suggested. "Then I'll take the twins to school after I get Henri to go up to the bungalow to tell Josh to get back here. Ivan can go over to the farm and hold the fort until Josh arrives."

Rachel didn't argue and within minutes Tom had taken control of the situation.

Ivan, who managed the Market Garden for Tom, was willing to assist and soon Henri was arriving at Trespershields to deliver the ominous message.

Josh and Judy's fond farewell was destined to be curtailed. The second part of Judy's disappearance was due to happen that afternoon. Disappointment was etched on both their faces.

Darcy jumped into action. "Okay, folks…change of plan. You've got fifteen minutes to say your 'goodbyes' then, Josh, you and Henri need to get back home. I'll take Judy to the station."

Josh looked at Judy…life could be cruel. They'd planned a blissful walk along the riverbank, then after a quick snack they would drive to the station in Durham. Instead, they spent their brief time sealing their kisses to memory.

Eventually, they pulled apart.

"Until we meet again, Judy. Soon…soon…we will be together. Oh, I almost forgot to ask. Do you remember your grandfather? Marcel thinks he may be at the bottom of this thing with my family."

Judy shook her head. "He died before I was born, Josh. I got the impression my father didn't get on with him."

"Do you recall seeing any family photographs? Do you have any other relatives on your dad's side of the family?"

Judy looked despondent. "No, Josh. There was only Aunt Edie, and she was a war widow with no family. I have no recollection of any family photos on my dad's side of the family. I'm not being much help, am I…but I really don't know."

They spent their last minutes locked in a tight embrace.

"I'll do my best to visit you, but if Bennie's out of action on the farm, then the workload will fall to me, so free time will be limited."

Judy caressed her boyfriend's face.

"It's only for a few months, Josh… we can write and make telephone calls."

"It will feel like a lifetime," moaned Josh.

***

As the family sat around the supper table, tiredness was etched on all their faces. It had been a trying day. Josh was exhausted. After returning from the bungalow at Trespershields, just before lunchtime, he'd taken over from Ivan.

When Nancy returned from the hospital, she gave Josh and Tom an update on Bennie's health.

"Well, it's as I feared – an operation is necessary. It's planned for tomorrow at the Infirmary in Newcastle. He's been ill for weeks, but you know my Bennie, he always makes light of serious issues, thinking they will go away if you don't acknowledge them. The doctor has indicated it's a bowel problem. They have no idea of the outcome, but he will be out of action for some time."

Nancy reached over the table and grabbed Josh's hand. "The good Lord must have known you'd be available, Josh. My Bennie says you know 'what's what'."

Josh swallowed, embarrassed by Nancy's comments. "Bennie always gets me to help him. I can do the ordering and the paperwork."

Tom sat back running his hand through his greying hair.

"No, Nancy…your job is to care for Bennie. You need to be at the hospital in Newcastle every day. We'll set up a rota, because I know you don't drive. Between Rachel, Darcy, Henri, Ivan, Josh and me…we'll cover it. Darcy might lend a hand with the paperwork." Josh spoke up.

"Isn't she doing some work for Marcel, Dad?"

Tom raised his eyebrows. "Oh, crumbs – I'd forgotten about that."

Tom and Josh reassured Nancy they would attend to the daily demands of the farm.

Tom informed the family about the medical issue at the Meckleridge Farm.

"It takes me back to when my brother, Jonty, had his accident many moons ago. I was summoned to help on the farm. Bennie was the farmhand in those days. I had the hotel to run, so Bennie stepped up and took over. There's a reason you are available, Josh…I'm expecting you to run the farm – Bennie's been training you, and that young farmhand will help you. Now Darcy, this is a family business, and we are going to need your help with the clerical stuff."

Darcy looked at her father. "But Dad, I've promised Marcel to do some undercover work."

Tom sighed heavily. "Your place is here, Darcy. I expect you to help even if it means working in your free time – Nancy will guide you."

Darcy was not impressed.

The peal of the telephone ringing interrupted her thoughts, and Darcy jumped up to answer it.

"Hello, Darcy – it's Judy. Just letting you know I've arrived safely. Francesca is just like you said – she's so friendly and I liked her immediately. Now, can I speak to Josh, please."

"Oh, Judy, I'm delighted to hear part two of my plan has worked – now we need to keep things under wraps for the next few months, only the immediate family will know of your whereabouts, but at least you will have some freedom." She handed the phone to Josh.

***

After supper, Tom returned to the attic, this time accompanied by Rachel and two torches. It was dark and dusty, but finding time in daylight hours was unlikely, so he took this opportunity. Under Rachel's direction they soon found the boxes pertaining to Bart Soames. Tom shone the torch, as Rachel searched the boxes – each was thick with dust and cobwebs. They examined three boxes. which dated back to Bart's time in Wales.

"One more box, then we'll leave it for tonight," said Tom, feeling as if he was swallowing dust.

"Ah…this looks promising," declared Rachel, pulling out a document folded in three. The ink was faded, but as she opened the brown tinged paper, Tom could just make out the words 'Land Registry'.

"By gum, Rachel, I think this box might contain what I am searching for. Let's take it downstairs and look at the contents in comfort."

Darcy replaced the telephone receiver and joined Henri in their sitting room.

"All set for Wednesday," she announced, snuggling up to her husband on the settee.

"Marcel is going to vacate the bedroom I used before and sleep in the box room. If you can take me over to Durham on Tuesday night, then I'll be ready to begin work at the quarry the next day."

"That's thoughtful of him," Henri replied, snidely.

Darcy sat forward and stared at him. "Henri Dukas, I do believe you are jealous of Marcel Duval!" she exclaimed.

Henri shrugged. "Darcy, I would be an idiot if I didn't suspect that man has a fancy for you."

Darcy glowered at him. "Henri, that's outrageous. I'm a married woman...don't you trust me?"

"Being married makes no difference to men like Marcel Duval, Darcy," Henri muttered.

She shook her head in disbelief. "Have I ever given you cause to doubt my love and devotion towards you? I vowed before God to love, honour and obey you in sickness and in health. I've done that...haven't I? We've experienced challenging times with your illness, then Leon's passing, but we've supported each other...haven't we?"

Henri was silent. Darcy was troubled.

"Henri...your silence is disturbing...speak to me, please."

Henri continued to stare into the flickering flames of the coal fire. Darcy was impatient.

"Henri, I love you...surely I am worthy of your trust?"

Henri fondled the edge of Darcy's neck and sighed.

"A healthy relationship is founded on trust, Darcy, but we must communicate our feelings... if we are to rely on each other. I am being open with you...I need you to know I sense something with Marcel. I'm not judging him or you. I'm just telling you what I observe. You are placing yourself in a potentially difficult situation and I expect you to behave in a trustworthy manner in all your dealings with Marcel."

Darcy swallowed. Was it true? Had Henri seen something in Marcel's eyes ..in his actions...did the man hold feelings for her? She blinked away her concerns.

"Stay with me on Tuesday night at Bertha's house," she suggested. "If Marcel 'sees' us as a married couple, it will help to dispel any designs he may have towards me. But I think you are being overprotective, Henri...this is a time to trust."

Henri enveloped his wife in a loving embrace...he had told her of his concerns...now he must trust her.

***

Relief was evident at Meckleridge when Bennie's operation was over – but it was short lived.

After visiting with the surgeon, Nancy was dealt a worrying blow.

"Nancy seems happy, but I'm not sure," Tom indicated to Rachel when he returned from the hospital. "Bennie needs to undergo radiotherapy treatment, which has serious implications."

Rachel looked pensive. "I think you should prepare Josh, Tom. He could be in this for the long haul. Is it what he wants in his life? He's being thrust into it and is doing well. But he sees it as a temporary arrangement. What if Bennie can't return to work? Should we be looking for a new Farm Manager...then Josh could work under him?"

Tom looked thoughtful. "We couldn't afford to hire another manager and pay Josh and Bennie, Rachel. The farm is profitable but will only support one manager and one farm hand."

Rachel reached out and squeezed her husband's hand. "Then we have a problem, Mr Smallwood. You need to put your 'thinking cap' on."

On Tuesday evening Henri took Darcy to Bertha's house in Durham. Marcel's aunt was delighted to be reacquainted with 'Rose Caudwell'. Darcy had a brief word with her and asked if Henri could stay overnight.

"Of course, my dear – it's unnatural for a young couple to be denied their married life. He is welcome to come over each night if he wants."

"That's kind of you, Bertha, he may do that," she added, hoping Marcel Duval would get the message loud and clear.

The next morning Darcy became 'Rose Caudwell', leaving her wedding and engagement rings at Bertha's. Marcel drove her to the quarry, on the outskirts of Durham.

"Remember your cover story, Rose. I am your boyfriend. You are undertaking this cashier's role in her absence."

Darcy was unsure of this aspect but agreed.

Arriving at the quarry office, Marcel introduced her to the owner.

"I'm around for a couple of hours each morning, then I return to lock up about five o'clock," he explained. "Now, I'll show you where everything is kept." Marcel stood back as Bill, the owner, showed Rose the layout of the office.

Marcel looked at his watch then stepped forward.

Without warning he took Rose in his arms, embraced and kissed her on the lips. She was so startled, she nearly lost her spectacles!

Chapter 22

Josh was summoned to his dad's office – it was a week since Bennie's operation.

"Take a seat – I want to have a chat," Tom indicated.

Josh was perplexed as to the formal nature of his dad's request.

"Dad…is something wrong?" he asked.

Tom leaned back in his chair and considered his son – twenty-one years old…on the threshold of life. He seemed too young to be making important decisions, yet by law he was a man.

"Josh, your mother and I feel this is the right time to bring this to your attention. The prognosis for Bennie is not good. His operation was successful, but he needs a course of radiotherapy treatment. In a nutshell, this indicates it's unlikely Bennie will be able to resume manual work – at least for the foreseeable future and maybe never."

Josh stared at his father – this sounded serious stuff.

"I know this is sudden, but you are in the ideal position to act as the farm manager. It would be on a temporary basis at first…but in a few months' time, when things are clearer in relation to Bennie's capabilities, I will need to appoint a new person to the role…and I would like it to be you." Tom sat back and steepled his fingers.

"However, your mother and I know you have not settled on a future career… so if you feel this is not to your liking, then let me know and I can begin to look for another manager."

Josh felt overwhelmed. His mouth was dry. "You mean… me…to become the Farm Manager…but, Dad, I have little experience."

Tom smiled – it was as he'd expected. "Josh, you are a young man with a strong work ethic. You have helped on the farm since you were a young boy. I've observed you since your return from your National Service. I think you have potential – with careful guidance, I am sure you could fulfil the role."

Josh was silent – he was just trying to get his head around his impromptu proposal to Judy, and now here he was being offered an ideal job. Both these things were a tremendous opportunity for him…but also a great responsibility.

His dad started to speak. "My brother and I were around your age when we were handed the Meckleridge Estate. I was just beginning a career as a botanist and Jonty was a teacher. I knew nothing about hotel management and Jonty knew very little about farming…but we did it…until Jonty was taken from us."

Josh had heard the family history before, but somehow it felt more relevant.

"Of course, at this stage it is all conjecture, Josh. We are praying for a complete recovery for Bennie, but if he is able to oversee things – he would be there to guide you. This conversation is about being prepared, Josh. I want you to be sure this is what you want to do with your life."

Josh was speechless and after thanking his dad he left his office. Helping on the farm had suddenly morphed into a potential career – it was a step into the unknown.

***

With the first week under her belt, Darcy felt she was making headway at the quarry. The accounting system was a shambles. It was easy to see how the business was losing money. Marcel had indicated the owner struggled to understand accounting and it appeared his cashier-cum-secretary had developed bad habits. The lady's absence had allowed somebody…Rose…to cast an eagle eye over the accounts and already she had spotted errors. Whether these were genuine mistakes or made to resemble them, she wasn't sure. She suspected a substantial amount of money was going adrift with the wages system, but she was not quite sure in what way.

Marcel was pleased with her progress.

"So, what's been keeping you busy, Marcel?" she asked towards the end of the second week. "Have you made any progress with Judy's situation?"

"Well, yes and no. After finding out Judy's grandfather's name – Ralph. I hoped for some enlightenment – but all I discovered was a death date. He died in 1929 in the workhouse. No indication of another address."

Darcy looked thoughtful. "The workhouse…that ties in with Judy's comment about her father and grandfather not being close."

"Yes. Now, I'm looking into Judy's father's war service. Another visit to the Durham County Records Office may give me a lead. Anyway, changing the subject…how do you fancy a visit to the dance hall? It's Wednesday…there's a dance on tonight!"

A loud bell should have rung out a warning, but Darcy allowed herself to be lured into the prospect of a few hours of distraction. What harm could it do? It was the ideal way to let go of some of her pent-up energy. Why sit making polite conversation with Bertha, when she could be jiving with Marcel?

Without another thought, Darcy joined Marcel that evening. Soon, Marcel was whisking her around the floor to the sounds of the big band music.

Their footwork was sharp and lively – both were energetic dancers.

As Darcy flopped into a seat, Marcel went off to fetch some drinks. Refreshed, they returned to the dance floor. The big band was ignited…the music was catchy… 'Pennsylvania 65-0-0-0,' they called, in unison with their revelling companions.

The cares of the day were trampled onto the dance floor.

***

As Darcy and Marcel were expending their energies dancing, back at Meckleridge, Tom and Rachel were scrutinising the box of documents they had retrieved from the attics.

"I'm glad I didn't become a solicitor," moaned Tom, grabbing his spectacles. "The jargon used in these formal documents is so hard to understand."

Rachel was scanning a file. "What exactly are you hoping to find? Maybe we don't have to read the details," she asked.

Tom looked over the top of his glasses. "Quite simply – who owned the farm before Uncle Bart bought it, and when he bought it."

Rachel nodded. "And how will this help us to understand why Bernie Dempster holds a grudge against you?"

"Rachel, I have no idea, other than a hunch. Someone in my family upset the man. I doubt if it was my father. A Church of England vicar was unlikely to cross paths with a Methodist lay preacher, so my money is on the wider family – Aunt Dora and Uncle Bart."

They worked in silence. Ten minutes later, Tom shouted with glee.

"Here it is," he declared.

Rachel moved over to sit beside him. Tom unfolded a yellowed, faded document. It felt fragile and showed a carefully drawn map, with demarcated boundary lines.

"I have a copy of a similar map in the filing cabinet in the office, from when Jonty and I inherited the estate. I'd forgotten all about it."

They perused the outline of their property and the adjoining farmlands. Tom pointed to some small, printed script.

"See this boundary line – this is where the Meckleridge House boundary met the farm boundary. Dora and Bart bought the house before the First World War, then during the war, Bart bought the adjoining farmlands and united them. Looking back, I think Aunt Dora saw the potential of land ownership to pass on to my family. As a vicar, my father didn't own land or property."

Tom laid the map to one side and unfolded another faded document.

"Here are the title deeds," he exclaimed.

He began to read – *The transaction took place between Ralph Bernard Dempster and Bartholomew Francis Soames on the 30th October 1916. Ownership of the property and lands known as Fairholme Farm were exchanged."*

The colour drained from Tom's face. He removed his glasses and stared at his wife.

"This is unbelievable, Rachel. This must mean, Bernie Dempster grew up on our farm…is this the root of the problem?" Rachel looked at Tom in bewilderment.

"It's possible, Tom…but why was it a problem?"

"That, my dear is a puzzle," he responded.

***

All eyes were glued to the mahogany box in the corner of the conservatory at Meckleridge House. The Princess Elizabeth had become Queen fourteen months earlier, when her father King George VI died. Now on the 2nd June 1953 she was being crowned Queen Elizabeth II. It was the first British coronation to be televised, and Tom Smallwood had been determined that the extended family would be able to view the spectacle in the privacy of their own home.

Darcy was sitting on one of the settees with Henri.

"Oh, my…she is beautiful and look at that coach!" she shrieked.

"I hear Winston Churchill was against the idea of the coronation being televised, but the Queen insisted," remarked Tom.

"Good for her," declared Darcy. "This is spectacular, I'm pleased I'm not at the quarry today," she commented.

Darcy had watched with nostalgia as the procession made its way down the mall, remembering her first published journalistic article, written about Princess Elizabeth's wedding day. Darcy was in awe of the spectacle and retrieving her sketchpad, began to draw her own sketches of the new monarch, signing them DD. Henri grinned and elbowed her.

"If ever you need a code name it could be 'Dee Dee'," he remarked.

Darcy smiled.

"DD," chuckled Chantal. "It's like Sam – his initials are CC…Conrad Carter."

"Oh, yes," recalled Darcy. "I remember how it made the search for Sam so much easier when we discovered his first name was Conrad – did you ever discover why he dropped his first name when he moved to England?"

Chantal smiled. "It's a good job he's on duty today, I feel as if I'm talking behind his back. It was all part and parcel of freeing himself from Evelyn. After they married, she had CC embroidered on his handkerchiefs, on the bed linen and printed on the top of their notepaper. He hated it so much, he determined to use his middle name when he left Scotland. Yet it's strange… he wanted his son to carry the family name."

Darcy grinned. "DD is better than Rose Caudwell – I think I'm getting a bit tired of her."

"How much longer for your undercover work, Darcy?" asked Chantal.

"Officially, next week, but the cashier is still not well enough to return, so it has the potential to last longer…but I haven't agreed to it, yet."

"Any news about the house?" she asked her aunt. During the weeks she'd been working undercover, she felt she was losing touch with the Carter family news.

"Yes, Darcy. This will come as a surprise…it's not being sold after all. It hasn't been an easy decision, but it just feels so right somehow."

Darcy looked puzzled. "What are you saying, Chantal?"

Her French aunt was beaming. "It means, Darcy, the Carters are going to move to Scotland in August."

Darcy looked aghast.

"Does this mean we are losing you again, Chantal?"

"Of course not, Darcy. We will only be in Edinburgh – you could visit for a day if need be – but we have lots of spare rooms for guests to stay."

"What about Sam's job?" asked Henri.

"Well, he has applied for a new job and is resigning from his present position at the end of July. Francesca has indicated he could always work as a locum at their practice in the meantime. It will bridge the gap, but Sam is a surgeon at heart. I don't think he will settle in general practice for long."

Rachel was listening and caught Darcy's eye.

"Did you know about this, Mother?" she asked.

Rachel nodded, slowly, and attempted a smile, but Darcy sensed a sadness in her mother's gaze.

"Yes, I was the first to know. It all seemed so far in the future when it was voiced…and now, it's all happening quickly." There was a crackle in Rachel's voice.

Chantal was keenly aware it was going to be a wrench for her sister.

CHAPTER 22

"The school year begins in August, in Scotland," Chantal remarked. "I'd hoped we could be married before we moved...but what's a few more months, after all these years?"

The door opened and Sam appeared. The twins bounded into his arms with excitement.

"We saw a queen in a pretty dress with a crown," announced Hope.

"There was a coach and lots of horses," added Con.

"Have I missed it all?" he asked.

"There's still the balcony wave," remarked Rachel. "It's been spectacular – something for these little ones to remember all their lives."

The door opened again

"Oh, look what the wind has blown in," cheered Darcy, "a soggy farmer Josh!"

"Quit the sarcasm, Darcy. Somebody's got to keep the place running. Any food, Mother? I'm starving!" he asked, sitting on the floor and receiving a waggy welcome from Lady.

Rachel jumped up. "Don't let me miss the balcony," she shouted, disappearing off to the kitchen.

"Have you got any help on the farm, Josh?" asked Sam.

Josh was tickling the dog's tummy.

"Well, George, the farmhand is shaping up nicely, and my pal Sid has been over a few times. He's doing an apprenticeship at The Works, but if he's on a 'six to two' shift, he comes over for a couple of hours and I appreciate his assistance. Oh, that reminds me, next time you see Marcel, Darcy, tell him Sid's grandma was telling him a bit more about Bernie Dempster."

Tom and Darcy eyeballed Josh. "What?" they asked in unison.

Josh smirked. "None of your business, you lot! It's between me and my private detective."

Darcy stood up, placing her hands on her hips.

"Josh Smallwood – you are the limit – it wouldn't hurt to tell us."

Josh didn't reply, just tapped the side of his nose.

***

"My brother has been talking to his friend, Sid," commented Darcy, as she and Marcel arrived at the quarry the following day.

"And?" enquired Marcel.

Darcy huffed. "My annoying brother is taking all this sleuthing very seriously – he wants to speak to his *private investigator* in person," she remarked, jumping out of the car.

No further comments were passed as Darcy and Marcel entered the wooden structure at the quarry. It was a rough affair – an office space, a tiny kitchen, walk-in cupboard and washroom.

Bill the owner greeted them. "Good morning!"

"Good morning, Bill. Rose has made excellent progress. Her job here is almost over – she has discovered the inaccurate entries in the books. When do you expect your cashier to return?"

The burly man removed his cap and pulled a face. "I'm grateful for your help. I wish I'd stuck in with my learning at school, then I wouldn't have had people fleecing me. I don't know when Jean is coming back – do you fancy working for me, Rose?"

Rose was immediately on her guard. "Sorry, Bill, I've got another job to move to, but I can stay until the end of next week, if that helps."

Bill thanked her, then Marcel performed his 'play acting' role, kissing Rose goodbye… for the owner's benefit.

Soon, Rose was alone. She began her sorting task, but this morning she couldn't settle. Why had she agreed to stay another week? Now that most of the sorting was complete, the work was dreary and lonely. Occasionally, someone would arrive to leave an invoice, or a workman would call in with a message. In the afternoon she heard a crunching on the gravel outside and looking out of the small window, noticed a small van parking in front of the office. Minutes later the door opened, and fear struck Rose Caudwell, as she looked up.

"Well, well, well…if it isn't Miss Rose Caudwell," said a familiar voice… it was Gordon Sinclair!

Rose froze, her heart beating fast – their last meeting hadn't ended well. She was troubled by the fact she was alone with the man.

"Oh, hello – we've met before, haven't we?" she replied, trying to sound businesslike.

"Yes, Miss Caudwell, we have – you and your detective friend caused me some trouble. I haven't forgotten, or forgiven, you and your interference. My uncle has banned me from his house and now I have no way to further my enquiries regarding my late mother's affairs."

Rose dismissed the comment. "Can I assist you today?" she asked, trembling.

"I was hoping to see Jean, where is she?" he asked, wandering around the office, picking up bits and pieces and infuriating Rose.

"Jean is unwell. Can I help? I have been doing Jean's job and know where most things are kept."

The look on Gordon Sinclair's face sent a chill down Rose's spine.

"You won't know about this, Miss Caudwell, Jean and I have a private arrangement," he replied, with a menacing look on his face.

He stood deep in thought, then commented abruptly. "I won't keep you any longer," he remarked and left the office.

Rose was still physically shaking when the quarry owner returned to the office later. She told him about the visitor.

"I don't know anyone called Gordon Sinclair," he replied, looking puzzled.

Rose decided to tell Bill she was acquainted with Mr Sinclair.

"It's not the first time I have met Mr Sinclair – our paths crossed a few months ago. I took an instant dislike to the man. I think his request to see Jean may not be above board, Bill."

Marcel arrived to collect Rose. She gave him an account of Gordon Sinclair's visit.

"Did he say if he was returning, Rose?"

She shook her head.

"I smell something fishy here, Bill, and I have no intention of leaving Rose on her own in case he returns."

Rose grabbed her coat, and they left the office. As they walked to Marcel's car he suddenly turned, stopped, then without warning kissed Rose firmly on the lips. Darcy stiffened.

"You only need to kiss me when there's an audience, Marcel," she retorted.

"Sorry, Darcy, but that was for Rose Caudwell," he jibed. "Sinclair is up to no good…don't worry, I'll be here if he returns. It's Wednesday…do you fancy a night of dancing to help you forget about that undesirable man?"

Chapter 23

It appeared that Darcy's undercover work was heading towards a natural conclusion. There was no way she was going to be left on her own at the quarry. Marcel dropped Darcy at Bertha's, intimating he needed to check something at his office.

She entered the little house in Baxter Street and flew up the stairs. She felt restless, so after releasing her hair and attiring herself in her own jacket, she ran back down the stairs…she needed fresh air. It was a warm June evening. After the rain of the Coronation Day, it seemed too good to stay indoors so she headed off towards the city centre.

As she walked, she mused…she would miss working with Marcel. The cathedral seemed to loom over the place no matter where she looked. She was trying to overcome an internal struggle. It had been creeping up on her over the time she'd been staying at Bertha's. It was hard not to admit it…but…she was attracted to Marcel Duval. When had his flirtatious role play turned into a reality? Those goodbye kisses seemed unnecessary in the beginning, but somehow, they had changed.

It's just a bit of flirtation, she convinced herself. Marcel finds me attractive...I find him attractive. It's totally innocent – it's all to do with my undercover work. Marcel is attracted to Rose Caudwell – not Darcy Dukas. But even as she said those words in her mind, she knew they were not true.

She stopped on the bridge and looked up at the cathedral. It seemed to ooze its solidarity...its faithfulness... its trust. Years of worshippers had trod a path to its doors, in faithfulness and trust to God. Am I walking a path of unfaithfulness? Am I untrustworthy? She questioned herself.

I adore Henri... he's everything to me, but I have needs...I enjoy being flattered. I love being swirled around the dancefloor until I'm breathless. Marcel offers me something Henri can't give me. Marcel is only a dance partner...yes, that's it. He makes me feel special, wanted even.

She walked across the road to the other side of the bridge. Oh, she felt so confused. The sun was shining; it was a perfect evening. She watched two young women walking across the bridge, giggling. A vision of Chrissie sprang to her mind. She'd intended to effect an attraction between Marcel Duval and Chrissie... instead she'd created an attraction involving herself. She vowed to do something about it...soon. But tonight... she would return to Baxter Street, get changed and after tea she would join Marcel for one final night of dancing.

She retraced her steps – had the glow of her marriage to Henri vapourised? Do we take each other for granted? Am I rebelling because baby Leon was taken from us? Darcy had many questions – but she was devoid of answers. She took a deep breath and entered the house.

***

Sam replaced the receiver and went in search of Chantal.

"That was the solicitor, I need to go up to Edinburgh on Friday. Let's see if we can make it a long weekend...can you swap your shifts?" he asked.

"Probably," responded Chantal.

Josh was washing his hands at the sink.

"Wish I could come with you," he muttered. "Seems an age since I saw Judy," he added dejectedly.

Sam turned towards Josh. "Why not? Surely you are entitled to a day off. You could get a lift with us in the morning, spend the afternoon with Judy, then get the train back at night."

Josh grabbed the towel to dry his hands. "It's a great idea, but it won't work," he sighed.

"What won't work?" asked Tom, walking into the kitchen.

Sam spoke up. "Chantal and I are going up to Edinburgh on Friday for the weekend. We need to leave early morning, as I have an appointment with the solicitor at twelve o'clock. I was just saying to Josh it would be an opportunity for him to spend an afternoon with Judy, then get the train back at night."

Tom rubbed his brow. "It's possible," he commented.

"How, Dad?" asked Josh. "Be realistic, we're planning on leading in the hay on the three barred field on Friday – it's Sid's day off and he's offered his services."

Tom looked at his son and shook his head.

"Do you want to spend the afternoon with your girl?"

Josh laughed. "Stupid question, Dad...of course I do, it's weeks since she went away."

"Then it's settled...go. Sid and George can do the lifting work, and I'll drive the tractor."

Josh stared at his father in disbelief. "Really, Dad…are you sure?"

"Yes, phone her, before I change my mind."

Josh was elated, but first he needed to speak to Marcel, and teatime may well be a good time to catch him.

"Josh," Marcel responded, hearing his voice on the telephone. "Your sister says you have some information from your friend Sid."

"Yes, Marcel. I think Sid felt guilty about him being the one to mention Judy and I were friendly. Anyway, it's taken a while but the other day he told me something. He asked his grandma if she knew anything about Bernie Dempster's background. She said the man should have been a farmer… not a funeral director. That was all, but I hope it might help your enquiries."

Marcel let out a low whistle. "Josh, that's a great help. I'm not exactly sure how this puzzle fits together, but I'm sure we are close. I'll try to pop over to Meckleridge on Saturday night. We need to pull together all the bits and pieces of information and see if any of it makes sense. See you on Saturday, Josh."

Darcy was descending the stairs dressed for her night of dancing.

"See if what makes sense…was that my brother?" she blurted.

"Yes, that was Josh with his information from Sid's grandma. It may be relevant – she reckons Judy's father should have been a farmer, not an undertaker," Marcel replied.

"I'll come over to Meckleridge on Saturday night. I know bits, your dad knows bits and Josh knows bits. We need to bring it all together...just like a jigsaw puzzle, to see if it fits."

Suddenly, he stopped mesmerised... and gazed into Darcy's eyes. The moment was electric.

"You are a beautiful woman, Darcy Dukas," he remarked. "Are you ready to dance your cares away?"

Momentarily, Darcy was jolted by Marcel's use of her full name...Dukas. Use of her married name reminded her of the vows she'd taken... important vows. Her cherished relationship with Henri was on a knife edge. If she continued in this vein...she could hurt her parents... hurt her family... hurt God...but most of all she would hurt Henri. It's wrong, she thought...morally wrong...but it's just for one last time.

They left the house and headed to the dancehall.

***

Rachel snuggled up to Tom as they lay in bed – he placed his arm around her.

"All set for your day on the farm tomorrow?" she asked her sleepy husband.

"I think I'm looking forward to it – spending a day out in the fields in the fresh air. I haven't been involved leading hay in, for many a long year."

Rachel chuckled. "No, Farmer Tom was not a role which fell naturally to you, unlike our Josh – he's suited to the job."

"Mmmm," Tom muttered, "I'm relieved. Our suspicions about Bennie's recovery seem likely. I think any future involvement he may have will only be sedentary. It will be Josh who will do the hard work."

"I'm pleased Josh is managing to see Judy again. I think he's in love."

Tom squeezed her. "You and your matchmaking, Rachel Smallwood. He'll probably have loads of girlfriends before he settles down."

"I wouldn't be too sure about that," Rachel retorted. "I've got a feeling she could be 'the one'."

They were each lost in their own thoughts for a few minutes.

"Well, only if we can unravel this problem with Judy's father. We must take a closer look at those documents we unearthed… and inform Marcel."

Rachel yawned. "Yes, he'll probably be over on Saturday night. In the meantime, I'm looking forward to having the house to myself tomorrow…how rare is that? You at the farm; Henri in the greenhouse; Josh and the Carters in Edinburgh and Darcy in Durham, doing her undercover work."

Tom's breathing changed…he was snoring – time for sleep.

***

Having made an early start, the Carters and Josh arrived at Francesca's house late on Friday morning. They left the twins, Josh and the luggage and headed to the solicitors, for Sam to keep his appointment. Francesca told them she would take the children to the zoo, so they did not need to hurry back.

Josh and Judy wasted no time walking to the local park and were soon cuddling and kissing on a secluded park bench. Their brief reunion was so anticipated, and they spent ages just gazing into one another's eyes.

"Not long now, Judy – I'm counting the days," Josh remarked. "Did you write to your parents?"

Judy cuddled up to Josh as he pulled her close. "Yes. Thanks to Francesca we managed to have it posted in London, by one of her friends. I wrote telling them I was safe and well and asking them not to try to find me. I told them I would contact them after my twenty-first birthday. It's my life, Josh. I have a right to choose my own friends."

"Was that letter I forwarded to you from the hospital?"

"Yes, thanks for that, Josh. They were very understanding and offered to keep my position open until September. But I can't return home to live, as long as I'm banned from seeing you."

"Marcel is following some clues…so he may soon shed a light on the problem. How's the accommodation with Francesca?"

"She's brilliant, Josh. She's arranged for me to help at a mother and baby clinic, three mornings a week. I don't get any pay of course, but I'm learning from the midwives, so I'm not going rusty. I'll be forever in her debt – but she dismisses any offers of money, saying she appreciates my company and helping her with household chores."

Josh pulled back and gazed adoringly into Judy's eyes. "I love you, Judy," he whispered bending to kiss her sweet, soft lips. He wanted time to stand still.

"Did you reflect on my proposal, Judy? Looking back, I realise it was sudden and perhaps inappropriate, but I wanted you to know how I felt about our relationship."

Judy caressed the side of Josh's face. "Josh, I want us to be together…more than anything… and I haven't changed my mind. We still have obstacles ahead, and we need to trust the problem my father has with your dad can be resolved."

"I hope it can be sorted soon, then we can enjoy a proper courtship, instead of this cloak and dagger stuff." Josh kissed her lovingly, oblivious to the other people in the park.

***

Chantal was sitting in the car, waiting for Sam. Their plan was to spend the afternoon at Matthison Hall, taking measurements and trying to plan their new living accommodation. Francesca was so thoughtful.

"I'd be delighted to entertain the children," she'd remarked, when they dropped the twins at her house. "I'm planning on taking them to the zoo today. It will give you and Dad time to begin organising things, ready for your move."

Sam returned to the car.

"That didn't take long – I was expecting a long wait," she commented, looking at Sam who was barely able to contain his excitement. "Are you all sorted?" she asked.

Sam waved an envelope in front of her. "More than sorted, my dear girl. In six weeks, my divorce will be granted!" he blurted, enveloping Chantal in a tight hug.

"Sam!" shrieked Chantal, in elation. "I can't believe it… it seems unreal…after all these years."

Sam took her hand and gently caressed her ring finger.

"I know I've said this many times – but I was never able to act on it. Chantal Martin, please will you agree to becoming my wife?"

Chantal gazed into Sam's eyes. "A hundred times 'yes', Sam Carter. Oh, I can't wait to tell Rachel – she'll have such fun planning and organising our wedding."

"Right, we need to get to our new home and begin taking measurements. If all goes to plan, we can move at the end of July then go back to Meckleridge for our wedding celebration. Our long-awaited hope is almost over, my darling."

Chantal was so happy. The relief after all the years of waiting was incomprehensible. Soon she would be able to marry her beloved Sam. They walked through the rooms of Matthison Hall, taking various measurements and planning the layout. She wanted to pinch herself to make sure it was real and not just a dream.

***

Time was dragging on that Friday morning. As promised, Marcel had stayed at the quarry with Rose, concealing his car behind a storage shed. Gordon Sinclair had not appeared on Thursday. To pass the time, he'd been rechecking the weekly outgoings from the quarry's account books. He noted some names did not have a tick beside them.

"What's the purpose of the tick on these entries?" he asked.

Rose explained the wage collection process – as each employee received their wage packet on a Friday afternoon, a tick indicated the receipt. The ones without the mark were for hand deliveries.

"Apparently, some men work different hours, and Bill gives them their wages separately," she added. "I leave those packets in the safe. Bill arrives at five o'clock, to help with the distribution."

Just before three o'clock there was a crunching sound outside.

"Quick, Marcel, I think our visitor has arrived."

Marcel took the cue and slid into his hiding place behind some shelving in the store cupboard, leaving the door slightly ajar to hear the conversation.

Gordon Sinclair entered the quarry office. Rose, wearing her glasses and her 'dumb' face, looked up. He was every inch a 'spiv'...smart suit, shirt, coloured tie and a trilby hat worn at a jaunty angle. His hair was neatly trimmed, and he sported a tiny moustache.

"Hello, Mr Sinclair – I told Bill about your visit and he..." Rose's voice trailed off, as Gordon Sinclair placed his hands on the desk and glowered at Rose, breathing his offensive breath into her face.

"I'm not interested in Bill, Miss Caudwell. My business is with Jean. I expect the wage packets are already made up and are ready for collection."

"How does that concern you, Mr Sinclair?" Rose asked, trying to appear extra dumb.

"I've come to collect my brother-in-law's wage packet... the poor soul is off sick. It bears the name James Johnson."

Rose tried to recall the ledger – she'd seen the name but had not set eyes on that individual. Gordon was agitated.

"Just fetch the packet, Miss Caudwell, and I will be on my way."

She stood up and walked over to the safe. Carefully, she entered the code and released the handle. As she reached inside, Gordon placed his hand on her shoulder, sending a cold shiver down her spine.

"No need to mention my visit to Bill – he knows Jean passes it on."

She rummaged through the brown buff packets and found the one with the name James Johnson. As she was about to hand it over, Marcel stepped out of the store cupboard.

"What the…?" Gordon snarled, catching sight of Marcel.

"Good afternoon, Mr Sinclair…we meet again. You seem to look after your relatives' finances. However, I must say this is rather irregular. I thought the wages for the quarry staff were distributed at five o'clock, when Bill arrived."

Gordon reached forward and snatched the packet from Rose's hand, then he pulled a small knife out of his pocket and flicked it open. Quickly, he hooked his elbow around Rose's neck.

"Get out of my way," he growled. "Miss Caudwell is going to take a little drive with me."

Marcel stepped towards the telephone.

"Don't do that, if you want to see Miss Caudwell again," he threatened.

"Marcel!" shrieked Rose in terror, trying to release herself from the man's grasp.

"Oh, a Frenchman…fancy that." Gordon spat out the words, pulling Rose towards the door.

Rose began to kick him, but her efforts did little to prevent her being dragged outside towards his van. Marcel jumped into action and followed, but Gordon pointed the knife at Rose's throat.

"Keep your distance and don't attempt to follow me or contact the police, M-a-r-c-e-l," he enunciated, sarcastically. "Miss Caudwell will be quite safe, if you do as I say," he smirked, pushing Rose forcibly into the rear of the vehicle.

Rose was screaming and hammering on the inside of the van. Gordon jumped into the driver's seat, and the vehicle sped away, but not before Marcel noted the registration number.

Chapter 24

Henri looked up from his workbench in the greenhouse. "What's she doing?" he asked himself. He could hear their spaniel whining outside the door. He pushed back his seat and ambled across.

"Hello, girl, what are you doing running free?" he asked, bending down to stroke the excitable little dog. It was unusual for Lady to be wandering around on her own. Both Darcy and Rachel were careful to exercise her on a leash in the grounds, only letting her run free on the lawns under supervision.

"Come on," he said. "Let's get you back to the house, I could do with a drink."

Lady followed Henri up the gravel path leading to the house.

His mind was elsewhere this morning. Hopefully today, his beloved Darcy would return from this undercover work in Durham. On the telephone the previous evening, she had indicated today was likely to be the last day. He'd felt uneasy this last week – nothing tangible, just a feeling...a wrenching uneasiness. He winced and caught his breath. His hip joint was causing him a great deal of pain recently. Was his condition worsening? If only he could see a potential cure to his problem on the horizon. It hampered so many aspects of his life. He and Darcy rarely discussed the problem…but it was always there.

Arriving in the kitchen, he called out. “Rachel, Rachel.” Silence. He hobbled into the hallway, shouted up the stairs and stood…silence. Maybe she’s upstairs lying down, he mused. He walked into the conservatory…empty. The lounge…the same. He checked the dining room and their lounge, but no sign of his mother-in-law.

Then it struck him. Both the back and front doors were closed…so how had Lady escaped? Perhaps the little dog had slipped her leash while Rachel was out walking her?

Henri stepped out of the front door, closing it behind him – it was so unusual for the house to be empty, but Rachel had commented at breakfast time how much she was looking forward to having a day to herself. He decided to check the Rose Garden, but just as he was turning in that direction, Lady took off across the lawn. Henri shouted, but the little dog was intent on her pursuit and was soon out of sight.

He used the little speed he could muster and gave chase, rounding the bushes at the bottom of the sloped lawn.

The sight which greeted him struck him with deep panic.

Lady was yapping, frantically wagging her tail… nudging a still form.

It was Rachel… crumpled…in a heap…on the grass, beside some laurel bushes.

“Rachel, Mon Dieu, what is wrong?” he gasped. Reaching her, he bent over and eased her gently onto her back. Her face was grey…her eyes were closed…she was still, so still. Henri patted her face.

"Wake up, Rachel, wake up...please wake up." Lady began to lick Rachel's face. Henri placed his fingers against her neck, praying he would feel a pulse...but found none. Rachel Smallwood's body was devoid of movement...devoid of breath...devoid of life.

Henri held his head. Quick. Action. I must get help. He rose to his feet, thinking what to do. Everyone was at the farm. Even Ivan and his sidekick from the Market Garden had gone over to the farm to help. Telephone, he thought. I must get back to the house and telephone the doctor and the farm.

With as much speed as possible, he returned to the house; thankfully, Lady followed. Stumbling through the door, he grabbed the receiver. The operator answered.

"Quick, ambulance, please. Meckleridge House – it's an emergency." He heard the connection being made but stayed on the line.

"Meckleridge Farm, please," he indicated...

Nancy answered.

"Nancy, it's Henri. Tell Tom he's needed at the house immediately." Nancy sensed the urgency in the Frenchman's voice and asked no questions. She replaced the receiver, grabbed the whistle, kept at the back door to signal a message. She headed off swiftly, blowing it repeatedly, as she went towards the three barred field. Every few minutes she stopped and let out three sharp blasts on the whistle... surely someone would hear and come running. But as she descended the slope to the field, she realised the whistle had gone unheard, lost in the tractor sounds and the shouting of the men. She was breathless but stopping, she filled her lungs and gave a long blast. Within minutes Sid was at her side.

CHAPTER 24

Henri was distraught…where should he wait? He should be at the house for Tom and the ambulance arriving, but he needed to be with Rachel. He locked the dog in their lounge and left the house. He could only trust his hearing. He was almost across the lawn when he heard the farm truck approaching. He lifted his arms and waved frantically. The truck crunched to a halt.

"Round the bushes," he called, pointing.

Tom and Sid jumped out and ran down the slope. Henri turned and followed.

Tom followed Henri's directions and ground to a halt, unable to approach his wife. Sid flew to Rachel's side and knelt, checking for signs of life. Slowly, he looked up, shaking his head.

Tom stepped forward, fell to his knees and cradled his adored wife in his arms.

"The ambulance is on its way," announced Henri, as he arrived.

"It's too late, Henri. My beautiful Rachel has gone," he whispered.

Sid went to wait for the ambulance.

Henri reached out, placing his arm around Tom's shoulders, as tears spurted from the grieving man's eyes.

"Rachel, Rachel…why, why?" he muttered.

Henri felt useless and tried to think straight. The family must be informed…but where were they all? Any other day the house would be full of family members bobbing around… but today…it was empty…like Rachel's life… empty and still.

***

No matter how hard she thumped and yelled, Rose was not going to free herself from the metal box in which she was travelling. It was dark and smelly, and she felt sick. The van was moving at speed, tossing her from side to side. What was happening…where was he taking her? Fear crept into the pit of her stomach as the enormity of her predicament took hold.

Suddenly, the van screeched to a halt, propelling Rose forwards. She reached out, grabbing at the side of the van's interior. The engine was still running. A sudden blaze of light invaded her metal prison, as the back door opened.

"Out. Give me your shoes and keep your mouth shut!" Gordon Sinclair yelled.

Rose obeyed and seconds later she was watching the little grey van disappearing into the distance.

She surveyed her surroundings…fields. Not one building in sight. What was she going to do? She sat on the edge of the road – surely a vehicle would pass soon. Untying her hair, she flung the braid and her glasses into the bushes.

"Be gone, Rose Caudwell… I never…ever… want to see you again," she declared. Think, Darcy…think, she told herself – I must be positive. The van had only travelled for minutes, so she must still be close to the quarry…I must walk back towards it.

Thankfully, it was a bright, warm afternoon – but the road was rough under her stocking clad feet.

Panic stricken, Marcel phoned the police, giving the van's description. Then leaving a scribbled note for Bill, he grabbed Rose's belongings and got into his car. She could be anywhere. He drove along the track leading from the quarry. He stopped at the junction…right or left? Gut instinct told him to take the road leading away from the city. Goodness knows where it would lead. It was deserted – no buildings, just fields.

Within minutes a moving object caught his attention... was it a person? As he approached, he saw two hands waving frantically...and there she was, Darcy Dukas, her loose hair blowing in the gentle breeze. The relief was enormous!

As he pulled to a halt, Darcy climbed into Marcel's car. They hugged as she sobbed into his shoulder.

"I wa – wa- nt Henri," she whimpered.

Marcel shut his eyes and swallowed...she belonged to another man.

The process at the police station took ages. They were both interviewed. Darcy offered to sketch a facial representation of her abductor. Time ticked by...there was no news of the missing van. Gordon Sinclair appeared to have vanished.

Soon, Bill the quarry owner arrived. "Gosh you're a welcome sight, lass," he exclaimed. "That note sent me into a frenzy – *Rose abducted. In pursuit. Police informed.*" Bill shook his head. "What happened?"

Marcel gave a brief account.

"Who was he – do you know?"

Marcel had limited knowledge.

"I've met him before, Bill. He's a small-time crook, intimidating people to obtain money. He was obviously on the fiddle, cajoling Jean to fall in with his little scheme. She was putting extra cash into that pay packet, but not enough to arouse suspicion. Then on an irregular basis, Gordon collected it. It's probably been going on for months. But this time he's crossed a line – abduction, use of an offensive weapon and threat. If they catch him, he'll be charged. But it's in police hands now."

Darcy turned to Marcel. "I want Henri…take me home, Marcel, I never want to be Rose Caudwell again!" she exclaimed.

***

Sid drove Tom back home from the hospital. He was a walking zombie. The formalities were sorted, and Tom was told to expect his own doctor to visit. Sid eventually guided a dumbfounded Tom out of the casualty department and into the farm truck. No words were spoken…the young man respecting Tom's grief.

An eeriness pervaded the house as Tom stepped into the hallway…something was missing…someone was missing. Nancy took over from Sid and led the grieving man into the conservatory, the radiance of the afternoon sun belying the darkness in Tom's soul.

"Sit down, Tom. I'll fetch a cuppa."

Henri passed Nancy in the doorway. He walked over to Tom and sat beside him, reaching out to hold his hand. "I've tried to locate everyone, Tom, but without success. I've left a message with Marcel's aunt to phone when they return from the quarry. Francesca's number is ringing out, so I can't contact Chantal, and I assume Josh is on a train."

It was unbelievable the family were so scattered and unobtainable. Tom stared at Henri, who was not sure if he was listening.

A croaky voice uttered, "Ring Peg."

Henri gasped. "Oh, goodness, of course," he exclaimed. Tom's sister, Peg, and her family lived in Lyon in France – Peg's husband was Henri's uncle. He stood and went into the hall to place a call to France.

Nancy returned with the tea tray.

"I've put a nip of brandy in that cup, Tom, it will help with the shock. Eeh, she was a lady your Rachel – a right, proper lady."

Tom lifted his head and stared into Nancy's eyes. "She's gone, Nancy, my beautiful Rachel…she's gone. How can I carry on without her?"

Nancy patted Tom's hand.

"You'll manage, Tom, she'll be there with you – it's the shock which will take some getting over, but you have a loving family."

The telephone rang – it was Marcel.

"Bring Darcy home quickly, Marcel," Henri demanded. Marcel detected an urgency in his voice.

"Yes, Henri, I will – you sound disturbed…has something happened?" he asked.

"I'll explain when you arrive," Henri responded and ended the call abruptly.

Darcy arrived home an hour later, unaware of the devastating news awaiting her.

A crunching on the driveway alerted Henri, allowing him to apprehend Darcy and Marcel as they entered the house.

"Henri," Darcy exclaimed, "it's so good to be home again. You'll never believe the escapade I've had…" she began.

Her husband took her in his arms. "Ma chérie, you must be brave for your father," he whispered into her hair.

"Brave…why…what's wrong?"

Henri pulled back and held both her hands tightly.

"It's your mother, Darcy…she…she's…"

Darcy jerked herself free from Henri's clasp and ran into the conservatory. The sight of her dejected father relayed the message.

"No, no!" she shrieked. "It can't be…please no…there must be a mistake. Dad, speak to me…tell me it's not true."

Tom Smallwood cradled his daughter as she fell at his feet and lay her head in his lap. The two sobbed in unison…a heart wrenching outpouring of mutual grief, despair and disbelief.

Marcel stepped out into the hallway to speak to Nancy, who supplied the details.

"What about Josh and Chantal – do they know?"

Nancy shook her head. "Josh should be on the train home, but he doesn't know. So far Henri has been unable to get a response from the number in Edinburgh."

Marcel thought quickly and grabbed the phone book looking for Francesca's telephone number. His eyes alighted on her entry, and he picked up the telephone. Maybe it wasn't his place to make this call, but the family needed help. This time there was an answer.

On hearing the distressing news, Francesca told Marcel she would inform her father. "Josh is already on a train to Durham; Judy left him at six o'clock. I could keep the children with me, if it would help, but that's up to Chantal."

After speaking to Nancy, Marcel left for the station.

***

As Josh alighted the train in Durham, Marcel was the last person he expected to see. His visit to Edinburgh had been significant. He was entering a new stage of life – responsibility. Their brief romantic interlude reinforced his love for Judy Dempster. He was so relieved they'd declared their love for each other, with the expectation that one day they could marry. He'd shared the information concerning Bennie's health and the possibility of becoming Farm Manager in the future. Now, they needed to trust that whatever Judy's father held against his family – it could be resolved.

"Marcel," he cheered, as he approached his friend. Perhaps Marcel was here with good news regarding his investigation. But as Marcel reached out and took Josh Smallwood's hand in greeting, his face looked serious.

"Josh, good to have you back home," he commented.

"I wasn't expecting you," remarked Josh, "I was expecting Henri or Mother to collect me." In truth it hadn't been decided, but he knew his mother would likely be the only person in the house that evening.

It was one of those moments, some would call it a 'sixth sense', but Josh knew Marcel was about to impart some life-changing news. He stared into his eyes.

"Something's happened, hasn't it?"

The Frenchman pulled Josh into a hug and whispered in his ear. "It's your mother, Josh. She collapsed on the lawn – we think late morning – she passed away before Henri found her."

Pulling back, Josh bombarded Marcel with question after question about the doctor, the hospital, his father, did Darcy know...did Chantal know...what was the cause?

Marcel tried to supply the answers, as they made their way on the twelve-mile journey from Durham to Malhaven.

On reflection, weeks later, Marcel told his Aunt Bertha he was sure he'd been guided to befriend the Smallwood family for this juncture in their lives. In the days following Rachel's passing, the family just fell apart… as if the glue which held them together had given way. The strong, resilient characteristics of everyone just seemed to vanish.

Where's Marcel? Has Marcel attended to this…or that? The family relied upon him. He made numerous phone calls, made the necessary appointments, helped to sort the funeral arrangements and became the resident taxi man. His Aunt Bertha came over from Durham each day, with a fresh batch of baking. She quickly made friends with Peg Thibault, Tom's sister.

When Marcel collected Peg from the station, she greeted her son Jonty's friend.

"This is a very sad situation, Marcel. My sister-in-law was a remarkable woman. She kept Meckleridge House running like clockwork – be it a hotel, convalescence home or extended family home. I will see to it that her legacy will live on. I will not leave my family to muddle through."

Marcel remembered Peg from his student days, and he was sure she would keep her word.

"Yes, Peg, Rachel Smallwood was a unique woman. There's not just a hole left with her passing…there's a crater."

The days were busy and demanding… but there was one aspect of Marcel's association with the Meckleridge folk that he had not anticipated.

Chapter 25

Darcy flew out of the front door in pursuit of her little King Charles spaniel. She knew where she would find her...underneath the laurel bushes, down the slope on the front lawn. It was the place where Lady had last seen Rachel, so it was only natural the little dog's instinct thought she was still there. It had happened many times over the last few days.

Sure enough, she was there but she wasn't alone...Josh was stroking her, sitting on the grass.

"Not you as well." said Darcy, sharply. "Every time Lady disappears, I find her here."

Josh looked up at his angry sister, his eyes bleary. "I've got an idea. I'm going to dig out an area around here, plant a little garden, get a wooden bench and call it *Rachel's Place*. It gets the sun from early afternoon until it sets. It will be a place to come, sit and reflect."

Darcy stared at her brother as if he'd gone mad, then ran further down the slope, stopped and let out a blood curdling scream.

The dog flew towards her. Josh jumped up. "Darcy... pack it in...someone will think you are in trouble," he exclaimed, but he knew the grounds were so extensive it was unlikely her outburst would be heard.

She turned and walked back to Josh.

"I am in trouble. That scream released the tension I have inside me. Why did she have to leave me when I needed her so much? How can I look after Dad? How can I cope with running this house? She was so perfect in organising things. She could manage a hotel, a family, keep us all in check. Her sewing skills; her baking; her mothering. Josh, I can't fill her shoes…they are too big!" she cried, flopping down on the ground.

"On top of it all, the Carters' move to Edinburgh makes things worse." She pushed her fists into her eyes. "I couldn't even give birth to a breathing baby and if by some miracle I ever did – what would I do? How would I cope?"

Lady crept onto Darcy's lap and began to lick her mistress.

"Don't you have any emotion, Josh?" she pleaded, her voice crackling.

Josh sat down cross legged, picking at some blades of grass. He remained silent, then lifting his head stared into the distance.

"I walked into the kitchen, yesterday and said, 'Is there a cuppa for me, Mother?' But it was Aunt Peg standing at the sink. I wake up each morning, thinking it's all been a bad dream, and she'll be there handing me a bowl of porridge at breakfast…I can't believe it. It hasn't sunk in."

The dog jumped off Darcy's knee, her keen hearing detecting approaching footsteps. Marcel rounded the corner of the bushes.

Darcy glared at him – since her mother's death she had refused to speak to the man.

CHAPTER 25

"Josh," said Marcel, "I've just spoken to Francesca. She asked me to tell you she and Judy will go straight to the church on Friday."

Josh stood up, alarmed.

"What? Judy isn't supposed to be coming to the funeral," he shouted. "What is she thinking about – I must try to speak to her," he added, running off up the slope towards the house.

Marcel looked at Darcy. The atmosphere was taut. He was aware of her attitude towards him since Rachel's death, but this was the first time they had been alone. He cleared his throat.

"Can I help you in any way?" he asked, tentatively, determined to end this 'thing' between them.

"Only by getting out of my life, Marcel Duval," she declared.

His jaw dropped. "Why? What have I done?" he asked, bewildered.

Darcy stood up, abruptly. "You caused it," she snarled. "We are being punished because of you…Mother was taken from us, because you came into our lives."

Marcel was shocked at her retort. He shook his head in disbelief. "Darcy, you are not making sense…please explain," he begged.

She spun around and lifted her hands in despair. "I started to have feelings for you…you…arrogant Frenchman…that's why she was taken…to punish me. It was a stupid infatuation…I love Henri. This foolish undercover stuff threw us together and somehow…somehow it happened. Henri trusted me…Mother trusted me. Don't you see, I'm guilty – guilty of causing her death. I couldn't be trusted and so I am being punished."

As she spoke her voice tone rose – it became a wail…it was high pitched …it was grief…it was guilt…it was despair.

Marcel stepped towards her. "Darcy, calm down," he began.

She was becoming hysterical. He lifted his hands and, placing them on her shoulders, began shaking her. She froze, then crumbled in a heap at the very spot where her mother had taken her last breath.

Marcel stared down at her.

"I'm sorry, Darcy. Sorry you thought about me in that way. I have never tried to come between you and Henri. I admit I have enjoyed your companionship. We became good friends, but it was only an assignment – you played your part to perfection. Please forgive me if I acted inappropriately outside of our cover."

"Coo-ee," called a voice heading down the slope.

Darcy gasped and rubbed her eyes, as Peg Thibault turned the corner.

"Henri is looking for you, Darcy," she called.

Then turning to Marcel, Peg asked, "Jonty phoned to say he and Sylvie will be arriving in Durham station at four o'clock – are you able to collect them?"

***

Tom was lying down on the bed. It had become a pattern since Rachel's passing. She had often enjoyed an afternoon nap on their bed – somehow, lying here, he felt close to her. This was the place where he let down his guard, especially at night. It was in the darkness Tom Smallwood shed his tears, but in front of his family he had not cried since the first day.

He constantly replayed that last day. It was so unusual for him to be out of the house for lengthy periods. Could he have helped her if their normal routine had been in place? He was usually having his morning cuppa around the time she must have collapsed. But Josh's visit to Edinburgh meant Tom was driving a tractor in the three barred field, oblivious to his wife's plight.

"Even if you had been holding her hand, you could not have prevented the massive heart attack she suffered," the doctor had informed him. Tom recalled a phrase his vicar father often quoted…*sudden death, sudden glory*. Rachel trusted God. She was a diligent church attender during their married life, and, like Tom, she knew trust in God was not about church attendance…it was about personal commitment.

Another wave of emotion enveloped him. He recalled the first day he had met her as a young teenager. Oh, how blessed he had been to love her from that very day. Yet, it had seemed impossible as their lives progressed that he would ever marry her.

There was a tap on his bedroom door.

"Dad, can I come in?" asked Darcy.

"Give me a minute," he called, dabbing his eyes with his handkerchief.

She entered the bedroom, his beloved daughter, Darcy Rose. She lay down on the bed beside him – he reached out and clasped her hand, tightly.

"Peg and Marcel have gone to Durham Station to collect Jonty and Sylvie. It's sad Uncle Pierre can't be here."

Tom squeezed Darcy's hand. This was a problem Peg's husband, Pierre, as a senior detective, often faced – being absent from family occasions.

"How are you coping, Darcy?" he enquired.

"Not good, Dad. I feel so guilty. I should have been here instead of galivanting around on a silly, idealistic notion that I was an undercover investigator."

Tom raised his other hand. "Stop, Darcy. No recriminations. I keep asking myself why was I driving a tractor? I thought I was helping Josh…you thought you were furthering your career. The doctor said none of us could have helped her…it was sudden…it was traumatic… it would have happened no matter where any of us were that day."

"But, Dad, I yelled at Marcel earlier and told him I blamed him for Mother's death – for taking me to that quarry."

Tom sat up and stared at his daughter. "Darcy…let it rest…that's a ridiculous line of thought…it has happened… she's gone…taken too soon. But she would not want us to live with 'what ifs'. Let's remember the good times with your mother."

A smile tinkered at the corners of his mouth.

"I must remember the last time she said she loved me… the last time we kissed…the last time we held hands…the last time we saw a sunset together…the last time we laughed at something. You don't know at that point it's going to be *the last* occasion. Bring your memories to mind frequently, Darcy… cherish them. We are privileged they happened. Appreciate them – we will get through this because it's what she would want."

A voice called for Tom from downstairs.

"What now?" he sighed, rising and gently kissing his daughter's forehead. "One day at a time, Darcy. I never thought I'd recover when my brother died…but I did…you too, will recover."

***

After spending a few more minutes on her dad's bed, Darcy left the room. She must take Lady for the walk she'd intended earlier. The door to Chantal and Sam's room was ajar – Darcy heard movement.

"Do you fancy taking a walk, Tallie?" she asked.

"Why not?" responded her aunt. "I feel so lost without the twins' demands, yet at the same time I miss them dreadfully." Chantal had agreed to leave her offspring with Francesca.

The two women set off across the lawns. Along with Rachel, they resembled each other in looks and stature. Lady headed for the laurel bushes at the bottom of the slope.

"Josh told me his plans for this place, Darcy…has he told you?"

Darcy nodded. They walked on and soon found the little dog.

"I told Josh he must ensure it becomes a 'happy place' – not a place of sadness. My sister would not have wanted any of us to come here to cry or be mournful. She was not a one for visiting cemeteries."

Darcy attached Lady's leash, and they began to walk.

"She's left us a hard act to follow," Darcy muttered.

"Yes," agreed Chantal. "My initial thoughts were to forget about our move to Scotland, but as Sam and I have discussed it, we think deep down your mother was at peace with the idea. When I spoke to Peg, she agreed.

Apparently, Rachel had written to Peg only recently, telling her about our decision. She'd said she was entrusted to look after Meckleridge House when she married your father and in a similar way, I was to be entrusted to look after Matthison Hall."

Darcy reached out and grabbed her aunt's arm. "Mistress of Matthison Hall, Tallie…just think, did you ever in your wildest dreams envisage that, when we first glimpsed the building all those years ago?"

Chantal smiled. "Never, Darcy…but Rachel also commented to Peg that one day you would take over the reins of Meckleridge House."

Darcy shook her head. "No, Tallie…I told my brother I can't do it. I don't know where to begin…I'm useless at housekeeping."

"Nonsense, Darcy. Seasons change. Think of it like this…she saw the potential in you…she trusted you to fill her place here at Meckleridge House. It won't be easy, but then trusting can be challenging."

They walked on in silence.

"I've got a suggestion for you, Darcy. Because you have a journalistic bent…why don't you write a journal to your mother, from time to time. Tell her how you are coping… what you are doing…what changes you are making. You've often said that writing is a powerful tool. No-one will ever read it, but I'm sure it will help you, not only to grieve, but to become the woman she envisaged you becoming."

The tears streamed down Darcy's face as she turned and hugged her aunt.

***

CHAPTER 25

As he opened his eyes on that late June morning, Tom knew instantly it was the day he would say his last goodbye to his beloved Rachel. Marcel and his family had done a splendid job of organising the funeral, sorting the details and only running queries past him when necessary. Their planning had been exemplary and had afforded Tom time to adjust.

He was so relieved for all their support – without it, he would have dithered, doubted and procrastinated…because it was for Rachel.

Along the corridor Josh was waking with a troubled mind. His worries were not related to the funeral, but to his girlfriend, Judy. Since rescuing her from her aunt's home in Bamburgh, her whereabouts had remained unknown to her family. There were six weeks until Judy's twenty-first birthday. Josh hoped she could remain undiscovered until that date. However, she was determined to attend his mother's funeral.

"My family will never know I've been to Malhaven for the funeral, Josh. I'll travel down with Francesca and the twins. We intend to go straight to the church. It's important for me to be at your side, supporting you. Francesca needs to leave after the refreshments so we will be back in Edinburgh by the evening."

"But what if someone sees you?" Josh had objected.

"I doubt the people who will attend your mother's funeral will know who I am, let alone that there is an estrangement with my family."

Josh still had concerns, but the prospect of Judy's companionship on this difficult day held sway.

The telephone shrilled – it was seven o'clock. Josh and Darcy met at the top of the stairs, as Marcel lifted the receiver in the hallway.

"Will one of you inform your father the vicar would like to see him at ten o'clock," he requested.

Josh went off to deliver the message, as Darcy asked, "Why? That's unusual, isn't it?" she asked bluntly. Since their conversation at the bushes, there had been no attempt from Darcy to communicate with Marcel.

"Darcy, I have no idea as to the reason, it wasn't my place to ask, I was merely passing on a message," he replied.

Darcy huffed and returned to her room.

Marcel wandered into the conservatory and gazed out of the windows overlooking the grounds. What was it about the young women around here? Darcy's attitude towards him and her cutting comments two days earlier, still rankled with him. How was he to blame? She was being irrational, no doubt a reaction to the shocking news – yet her disdainful looks and refusal to converse, were still apparent.

He liked visiting Meckleridge, enjoyed his friendship with Josh and hoped this issue with Darcy would improve.

Then there was Chrissie. Her rebuff weeks earlier, had not abated either.

As part of his funeral organisation duties, he visited the florist's, Leveridges. He'd hoped Chrissie wouldn't be around, but she was the one tasked with organising all the floral arrangements for Rachel Smallwood's funeral.

He'd met with her on three occasions and each time she'd been businesslike, but abrupt. Marcel was not one to be easily offended and decided to try to meet her, after today was over. There was something intriguing about Chrissie and he thought it was worth another attempt.

Tom and Peg were equally surprised at the vicar's request. The plan was to meet the cortege outside the church. Rachel always disliked the ritual of 'lying in state', telling Tom she did not want it for either of them when their time came. The service was to be held at 2pm. Francesca was taking the twins to the farm, where Nancy would look after them, then driving to the church. Bennie was now discharged from hospital, and Nancy needed to be at home to care for her invalid husband.

"This is highly irregular," commented Tom as he entered the church with Marcel.

Tim Dobson, the vicar, was no stranger to the Smallwood family. He had officiated at Tom's brother's funeral; Tom and Rachel's wedding; Darcy and Josh's christenings; Tom's parents' funerals; and Darcy and Henri's wedding.

The vicar walked down the aisle and shook Tom's hand firmly. "Tom, thank you for coming, please sit."

Tom followed his direction, noting the colourful vases of flowers already in position at the front of the church – Darcy and Chantal's suggestion, no doubt.

The vicar coughed. "There is a problem, Tom, but I think I have resolved it. However, I didn't want to explain this on the telephone," the vicar began.

"Last night the staff from Barclays Funeral Services were attending a function at a local hotel."

Tom stared at the vicar, perplexed.

"Unfortunately, they were all taken ill and after the event, some of them were hospitalised. The result is Barclays are unable to perform their duties today."

Tom's eyes widened.

"I received notification of this distressing situation at six this morning, but thankfully, I have arranged for Dempster's Funeral Services to take their place. It was amazing they were able to do this at such short notice. No-one will be any the wiser. Your family are to meet the cortege outside the church as planned."

Tom's face turned ashen, and Marcel grabbed his hand.

"Is there a problem?" asked the bewildered vicar.

Chapter 26

Receiving an early morning call from the hospital was all in a day's work for Tim Dobson. However, the request that morning was unusual. In his many years in the clergy, he'd become resourceful. After listening to the sad tale of the food poisoning incident, he telephoned Dempster's.

He'd met the owner professionally before, but his response was strange.

"Aye, vicar, I'll help. Our good Lord works in mysterious ways his wonders to perform."

Tim knew this was a quote from a hymn penned by William Cowper in the 1700s. He was also aware of Bernard Dempster's reputation for being solemn, stern and well suited to his occupation. He decided not to pass this comment on to a gentleman like Tom Smallwood.

Marcel drove Tom back to the house.

"I trust this change of arrangements won't cause a repeat of the last time you encountered Bernie Dempster, Tom."

"I sincerely hope not, Marcel. I will not have issues surrounding my dear wife's funeral."

But as they travelled back, Tom sensed some clouds from the past were surely heading to St Cuthbert's Church in Malhaven that afternoon.

"I did continue my enquiries into Bernie's war service, but with the situation at the quarry, I was not able to pull things together," Marcel explained.

Darcy's ordeal at the quarry had paled into insignificance with the news of Rachel's death.

Tom seemed miles away, but the comment jerked his mind. Was it only two weeks since he and Rachel made that discovery in Uncle Bart's boxes and Rachel had suggested a get together with Marcel to pool their findings?

"Oh, Marcel, I did a bit of digging around in my uncle's old papers but…" He felt a lump forming in his throat and coughed. "It seems so trivial now – I discovered my uncle bought our farm from Bernie's father in 1916."

"What?" yelled Marcel in surprise.

Tom nodded. "It's likely Judy's father grew up on our farm."

Marcel gave a low whistle and turned into the winding drive of Meckleridge House. "Tom, I think we may have found the root of the man's problem!" he exclaimed.

A figure was walking towards them on the driveway, waving two hands in the air.

"What on earth is he doing?" asked Tom, as Marcel brought his car to a crunching halt in front of Josh. Tom wound down the window.

"A warning, Dad, you've got a visitor, and you'll never guess who it is," Josh announced.

"Bernie Dempster, I imagine," Tom replied to a shocked Josh.

Darcy was standing in the hallway as Tom entered the front door.

"Dad you've got…" she began.

Tom interjected. "I know, ask Peg to make some tea please. I want you and your brother to join us," he responded, striding towards the conservatory.

Darcy looked shocked and reached out to grab her father's arm.

"Stay calm, Dad," she remarked.

Bernie Dempster stood.

"Tom," he began. "May I offer you and your family my sincere condolences." He shook hands with Tom, as Darcy and Josh entered the room.

"Thank you, please take a seat," Tom replied, indicating one of the settees.

"I am sure the vicar has apprised you of the unfortunate situation with Barclay's," Bernie announced.

Tom sat opposite the undertaker and a baffled Darcy and Josh stood behind his armchair.

"This is an awkward situation. I realise the last time we met, I was rude to you and your dear wife," he coughed.

Josh felt anxious – why was Judy's father here?

"My behaviour was out of order that night and I need to apologise. It was related to a personal bitterness concerning a situation you had no knowledge about, or control over." There was a pause as the big man shuffled about, obviously trying to form his words appropriately.

"There was no way I could walk up that church aisle in front of your deceased wife's coffin, without seeking amends."

Peg pushed open the door, carrying a tea tray. Josh was perplexed…what was going on? As if sensing Josh's bewilderment, Bernie Dempster looked directly at Josh. "Young man, this concerns you as well as your father."

Peg handed around the cups of tea, after asking the unusually subdued man if he needed milk or sugar.

"I will try to say my bit quickly, as we have limited time," Bernie continued. "Fairholme Farm, or Meckleridge Farm as you know it, was my birthright."

Josh's jaw dropped.

"I wasn't obliged to serve my country as a soldier, because farming was a reserved occupation…but I was a young man with a fighting spirit and refused to heed my family's request to stay at home."

Tom lifted his eyebrows and Darcy sat on the arm of his chair.

"I was unaware of a habit my father developed after I left home. He took to gambling…why, I have no idea. It became an addiction. He did not expect me to survive the blood bath of World War 1." His voice crackled. "In order to clear his debts, he sold the farm to your uncle." Bernie pulled out a handkerchief to mop his brow, took a drink and continued.

"When I returned from the war unharmed, I was devastated to learn what he had done. He was depressed and penniless and what should have been a joyous homecoming for his son and heir, turned sour. At that point I determined to live a vice-free life, I built up my business from scratch, joined the Methodist Church, met and married my wife. However, deep down I was resentful, and sadly I took it out on my daughters. I admit my thinking has been warped." He stopped and finished his tea.

Darcy glanced at the clock.

"That night when I heard where Judy was, and the fact she was sweet on the son of the family who took away my inheritance…I'm ashamed to say, I exploded. Over the months since Judy disappeared, I have done a great deal of 'soul searching'."

Darcy was impatient – when would the man stop talking?

Bernie stood up. "I must make haste. I am trusting you will accept my apology, Tom." Then looking at Josh he added, "I suspect you know the whereabouts of my daughter Judy, young man. If you do…then I ask you to tell her about this visit and try to persuade her to return home. Her coming of age will be happening soon – I will not stand in the way of her choice of friends." He reached out and shook hands with Tom again.

"See you at the church," he added, then turned and walked towards the door.

***

Josh was trembling. He was standing inside the gates of St. Cuthbert's Church in Malhaven, but his mind was elsewhere. Soon, his dear mother's funeral would take place. Aunt Peg, in her usual organised manner, had taken control after the unexpected visitor left earlier that morning. His clothes were neatly pressed, ready for him in his room – a snack lunch was provided in the kitchen. Yet, no amount of careful planning could avert the collision Josh feared was about to take place.

It wouldn't be a clashing of metal and a screeching of brakes, but a clashing of opinions and a screeching of raised voices…a scenario his mother did not deserve.

Judy would be frantic at the sight of her estranged father leading the cortege – he had been unable to warn her. His only hope lay in the apologetic man, who he'd seen that morning, behaving in a civil manner befitting of the occasion.

It was a first for Josh – he'd not been to a funeral before. He was to be a underbearer along with Jonty, Marcel and Sam.

Josh heard the engine, then saw the hearse descending the hill, with Bernie Dempster leading the way. Where were Judy and Francesca? They had not passed him. Jonty nudged his arm, and they walked to the rear door of the hearse. On the opposite side of the road, the family alighted from the vehicles…it was out of his control now.

The strains of the hymn *Love Divine*, Rachel's favourite hymn, reached Josh's ears. The vicar led the way followed by Bernie Dempster, Rachel and her pallbearers and the family. If anyone had asked Josh Smallwood to relay the service Tim Dobson conducted, he would have been unable to give any detail. Judy's whereabouts were uppermost in his mind.

As the service ended, he joined the other pallbearers and hoisted the coffin onto his shoulders. The congregation began to sing *Amazing Grace*. He heard his father's deep baritone voice singing the lyrics – how could he sing, he pondered.

The cortege arrived at the font, located near to the church entrance, the group needed to take a right turn. At that moment the church door opened and into the foyer stepped Francesca and Judy.

"Dad," whispered a shocked Judy, stepping swiftly to the side, to allow the entourage to pass.

Quick thinking Darcy stepped out of line and pulled the two young women to her side, as Henri paused and allowed them to walk in front of him.

CHAPTER 26

The procession wound its way into the graveyard. Under Bernie's directions the groundsmen took over from the underbearers, and Rachel's coffin was lowered into the open grave… but Josh knew his role was not complete and he was shaking.

In her usual exuberant fashion, Darcy had suggested the family should say their own personal words of goodbye to Rachel, before the committal.

There didn't appear to be a dry eye in the small, private group. As Josh stepped back from the open grave, Judy joined him and slid her hand into his – words of explanation would come later. Josh squeezed Judy's hand. The tributes were personal and heartfelt.

Darcy spoke first. "Mother, thank you for bringing me into this world and guiding me on this tempestuous path, called life. I will always cherish your words of wisdom. You have taught me how to climb mountains and face challenges…I will miss you so much." Tears ran down her cheeks as Henri placed his arm around her and she leant her head against his shoulder.

Chantal spoke next. "Dear Rachel, I think I sensed your presence before I knew you existed. Thank you for being the best sister possible." Sam stood at her side.

Josh swallowed and fumbled in his pocket for his note containing his words, but he was unable to read them, as tears blurred his vision. His voice crackled, "Mother, I love you. Goodbye." As he spoke the last words, Judy tightened her grip on his arm.

Contrary to the assembled family's expectation, Tom Smallwood spoke in a loud, clear, controlled voice. "Dear Rachel, you taught me the meaning of love and how to trust. I loved you from the first moment I saw you. You have been and will continue to be, my everything. Today we are parted, but only for a little while. My darling, Rachel… continue to blossom." Peg handed Tom a single yellow rose, cut from their Rose Garden that morning – he dropped it on top of the coffin… its significance known only to a few.

The vicar conducted the words of committal and prayer.

Josh sensed a movement from behind – it was Bernie Dempster. Judy froze. Her father placed his hand on her shoulder and bent forward.

"Please forgive me, Judy," he uttered. "Love is too powerful an emotion to deny."

Judy felt her legs were about to give way - she was visibly trembling in disbelief. He turned and followed his employees, walking away from the graveside. Judy collapsed into Josh's arms, her sobs causing her body to heave.

"Sssh," comforted Josh, "I'll explain it later."

The walk to the church hall was short, but somehow Josh managed to relay the account of her father's presence at the funeral and his explanation and apology, to Tom, given that morning.

"I'm not going back home, Josh," Judy insisted.

The funeral tea was a sad but essential event. Bertha and Peg had provided a wonderful spread in honour of Rachel Smallwood. It gave Tom a chance to chat to the many townsfolk he'd befriended over the years. Josh couldn't wait for the formalities to end, but eventually the family were ready to make their way home.

"Judy," boomed a voice, as she was collecting her coat. For the second time in a few hours Judy froze. Darcy noticed Bernie Dempster's arrival.

"Mr Dempster," she called, stepping in front of the big man. "This is a private function."

Josh, Henri, Marcel and Tom appeared at her side. Bernie held up his hand to stop their advance.

"I come peacefully. There is no need to fear my presence. My wife begged me to try to persuade our daughter to return home."

Judy shook her head. "No, Dad, tell her I will visit after my birthday," said Judy. "I also need to inform you that Josh and I are courting. It's my choice, Dad," she declared.

Bernard stepped towards Josh. "You have my blessing," he added, reaching out and shaking Josh's hand.

There was a quietness in the room. All eyes seemed glued to the group. For over thirty years this man had carried a burden of resentment and bitterness.

Darcy spoke. "I think my mother has brought something into this sad situation. Without her knowing, her death has brought peace and an end to a bitter resentment. Each of us has learned from her words of wisdom in our lives and although she will never know, the fact that Mr Dempster could not attend to his duties today without making his apology, speaks for itself."

Nods of agreement were in evidence.

Bernie looked around the group. "I said to the vicar this morning '*God works in mysterious ways his wonders to perform*'. I think this has been one of those occasions."

Tom stepped forward and shook Bernie Dempster's hand, for the third time that day.

***

In August, Judy celebrated her twenty-first birthday. The day before a nervous young man visited Dempster's Funeral Parlour. He asked to speak to Mr Dempster. One letter had been sent by Judy to her parents, stating she would visit them on her birthday.

"Now, young man, what can I do for you today?" The big man smiled.

"I have come to ask for permission to marry your daughter Judy, Mr Dempster," Josh replied. "I know she will be twenty-one tomorrow, but I wanted to make my request in person and tell you I love her very much. I am a young man with good prospects …the undermanager of a local farm, which in the fullness of time I will inherit."

Bernie smiled. "Eeh, lad…now there's a miracle I never expected to witness," he answered. "It's as if it was always meant to be. Of course, you can wed her, and I trust you will make her happy."

The next day Judy's birthday was celebrated in style at Meckleridge House. Bertha baked pies and cakes, and together with Chantal and Darcy they provided a tasty spread. It was a double celebration, as everyone admired the dainty diamond engagement ring, Josh had given to her as her birthday present.

Before the party Judy kept her promise – she and Josh visited her parents' home to show them the ring. Her mother and sister were overjoyed and added their congratulations.

After the cake was cut and the young couple's future was toasted, Chantal pulled Bertha and Darcy to one side.

"I think we can say, ladies, we provided a meal equal to my sister's standards tonight." She paused and smiled, as they agreed. "Would you both be willing to do it all again next month? Sam and I have set the date!"

Darcy's eyes widened and she hugged her aunt.

"There will only be a few guests, similar to this occasion."

Darcy wiped a stray tear from her cheek.

"It's so sad Mother hasn't lived to see your wedding day, Chantal, but if Bertha is willing to help me, I'm sure we can do the honours."

***

FOUR WEEKS LATER

Josh was nervous – it was the second time in a few weeks he'd been asked to speak publicly. But unlike the previous time this was a joyful event – he was best man at Sam and Chantal's wedding.

He watched the assembled group. It was hard to believe it was only a year since his return from completing his National Service… so much had changed for all of them in that year… and more changes lay ahead.

The previous evening, after supper, his dad had asked to speak with him privately.

"Josh, I must impart some sad news." Josh had tensed, as his dad continued. "I expect you have noticed Bennie's health deteriorating, which means the mantle has fallen on your shoulders sooner than we expected."

Josh nodded, it was as he thought, but until the words were spoken, it seemed distant.

"Josh…you are now the manager of Meckleridge Farm," Tom announced,

"I'm not sure I'm ready, Dad," he'd responded.

His dad had placed his arm around Josh's shoulder. "You are, my son, trust me...you are."

He'd looked up into his father's eyes.

"Many times, during our lives, we are called upon to trust. When you trust someone, you believe you can depend on them. I recall the day I asked your mother to marry me – we had history, and I took a risk... a season of trust ensued."

His dad had called them 'seasons of trust', which had given him an idea. Now as he was about to make his little speech, he looked at his family.

His aunt, Chantal – she looked radiant, yet she'd walked through a 'season of trust' when Sam was reported as missing in action. She'd held a confident expectation that there would be a good outcome...and here, today, it was being fulfilled on her wedding day.

His gaze fell on his sister, Darcy, and her husband, Henri... they also had travelled their own 'season of trust', since their first-born child failed to live. Ahead lay a new season...an expectation of a cure for Henri and a belief that one day, they would have a longed-for baby.

He rattled a spoon against his glass to call for silence.

"Life is full of seasons of trust," he began. "We trust people and situations to have positive outcomes...but it comes hand in hand, with bumps along the road. Each of us here today has known or is experiencing, our own 'season of trust'. Sam and Chantal doubted this day would ever dawn...but it did. So, if you find yourself doubting...look to this couple and take heart...miracles do happen! Please join me in wishing, Sam and Chantal a long, happy married life...to Sam and Chantal."

Josh raised his glass, and the small group joined him, repeating the toast.

"When did you become so eloquent?" jibed Darcy to her brother, who winked at her.

Marcel looked around the group, who he now regarded as his adopted family. "Can I make a final toast, please. I was truly blessed the day I met the Smallwood family. I want to thank you all, for accepting me and welcoming me into your home. Since then, I have learned a great deal about trust. Trust is a bedrock of reliability… trust takes time… trust can and will be tested. So, everyone… let's raise our glasses once more. Here's to trust," he remarked.

Epilogue

The sound of exuberant voices led Darcy from the front door of Meckleridge House across to the lawns. She stopped and gazed in amazement at the sight before her eyes. To any other woman the spectacle of a father and son kicking a ball around a grassy area, would be commonplace. But for Darcy Dukas it represented a miracle…a miracle of hope…a miracle of trust. Her husband, Henri, was living proof of those two powerful emotions.

Ten years ago, after her mother, Rachel, had passed away, Darcy grasped at hope and trust. They filtered into every corner of her life. Many dark days followed when she questioned her ability to cope, to become mistress of Meckleridge House. When Chantal and Sam moved to Scotland, she had felt so low. Her mother's efficiency left a gaping hole – one which Darcy could not fill. Yet, she became resourceful and recognised the areas where she needed assistance. After Bennie died, Darcy asked Nancy to become their housekeeper. She remained at the farmhouse until Josh and Judy married and made it their home, then Nancy moved to 'live in' at Meckleridge House.

Nancy taught Darcy many things about housekeeping, but her role enabled the young woman to pursue her journalistic call. She had now penned successful articles in local and national newspapers, focusing on human interest topics.

Darcy's hope and trust in becoming a mother again, was also rewarded. She smiled at her eight-year-old son, Jake, deftly showing off his ball skills.

But to Darcy, the greatest trust miracle had taken place earlier that year. Sam, now a surgeon in Edinburgh, had kept abreast of the pioneering work regarding hip replacement. Henri had been invited to undergo tests and had been one of the earliest patients to receive a new hip via this new medical procedure.

The months surrounding the operation were tense and fraught, as Henri spent many weeks away from his family. But the joyous day of his homecoming eventually arrived.

Jake caught sight of his mother and ran to greet her.

"Papa says I am bound to score the most goals on Saturday – more than the others," he shrieked, excitedly. Darcy hugged him.

"Nothing like belief in in your own abilities," she laughed, as Henri jogged to her side and embraced her.

The 'others' were his two cousins, Richard and Peter – Josh and Judy's sons, and Philip – Marcel and Chrissie's boy. They were all members of the local junior boys' football team and rivalry between them was rife.

"I'm off in search of Dad," she announced, leaving her husband and son.

As she walked, Darcy was reminded of Marcel's toast at Sam and Chantal's wedding party. Marcel had referred to trust being the bedrock of reliability and said that it was often tested. Poor Marcel's trust was certainly tested back in those days.

She gradually forgave Marcel, but it took time. After Gordon Sinclair's conviction Marcel's business struggled, but he'd persevered…she smiled – it still bore the name DD's!

But he was certainly tested where Chrissie was concerned. She rejected Marcel 's attempt at a friendship for many, many months. She'd been hurt in the past and doubted she would ever trust a man again.

The more Chrissie rebuffed Marcel, the more tantalising she became to him.

Eventually, with gentle nudging and encouragement from Darcy, Chrissie relented, and Marcel and Chrissie became a loving couple as Chrissie learned to trust again.

Darcy rounded the corner of the bushes, where her dad was sitting on the bench at 'Rachel's Place' where he spent hours, if the weather was suitable.

Tom greeted her with a beaming smile, as she sat down beside him.

"Are you coming to the Football Tournament on Saturday, Dad?" she asked.

"I wouldn't miss it – my three grandsons will hear me cheering them."

Darcy's reflections that morning bubbled within her, and she grabbed her father's hand.

"Thank you, Dad, for all you have taught me about life – love… truth…hope…and trust." She stopped, her voice crackled, and tears of happiness streamed down her cheeks.

Tom placed his arm around her shoulder. "Hey, what's brought this on…has something happened?" he enquired.

She wiped her eyes with the back of her hand and continued. "No, I've just been reminding myself… when things seem against us, and we are about to give up… that's when we have to trust the most."

Tom squeezed his daughter as she rested her head on his shoulder. They sat in silence, each reflecting.

"Yes, Darcy… as Josh once said…there will be bumps on the road of life…but then there's trust."

Author's Note

THEN THERE'S TRUST is the third book in the Blossoming series. BLOSSOMING OF TRUTH tells Tom and Rachel's story and HOPE ON HOPE follows the early lives of Chantal and Darcy. However, each book can be read as a standalone.

THEN THERE'S TRUST is the product of 'an itch I needed to scratch'. The characters from the previous two books were calling me to continue their story. I trust you have enjoyed reading the next instalment of their lives as much as I have enjoyed writing it.

Exploring the themes of truth and hope in the previous books led naturally into the theme of trust in this third book.

Once again, the book is set in a fictional corner of northwest Durham but is based on the town where I have lived all my life.

Moving into the 1950s felt comfortable, being the era into which I was born. It also afforded opportunities to chat to people about their living memories.

BLOSSOMING OF TRUTH, HOPE ON HOPE and THEN THERE'S TRUST bring the Blossoming series to its conclusion, but ideas continue to formulate…so watch this space!

Best wishes,
Susan Gray

If you have enjoyed reading THEN THERE'S TRUST, please leave a review on Amazon or Goodreads.

www.goodreads.com/author/show/42479536

Please follow me on social media:

www.facebook.com/susangrayauthor
www.instagram.com/suangrayauthor
www.x.com/susangray275384
www.tiktok.com/@susangrayauthor

Acknowledgements

'Thank you' are two small words, which sometimes fail to express the deep level of gratitude I wish to convey. Since my writing journey began six years ago, I have been amazed to have family, friends and acquaintancs who have helped me with their words of encouragement and advice, unwavering support and technical 'know how'!

Each book project brings new challenges. Having someone there with which to bounce ideas around has been invaluable. My husband Vic and cover designer Ruth are both so patient with me…I would be lost without them, and I value their input greatly.

I wish to extend a big thank you to all my readers and everyone who has spread the word about my books…your loyalty is much appreciated.

I also want to add a note of gratitude to my draft readers for their assistance, and to the authors I have connected with on social media – it's good to share experiences.

Finally, my thanks go to UK Book Publishing for working with me on this fourth publication.

About the Author

Susan Gray's late onset career began in 2020, when she wrote her debut novel SPANISH HOUSE SECRETS. It was a dream fulfilled to hold a copy of her own book.

Her plots are inspired by 'life'...unearthing hidden family secrets and unpacking themes such as forgiveness, truth, hope and trust. She seeks to entwine the genres of mystery and romance, and her books are character driven.

They are set in the beautiful landscapes of northeast England where she lives with her husband.

When not writing she enjoys reading, crafting, puzzling, catching up with friends over a coffee and travelling.

She has written eight books, four of which are now published...SPANISH HOUSE SECRETS, BLOSSOMING OF TRUTH, HOPE ON HOPE and THEN THERE'S TRUST.